S0-BIG-298

KALYANA

WAYNE PUBLIC LIBRARY
PREAKNESS BRANCH
1 HAMBURG TURNPIKE
WAYNE, NJ 07470

JUN 0 8 2017

JUN 6 2017

KALYANA

RAJNI MALA KHELAWAN

Second Story Press

Library and Archives Canada Cataloguing in Publication

Khelawan, Rajni Mala, author
Kalyana : a novel / Rajni Mala Khelawan.

Issued in print and electronic formats.
ISBN 978-1-927583-98-2 (paperback).
—ISBN 978-1-77260-002-5 (epub)

I. Title.

PS8621.H45K35 2016   C813'.6   C2015-908406-7

C2015-908407-5

Copyright © 2016 by Rajni Mala Khelawan

Edited by Christina M. Frey and Patricia Kennedy
Designed by Melissa Kaita
Cover photographs © iStockphoto

"Kabhi Kabhi" written by Majrooth Sultanpuri
© Published by Saregama Music United States
All rights reserved. Used by permission.

Printed and bound in Canada

*Second Story Press gratefully acknowledges the support of the
Ontario Arts Council and the Canada Council for the Arts for our
publishing program. We acknowledge the financial support of the
Government of Canada through the Canada Book Fund.*

Published by
SECOND STORY PRESS
20 Maud Street, Suite 401
Toronto, ON M5V 2M5
www.secondstorypress.ca

For my mother, Shanti Kumari Singh

FIJI ISLANDS
Red hibiscus and bougainvillea hedges

My mother once said that everyone in this world is granted one beginning and one ending. Life is made up of what is in between: the connections, the discoveries, the triumphs, and the losses. Some of these inspire us, some mold us, and some destroy us. Yet no experience leaves our spirits untouched.

KALYANA.
One simple word, but its meaning carries the weight of the universe.

Blissful.

Beautiful.

Blessed.

The auspicious one.

It encompasses all that is good, all that is pure, and all that is true. And all that is without suffering, without pain. Kalyana. That is my name.

My mother had gifted me with my name long before I was conceived, she claimed. Although she never would tell me directly where the birds had met the bees, I once overheard her tell the story to my *mausi*, my aunt and her sister.

It had happened in the middle of the day, at ten past the noon hour, in an old hut by the Pacific. The windows were open, my mother said, and the warm breeze blew in the salt of the sea. "Kalyana happened then." Her voice was firm,

5

certain. She sat calmly at the dining table, picking pebbles out of a bowl of uncooked rice.

Manjula only rolled her eyes, pursed her lips, and shrugged her shoulders.

"Yes, Kalyana happened then."

"And how would I know what happened, Sumitri? I am still without a husband."

"Yes, yes, Manjula. I know you're still without a husband." My mother smiled. "Kalyana happened after a brush of blissful, passionate embrace." Then, turning sour, she said, "Unlike my son, who happened right after the burst of pain."

"Pain?" Manjula, wide-eyed, awaited her education.

"Oh, *Kutiya*. There's always pain the first time." She paused for effect before continuing. "And blood."

"Blood?" squeaked Manjula.

My mother eyed my aunt conspicuously before whispering, "It's only a little bit of blood."

"Oh my God! Pain. Suffering. And blood. How can that be? Isn't it supposed to be God's gift of pleasure to mankind?" Manjula wrestled with her breathing, blushing as she whispered, "Do men suffer also when the birds meet the bees?"

My mother playfully slapped her sister on the arm. "Manjula, have you lost your mind?" she smirked. "Only women bleed!"

1

M Y MOTHER often told me that while suffering hides deep within, unnoticed and unseen, pain is marked by a release of blood. I did not understand how this pain and blood could ever end in a state of emotional bliss. But my mother was insistent.

Blood and pain, she said, marked the passage of a woman's life. It happened to a new bride on her wedded bed; it happened to a new mother in a birthing tent. This was something men could never share or understand. "It is this blood, Kalyana," she would say, looking deeply into my eyes, "it is this blood that bonds one woman's soul to another."

There was blood when I was born, she said, buckets and buckets of it. And pain, much pain. My mother would tell me how she had howled and screamed for the gods' mercy, how she had begged to be reincarnated as a man.

And yet some women, she said, had become like men without the assistance of the gods. On the day of my birth, she told me, the women of a faraway land called America had gone mad. They had taken off their brassieres and destroyed them in a bonfire in the center of the town, chanting and circling the flames like mad, ancient cavemen. Later, after all the brassieres had turned to ash, the women had stopped cleaning, cooking, and shaving under their armpits and rebelled against their husbands. They had buttoned up white shirts, strapped on belts over their khaki pants, and gone to work like men.

My mother had heard all of this on a transistor radio, the same one that she kept tucked into her pocket. But this did not keep her from retelling the story, adding her own particular flavor. For extra effect, my mother would seal the tale by raising her right arm and pointing to her clean underarms with her left index finger. "The hairs grew out long enough for braiding, Kalyana," she would say. "Eeeeww!" And she would scrunch up her nose.

She would tell other stories, too, stories from our past. My grandmother, she said, was born on SS *Sangola*, a merchant ship of the British India Steam Navigation Company. She arrived in an unusual way: head first, like a bag of stones, with her umbilical cord wrapped around her neck. My mother would pronounce SS *Sangola* like the British, exaggerating each syllable for dramatic effect.

This journey, she always claimed, had been the ship's third time on the great oceans, bringing Indian laborers from the heat of Calcutta to the plains of Fiji. Just like the birds that migrate south in search of the warmth of the sun, leaving behind the harshness of winter, so the Indians came to Fiji with *lotas* filled with hope, fleeing the chill of poverty.

The laborers, my mother said, were numbered carefully: 1,151 set sail. Yet 1,152 laborers landed on the Fiji sands on

February 1, 1909, and my mother insisted that my grandmother had accounted for the extra number. She was sure
about this detail, too, as she was sure about everything else.

My grandmother had tumbled out of her mother's womb
onto the grimy wooden decks. It happened on the dark-
est night of the century, twenty-three days before the ship
reached the Fiji shores. To conceal my great-grandmother's
nakedness and suffering from the curious eyes of the men,
all of the women on the ship had gathered around her in a
circle, fat penguins holding up great veils of saris. Only my
great-grandmother's screams of agony had pierced through
the thin material, followed by the women's shouts of joy. My
grandmother's small head, covered with thick black hair—a
trait of all Indian women—had emerged like a turtle's head
out of its shell.

Upon hearing the sounds of joy, the men had hopped on
the decks as the steamship parted the seas. A pundit on the
ship blew the conch shell amidst the jubilation; its reverberation echoed across the waves of the Pacific Ocean, causing
the small creatures living below the seas to dance and swirl.
Even the Surgeon-Superintendent, the most important man
on the ship and the Indian people's protector and boss, had
come out of his cabin with his hands on his hips and a grin
planted across his thin, pale face. He had stood and watched
the celebration, though from a necessary distance.

My mother also said that, on those same decks where
my grandmother had taken her first breath, the Surgeon-
Superintendent had killed an immigrant snake. It had
happened like this: When the Indian men and women were
boarding the ship from the docks of Calcutta, a *naag*, a king

cobra, had followed their scent and the sound of the conch shell and crept aboard the ship like a hidden stowaway. During the voyage the passengers would occasionally catch a glimpse of the black, slippery creature making its way from one corner or hole of the cabin to another, slithering in and out among the barrels of food and water stacked on the decks.

The Surgeon-Superintendent had received the news of this extra immigrant, one whose potential as a hard-working laborer was limited. He had not believed that the snake had followed the scent of the laborers or the sound of the conch shell; rather, he was convinced that it was the snake charmer who had smuggled the snake on board in the round wicker basket that he kept carefully covered with a red loincloth. The Surgeon-Superintendant would spend his days afflicted with worry. What if the snake were to strike one of his laborers dead in the middle of the night? Every uninjured head delivered safely to the shores of the Fiji Islands entitled him to an additional payment.

The yellow-haired man had set out to capture and destroy the unwelcome guest. This to the horror of my ancestors, who had stood there shuddering in their *dhotis*, shaking their heads. They had worshipped the very presence of the king cobra, a garland of Lord Shiva. Its company on the ship would have been taken as a blessing, a symbol of good fortune.

The snake charmer was summoned and made to sit in the middle of the deck and play his *pungi*. The sweet melody attracted the snake to the deck. It coiled up in front of the charmer and, mesmerized by the tune, swayed gracefully.

At this point I could caress fear with my fingertips, for I well knew what would happen next.

The Surgeon-Superintendent had grabbed a blackened steel pot by its handle and beat the snake on the head, smashing it into the ground. Venomous blood splattered the decks and the Surgeon-Superintendent's white shirt, staining both. My mother would look me in the eye confidently and insist that even the king cobra wasn't beyond the wrath of pain; the snake had hissed in agony under the hold of the pot for nearly a minute before its spirit evaporated into the dark waters of the universe, releasing it from suffering inflicted by man.

As the king cobra lay lifeless, its yellow belly up in the air, the laborers gathered around it. They chanted verses in Sanskrit and prayed for the light-haired man's soul until the strike of his whip sent them sprawling to throw the snake's remains overboard. Two days later, the distraught snake charmer followed his beloved snake into the depths of the sea.

Later that year, a big steel pot had fallen on the Surgeon-Superintendent's head, cracking his skull in a hundred places and killing him instantly. It was more than a few days before his body was discovered, my mother would insist. His face was unrecognizable because of all the dried blood, and he stank like cow's dung.

Of all the stories my mother told me when I was young, this one alone stirred recurring nightmares. I was transported back to the SS *Sangola*, in the middle of the ocean. The ship was swarming with countless king cobras, slithering all around me. I could hear low growls under their hissing calls. They were coiled in front of me, wearing red maharajah crowns, while others held back, draped over the barrels, hanging on the masts. Trapped, I shivered, chanting prayers, my knees clutched to my chest. I stayed huddled in a corner of the deck as the sensation of slithering serpents crawled up my legs and across my body.

Then my mother would miraculously appear. She would hit the snakes on their heads with a blackened steel pot. Black blood and gore would paint the walls and decks of the ship as the pitiful snakes collapsed belly up, one by one, until a stream of yellow carpeted the ship's floors.

The nightmare would end as my screams awoke the house. My mother would pick me up from Manjula's thin mattress and take me to hers, placing me in the center and tightly tucking around me the white mosquito net that hung from the ceiling. My father would rise and go to our small kitchen to boil milk on the green kerosene stove.

Then my mother would stroke my back and tell me more stories, tales of Krishna, the mischievous deity. Krishna, she would say, was born in the dead of night in the middle of a jail cell, while the gods cried buckets of tears and the wind howled louder than a lion. The whole village of Mathura was in turmoil when Krishna was born to Devaki and Yasudev. The thunder rolled with an immense ferocity and the lightning struck the four corners of the world.

"Why was Krishna born in a jail, Mummy?" I would always ask.

"Because Devaki's evil brother, the King Kansa, had imprisoned them for life."

"What was her crime, Mummy?"

"She didn't commit a crime. King Kansa was an evil soul!"

"How can she be in jail if she didn't commit a crime, Mummy?"

My mother would pause thoughtfully. Then, in a measured voice: "That's because life is sometimes like that, Kalyana. Life can be unfair."

As she spoke, a softness would come into her voice, and she would lower her eyes to the ground. I never understood the pause or the sigh. It was only later, much later, that I came to realize how well she knew the meaning of this, yet how well she had hidden it throughout most of her living years. Later, I came to understand exactly how life could be unfair.

My mother would shake herself a little and continue the story. Evil King Kansa had been given a prophecy that his sister's eighth child would bring him judgment in the form of death, ending his evil rule over the kingdom of Mathura. To defy this fate, King Kansa had imprisoned Devaki and Yasudev, killing every child born to them.

Krishna was Devaki's eighth child. Yet although he was born within the confinement of a cold, concrete cell, he came into the world wholeheartedly and mischievously, tickling his mother's insides and sending her into quiet hysterics. He entered life twinkling like a star and smiling beyond understanding. The skin he wore was the shade of deep ocean blue.

The exact moment that Krishna emerged from his mother's womb, Yashoda, the Queen of Gokul, gave birth to a daughter. Unlike Krishna, this child plummeted into the world with a thunderous roar, shaking the earth and raising the ocean waters. People said she was born without blood and gore, in the comfort of her father's kingdom. They said her skin glistened with a honey-like liquid, making her whole being shine like melting gold.

At this moment, Devaki's jail cell was illuminated with

a blinding light. The guards succumbed to a hypnotic sleep as the cell door mysteriously unlatched and opened wide. Yasudev, following divine instructions, picked up his new-born baby, placed him in a wicker basket, and started a journey across the Yamuna River to Yashoda's village.

At this point, my father would return with a stainless-steel glass of warm milk and honey. He would untuck the mosquito net and crawl into bed. I would guzzle the milk, wishing for still more sweetness as I hung onto my mother's every word.

"What happened next, Mummy?" I licked the edges of my lips.

"The Yamuna River raged and her waves threatened to swallow Yasudev and baby Krishna whole." My mother would fix her penetrating stare upon me, and my heart would skip, the hairs rising on my arms. I knew what would follow: "And it was then that the five-headed snake from below the waters emerged."

"Five-headed snake!" I would shiver in the night air.

"Sumitri, you are frightening her," my father would say. "The child is scared of snakes and is ridden with nightmares about them, and here you are telling her stories about snakes with five heads!"

"Rajdev Seth, it's not *snakes*," my mother would say. "There was only one five-headed snake. And it was a good one."

My mother would throw me a conspiring look and try to speak the next series of words as fast as she could before Father could demand that she end all stories for the night.

"The snake's five heads shielded baby Krishna from the

water, and the snake itself was Yasudev's guide, allowing him
to—"

"Sumitri…"

"Snakes are not to be feared, but to be embraced. They
are your guides. Kalyana—"

"Sumitri!" My father would tell my mother to go back to
sleep, bringing the story to an abrupt end.

Even though I had no desire to wrap my arms around
any snake, whether it was wearing a crown or had five heads,
I desperately wanted my mother to go on and finish this story
rather than leaving me unsatisfied and hanging once more. In
an ironic way, it was the ultimate temptation: I simply had
to hear the story again, even with its five-headed snake, just
so that my mother could at last explain to me how the story
had ended.

My father would then take over the telling of tales,
kissing my cheek and soothing me with funny stories. My
favorite was the one about the elephant with the itchy back.
The elephant would go and sit close to a large tree, so that
he could rub his back on the thick trunk, shaking the tree so
hard that it made a little bird's nest fall to the ground, cracking the mother bird's eggs. The elephant did this every week,
to the bird's anguish.

My father would pause and ask me how the elephant
would rub its back on the tree trunk. I would wiggle my back
on the bed, shaking it. "Like this, Daddy?"

Then one day, my father would continue, the bird came
down from the tree and asked the elephant to stop shaking
the tree and making her nest fall to the ground. The elephant,
looking at the little bird, said, "I am much bigger than you.

What can you do to me?" He went on scratching his back on the tree.

Then the bird, screeching raucously, flung herself toward the elephant's ear and pecked at it until the tormented elephant promised to never rub his back on the bird's tree again.

"And so you see, Kalyana," my father would say as he tucked the blankets around me. "Even though the bird was little, she was not without power."

He would ask me again to show him how the elephant would rub his back on the trunk of the tree, and once again I would shake the bed and giggle. Eventually I would pull the blanket over my head, snuggle deeply beneath, and fall asleep, thinking about the elephant and the little bird.

2

I COULD SEE the sun rise from our kitchen window. It always started with a speck of deep orange far in the distance. Slowly the speck would become larger and larger, at last spreading across the sky in a brilliant fan. Then it seemed as though all of Fiji would light up. Birds would chirp. Caterpillars would awaken, stretching and yawning, wriggling their little bodies along leaves and twigs. Frogs would croak to clear their throats. Butterflies would spread their wings as the lizards disappeared into their holes. And the newspapers—they would lay claim that theirs was the first newspaper published in the world that day.

When I was younger, I thought this meant that *The Fiji Times* was the first newspaper ever published in the world. Mother had always said, "News reporters, Kalyana, have the best job in the world. Through the mighty power released from their pens, they can bridge the gap between solace and pain." Because of mother, I never doubted that news reporters were important people who were granted the duty to change humanity and erase its suffering. It made me so proud to have been born in a country that had discovered the business of printing news, the trade of exchanging stories. As I grew older though, I began to realize that I was terribly wrong: *The Fiji Times* did not discover the business of printing news; it was merely insisting that Fiji was the place that saw the first light of day.

Worse, years later, when all the timekeepers joined together to measure exactly which place on the globe saw the first morning light, a small island by New Zealand took the centuries-old title. The Fiji Islanders wept and scrambled to modify their timekeeping sheets, but alas! The truth was clear: Fiji was not the place where the first day of the entire world began.

It was like the Fijians had believed in something all their lives and then had it snatched away from under their feet, leaving their hearts and minds in chaos. Pillars supporting them had crumbled, toppling them unfeelingly toward the ground. My mother shook her head and clucked with disapproval as I devoured chocolates to bring the light back into my days.

First or second, however, the sun inevitably did rise upon Fiji. So did my mother, always the first to awaken in the household; none could contest that.

Manjula, my aunt, awoke second. My father rose third, and my brother, Raju, always woke last, whether it was the weekend or mid-week or a special occasion like Diwali or Holi or Raksha Bandhan. I would awaken mostly after Manjula, but sometimes after my mother.

Manjula was a great help to my mother. If my mother turned flour into dough and made *rotis* over the open fire,

Manjula swept the floors or soaked and cooked dhal and rice for lunch. If my mother pounded the clothes on the rocks and hung them outside on the line to dry, underwear, brassieres, and all, Manjula chopped the wood and heated drums of water for bathing. While my mother sprinkled spices over the chickpea and *masala* curry and stirred onions into a pot of tomatoes for dinner, Manjula gathered crisp garments from the clothesline outside and ironed them without a crease.

Occasionally there were other chores. The concrete stairs had to be scrubbed to rid them of the green mildew that kept appearing in the warm humidity of our island nation. The brass and steel pots always seemed in need of shining. My father's black leather shoes had to be polished every week to keep them sparkling and clean; I could see my reflection in them when Mother was done.

The drapes must be washed and the comforters put out in the sun to air. The doormats had to be beaten on the side of the concrete wall until they released a cloud of dust so thick that I sneezed ten times in a row. Sometimes, my mother or Manjula would take the green leaves of a coconut branch and gently slice them, leaving the mid rib intact, so that a cluster could be bundled and used as a broom. The remaining leaves would be woven into the baskets where my mother kept potatoes, onions, garlic, ginger, and eggs.

Then there was the food for storing. Roots must be pounded into masala, and dried coconuts grated and soaked in a large pot. When I had small feet, I was allowed to foot-crush the mixture so that all the goodness was squeezed out of the coconut. The milk would sit in a pot overnight, the oil and water slowly separating.

Manjula could not wait to pour the coconut oil into long-stemmed bottles and line them up on the windowsill. She would rub oil on her body, her hair, and her scalp. If I even approached the bottles, she would watch me closely as I poured a tiny pool of oil into the palm of my hand. "Enough. Enough. Enough. What are you doing?" she would rasp. "You don't need that much. It'll spill all over on the floor and leave a stain."

I would dart a furtive look toward her and linger around her precious bottles yet a little longer. Standing there, the tiniest smile playing around my lips, I would uncork this one and unscrew another. I would inhale the pungent aroma of the clear, yellowish oil, letting the scent pass through my body as though it were the last breath I would take on this earth.

Manjula would stand close to me and keep an anxiously watchful eye. Perhaps she feared that the bottle would slip from between my hands and crash to the ground, breaking glass and creating yet another chore for her. Or maybe she was simply afraid that all of the world's coconut oil would somehow evaporate into the atmosphere, leaving her vulnerable to her constant headaches.

Often Manjula would say that only coconut oil could cure a woman's pounding headache. My mother had laughed then. "Why would you need to develop a headache?" she said. "You sleep with Kalyana, fool!" Sometimes Manjula would roll her dark eyes and playfully slap my mother on the back. On darker days she would storm out of the house and head for the ocean.

I did not understand this talk of headaches and sleeping.

But even as a small child, I could see that Manjula's temper was like the waves of the mighty Pacific. It rose and fell as the tides came in and out.

Our house was a one-level wooden dwelling on stilts, complete with a concrete porch and a tin roof. It had only three bedrooms: my mother and father occupied one together, and my brother Raju slept in another. The third room was the one Manjula and I shared.

Manjula did not want to share a mattress with me. When I turned four, my mother had removed me from the bed she shared with my father and placed me in Manjula's—to the absolute dismay of my auntie. For three whole months, my mother told me, Manjula had walked around the house with a long face and puffed-up cheeks, refusing to acknowledge my mother's stories or my brother's requests for almond milk and chai. In the end, though, it did her no good. My mother never even considered relenting, and Father was similarly determined to ignore her shameful protests.

Manjula would frequently tell me that she wished I had been born a boy; that way, Raju would be the one sharing his room with me. Then she could continue to spread her legs and arms wide in the middle of her thin foam mattress and moan in the solitude of night. I never understood then what she meant, but during those years with me she must have yearned for her imaginary midnight lover.

Our room was filled with toys that my father had bought for me: stuffed animals and dolls with golden curls, crystal-blue eyes, and pink cheeks, and real china, toy trucks, and a red tricycle. Then there was the magnificent wooden dollhouse that my father had built for me himself. My most prized possession, however, was a miniature stove. I have never forgotten how I acquired it.

I was only five years old when, in the midst of shopping for food with my mother, I spotted a tiny model of a gas stove. It was stainless steel, with black plastic burners and golden plated plastic knobs. It came with its own matching pots and pans, though I no longer remember the colors.

The moment I set my eyes upon it, my heart fluttered and butterflies sprang around in my tubby belly. I dreamed of mixing marigold flowers with frangipani in those tiny pots, pretending that they held an array of Indian curries, and I pictured myself preparing mud pies and changing the knobs on the stove while squatting in front of it, just like my mother. I could even set it in my dollhouse, in the miniature cupboards right beside the sink.

I started off with a direct request to my mother. "I want this, Mummy."

"No."

I unleashed a series of pleas in varying tones and pitches. She batted her long eyelashes and rolled her large Indian eyes. I told her that if she got me the stove, I would wash all of the dishes after dinner. Her reply was quick: if I washed the dishes, she would have to rewash them. I told her that I would never, ever, ask her for anything again. She told me that she didn't believe me. I told her that I had been a good daughter since the time of my birth and was entitled to this baby stove. She turned around and started talking to the cashier.

Then I loosed my final strategy: I started wailing loudly in the middle of the store. People stared more at my poor mother than at me, though I was far too wrapped up in my own anguish to know or care.

My mother lifted me up from the ground as I thrashed my legs like a two-year-old child, and she and I left the store—me huffing, puffing, and screaming like the wolf in the story about the three little pigs. My mother was the brick house that wouldn't fall down.

I came home and went to bed. It was as though my mother had taken a sharp knife and made a small slash on the center of my soul, her first offense. But then again, who was keeping score? I was sure that because she, my protector and my giver, couldn't see blood, she must have thought that I was not in pain. But oh, my merciful gods, I was suffering. My tears were an endless river. My eyes were reddened, swollen, and hollow, and the beat of my heart was dull and muffled. There was no longer a fluttering rhythm in my chest.

When the clock struck five, I emerged from my room like one raised from the dead. I paced in front of the door, eyes to the ground and hands behind my back. When at last my father arrived home from his wood-carving shop, I let out my loudest wail and rushed towards him. He lifted me in his strong arms while I told him all about my mother and the miniature stove. He then did what I think all fathers should do: marched right back out to the store and bought the toy. I think that at that time my father's biggest fear was that the store would close before he could reach it.

When he saw the package, my brother shook his head. Manjula had no comment, but she pounded the dough more fiercely than usual; I was surprised that the rotis still rose and came out soft and tasty that night. And my mother, well, she fell angrily silent for the remainder of the day. But I loved my stove, and I think after that it was hard not to love Father best of all.

From time to time, Manjula would hide my miniature stove. I would find it in the strangest of places: underneath the mattress or behind the old dresser. Buried deep under petticoats and hemmed skirts in the wooden drawers. I would often catch Manjula kicking my toys around the room, too. She would always claim that it had been an accident, although I was fairly certain that there had been no accident at all. Over the years I grew to know every hiding place of Manjula's during the hours spent searching for my beloved stove.

Manjula also had a prized possession in the room we shared, a framed photograph of bees and birds flying around each other. My mother had given this to her on her thirty-first birthday, and it hung over the old brown dresser in our room. Manjula would stare at this picture often, the corners of her lips strangely turning upwards, while a glazed look would come over her eyes. It seemed as though she were entering a foreign land in an ultimate dream. It was engaging and entertaining, because I knew what she wanted: she was wishing that the bird would mount the bee. Or is it the bee that mounts the bird?

Lust's gripping thirst was palpable on her reddened lips. Its hunger was evident in her small, dark eyes. It was a great wonder that the men of the village didn't flock to her, considering the aura that she exuded with each mincing step and flirtatious flip of her hair. Even though my mother and she did not share physical similarities, she had a pretty face and enough dips and valleys on her body to make any warm-blooded man's heart stir.

Yet Manjula's one flaw seemed to mask everything else: Her left leg was shorter than her right, and she walked with a noticeable limp. Neighbors snickered and whispered whenever Manjula tramped down the gravel road leading to the ocean, and they were not discussing the flutter of her dark hair as the warm breeze floated through it. It was said that not only were her legs two different lengths, but that she was also missing both her big toes. Everyone was certain that she would die an old maid, untouched and innocent.

The ruthless neighbors weren't far from the truth. Gray hairs were already making an appearance around the edges of her square face, and fine lines had begun to grow at the corners of her eyes. For a woman, the thought of dying unwed and childless was next only to the thought of dying alone. Both were undesirable conditions. But I was more concerned about my auntie dying without a last name.

In those days, Indian women received only a middle name, awaiting marriage to begin using the surname of their husbands. My mother had only a middle name until she married my father when she was just sixteen. Sumitri Mani married her twenty-eight-year-old husband and became Sumitri Mani Seth. I also carried just two names, a first and a middle: Kalyana Mani.

If Manjula never found a husband, she would die only

as Manjula Mati. Even then, this was unthinkable to me. For of all the possessions in this world, your name is the one thing that is yours alone. It is that which separates you from another, something respected, something to protect. To carry only an incomplete name? What a tragedy!

Manjula, however, did not seem concerned about her lack of a last name or even about the neighbors' snickering and whispering over her missing big toes. Every evening she would hobble down the dusty gravel road to the ocean with her head high and her torso straight. She always wore long, colorful petticoats that she sewed for herself on the old wooden Singer sewing machine that my father had bought for my mother and that my mother had never used. I can still remember the sound of the machine rumbling deep into the night as Manjula sat in a tall chair in front of it, pedaling with her longer leg, her hands feeding yards and yards of fabric under the bobbing needle.

Sometimes Manjula would sew things for me, too. It might take some bribing, but eventually she would succumb to the feel of a crisp bill in the palm of her hand. My indulgent father would easily hand me ten dollars, and Manjula almost always settled for five out of the ten to finish the task of sewing me a dress of my choosing. She could sew cap sleeves, half-sleeves, high collars, low collars, or V-necks. If it was a more complicated project, like a frill at the collar or a flare at the arms or even a pleated skirt, she would demand seven dollars, to my utter dismay. Yet I would almost always lose negotiations, as she would refuse to lower her rate, knowing that I wanted that dress far more than the extra dollars I had to pay. I would consider my expenditure worthwhile when later I twirled and paraded around the village in my new frock.

News of her talents traveled far and wide, and soon every month Manjula had a new villager bringing printed and plain material, asking her to sew this dress or that skirt. I never understood how she did it without patterns or instructions, just exact measurements. She never forgot to charge a minimal fee to everyone and demanded payment up front. Although I discovered many of her hiding places over the years, I never found out where she stashed her money or what exactly she did with it. But she always delivered.

Though Manjula constantly kept her legs and feet covered with long petticoats, I always wondered whether the rumors were true. Could she truly be missing both her big toes? I often would try to stay awake until she fell asleep at night, hoping for the chance to lift up her *lengha* while she slept. I needed only the quickest glance at her feet to satisfy my curiosity for all time. But long before she would close her eyes, mine would become heavy with sleep, and before I knew it I would be lost to a world of dreams.

I never dared to ask Manjula about her toes, for I knew well what she would do if I did. She would backhand me across my face, leaving a red mark across my cheeks and making them swell. It would be done in haste, without thought to the consequences. Then I would need to lie to my father, saying that a hornet had stung me on my cheek, making it balloon like a pufferfish.

If my father came across the truth, then he must take a belt and beat Manjula as she huddled in a corner of the house, screaming and wailing for mercy. None would be bestowed on her, I knew, for I had once already seen my father beat her like this. Even though there was no blood, I was sure that there was pain. And I somehow knew that this suffering was unlike the one of which my mother frequently spoke.

The day Manjula was given her beating was the one day I remember my mother had no more stories left to tell. A heavy kind of silence fell upon our thatched-roof house, a brooding blankness so thick that at times I could almost feel the room stand still. I don't remember Manjula's crime any more. But I have never forgotten her punishment.

It made me think of Tulsi across the street and the suffering she endured at the hands of her husband, in front of her old widowed mother-in-law and her three grown boys. Her screams begging him to stop would vibrate through the village, and my father would turn up the news on the radio to drown out her cries. Manjula would disappear into our room for hours. My mother would bang pots and pans, heaving and cursing under her breath. She would slap the dining table and shake with fury. I was sure that she wanted to cross the street and stride into the neighbor's house, pulling the husband out by his ear and dumping him in the ocean, throwing the sharks a glowing feast.

But it never happened. Not at the hands of my mother and not from anyone else. The whole village would see Tulsi's bruises and black circles of horror around her eyes and yet turn away. To interfere with a man who was in the midst of disciplining his wife—regardless of her crime—was a distasteful concept. It was unthinkable.

3

IF SNAKES haunted my nights, my brother Raju troubled my days. My mother said that he was trouble even in her womb. He would kick, roll, and tumble inside her belly, making it difficult for her to catch even a wink of sleep. It was only when he slid out of her womb gently and easily that Raju gave my mother a moment's respite. Her blood didn't come in buckets that day, but only dribbled like a leaky faucet. From that day onward he was her baby Krishna and she was his Yashoda, the devoted mother who never saw the mischievous ways of her divine son.

Raju was about six years older than me, but definitely not wiser. His full name was Rajendra Seth. It was my mother who had first begun calling him Raju, and somewhere along the way his long name had disappeared. All that remained in memory was the twisted and shortened version: Raju Seth.

Raju tried to shorten my name too: from Kalyana to "Kali." He always hung out his tongue right after he bellowed "Kali!" and his antics inevitably sent Manjula into hysterical laughter. My mother would simply shake her head and tell Raju to take the rubbish to the bins outside.

Kali! Of all the words he could have chosen.

In Hindi, "Kali" signified two things. First was the Goddess of Destruction, a terrifying being who showed no mercy when she slit the throats of men and used their heads as her throne. She had blue skin and always hung her tongue outside her mouth. What was even more troublesome was that she wore a skirt of dismembered hands; in one of her four arms she carried a severed head with fresh blood dripping to the ground. Shockingly, she was often shown standing on the prostrate body of the powerful Lord Shiva himself.

My mother said that being called Kali was not a curse, for Mother Kali was symbolically a destroyer of ego. This, she said, was why Kali carried a sword in one of her four hands and a bowl of sweets in another. To those removed from the illusion of ego and immersed in the pursuit of spirituality, Mother Kali appeared sweet and affectionate, overflowing with a mystical love. My mother also said that Kali hung out her tongue because she enjoyed all of the world's tastes and cuisines—just as I did. She would then grab my fattened cheeks and squeeze them, causing me to scream and wriggle away.

Talk of the mighty Goddess Kali drew four peculiar old women to our living room for some *telanwa*—good, old-fashioned Indian gossip, though without the usual fresh scones, jam, and bubbling pot of tea—though only I could see them. My mother called them my imaginary friends—a symbol of my childhood, my innocence.

The first old woman blew in from the East like a strong,

cool breeze, plunked herself in the hollow of the sofa, and sat there, strong and sturdy. The second, moving with the fluidity and clarity of water, eased comfortably under the window. The third, burning hotter than the flames of fire itself, shuddered wildly like a fakir in the middle of the floor. And the fourth old woman, the one possessing the knowing confidence of a matriarch and bosoms large enough to feed ten dozen newborns, stood hunched at the entrance like the mighty Kali herself, carrying the weight of the world upon her shoulders. I called the fourth old woman "the Mother."

Each of the four old women tossed Raju's teasing comments back and forth in the air like a football, the colors of their auras—yellow, blue, red, and green—mingling into one form. Our small living room seemed to glow fiercely with their energy. The old women remarked enthusiastically that Shiva was Kali's husband, and yet she stood upon the powerful God himself, dissolving his power. Raju was a mere fool. The first old woman would poof her cheeks, urging me to blow hot air onto Raju's face, and when I followed suit it would make the other three women roll over on the floor, laughing hysterically.

Even though their lively presence would make me crack a smile, however, I could never see past the tongue, the blood, and the severed head, and refused to embrace the name "Kali." But some nights, trying not to hear Tulsi's piercing screams penetrating the quiet village, I would secretly wish that the spirit of Mother Kali would possess her body across the street. For how else could she find the courage to mightily step on her husband's head and dissolve his power?

The other thing the word "Kali" signified was not much

prettier than the first; it simply meant "dark-skinned." Whenever a child left her mother's womb and entered this world, the first question on everyone's mind was, "Is the child fair?" Not fair like the British, but sweetly brown like caramel. If the child was born with dark skin, like black olives of the Mediterranean, midwives circling the new mother would sigh and say, "What a pity!"

Fiji Indians practiced their own system of caste differentiation. While in India the levels were based on a family's occupation, in Fiji classes came to be defined by the shade and tone of the skin. Those with fairer skin were at the top of the chain and were, like the British and the Americans, a symbol of soaring superiority.

I put my arm up against Manjula's once, to compare our colors. She pushed my hand away abruptly and swiftly, shaking her head and frowning angrily. "Fool," she muttered under her breath.

"What a pity!"

I am sure that's what the four old women said when Manjula was born. She did not look like any one of us; her skin shade was darker than all of ours put together. Often I would wonder if Manjula's fate was tied to her skin and not her limp.

The white men made the decisions, had always made the decisions, it seemed. Whether in India or Fiji or especially in Africa, men with lighter skin had delegated futures, choices, and even life and death to those much darker than they. We were fairer than the Africans, and perhaps that is the reason that we escaped the branding and the shackles, but not the ill treatment.

I also knew that white men had done things that we could only marvel at. They had landed on the moon. The moon! They had landed on that white, round sphere itself. My mother said she was stirring custard on the kerosene stove when the news came that an American man had landed on the moon. Soon after his feet touched the rocky surface, this man declared, "That's one small step for a man, one giant leap for mankind."

For mankind he said, but this was hard to imagine. The American man—my mother didn't remember his name—had traveled to the moon, and here we were, still fighting for independence from British rule.

I did not want to be called "Kali."

What I wanted made no difference to Raju, however. He would hop about on his two thin legs, both fists up in the air, shouting "Kali!" and punching my arm.

I was sure I would be black and blue the next day. "Ma!" I would scream. "Look at what *bhaiya* is doing!"

Mother would come running. "What are you doing, Raju? Why are you tormenting your sister?"

Raju would continue jumping around like a fool, tight fists punching the air. Jokingly he would tell my mother that when I was older and married like every other respectable woman—at this point he would slip a sly look towards Manjula, who would purse her lips and leave the room—then I would stand strong and take my husband's beatings.

I told Raju that my husband would never beat me. If he dared, then I would deliver one swift kick to his buttocks and he would go sprawling down the porch steps into a muddy puddle. I would morph into a beautiful butterfly and fly away.

Raju looked at me, confused, as my mother chuckled and shook her head. "It would be one small step for you, and a giant leap for womankind," she said.

Raju still looked puzzled. "Then you would be divorced like the *goras*."

The gossip in Fiji was that after these women in Britain and America started wearing pants and going out to work, they began painting flowers on their faces and living with men who were not their brothers, fathers, or husbands. Sometimes they were divorced and took another man, and sometimes they would even enjoy all the sinful pleasures of marriage without any marriage at all! The villagers would cluck with disapproval, and it baffled me, too. To live with a man without the pundit chanting Sanskrit prayers over an open fire, without receiving your father's blessing, and without watching your mother's tears of happiness? To miss the feasting and celebrating with the whole family, yet to live in harmony and bliss, without shame, with a total stranger? My mother called it "shacking up" or "living in sin," but sometimes she called it "a movement." A movement? My mother said that's what the *goras* called it. She must have heard that on her transistor radio, too.

The four old women cohesively agreed that it wasn't a movement, no indeed. This had happened because the women in America and Britain were under the influence of clear liquids and magical herbs that made lions appear in streams, flowers sway in the winds, and walls heave. The four old women said that sometimes these magical substances made people dream that they could fly; some poor souls, thinking that they had wings, jumped right off the roof and cracked their skulls into a million pieces.

I never wanted to touch these strange liquids and herbs, let alone taste them. Still, what was this movement? I was curious.

The only day Raju didn't torment me as he usually did was on the full moon of the first monsoon month. This was when we would observe an ancient Hindu festival symbolizing the bond of protection between brothers and sisters. It was called the Raksha Bandhan.

On this day, Raju would awake with my interests in mind. When he broke a twig from the tree to clean his teeth, he would snap one for me as well. The twig was five inches long, and my brother would also bring me a lump of charcoal and leave it on the dresser by my mattress. When I awoke, I would chew the tip of the twig, shredding it and using it to brush my teeth. I would then take the block of charcoal and give my teeth a polish, making them flash whiter than a jasmine flower. When I was older, the twig turned into a toothbrush and the lump of coal into toothpaste, but Raju would leave them on the same dresser. The twig and coal could only be used once and thrown away, but the toothbrush and toothpaste would last for several months to come.

Raju would put on a crisply ironed flowery shirt and brightly-colored bell bottoms. He would don a flashy tie that Mother had bought for him just for this occasion. Then, sitting on Manjula's sewing chair, he would swing his legs and wait.

Legend held that when Krishna cut his finger in the war against an evil entity, Draupadi, a mortal woman, tore off a strip of cloth from her sari and wrapped it around Krishna's finger. Krishna, touched by her warm gesture, vowed to protect her like a brother. And years later, when her five husbands lost her to their archenemy in a roll of the dice, Krishna fulfilled his promise. When the evil Karavas attempted to unravel Draupadi's sari in the middle of their courtyard, shaming her husbands and challenging her honor, Krishna divinely elongated the sari to spare her from any indignities. On Raksha Bandhan, my brother must imitate this compassionate, brotherly side of the usually mischievous deity Krishna.

In anticipation of this yearly ritual, I would place incense, sweets, sandalwood paste, and a *diya* on a clean brass tray. Lighting the incense sticks and *diya*, I would circle my brother, who would sit through the ritual, gleaming at this unusual attention. I would put down the tray and tie a store-bought *rakhi* or Raksha Bandhan on his wrist, asking him for his devotion and protection. He would place his hand on my head, blessing my request with a silent acceptance. I would end the ceremony by putting some sandalwood paste on his forehead and offering him the sweet Indian candies he loved best. Then he would pull out a wrapped box from behind him.

This part of the ceremony was always my favorite. When I was younger, he would buy me dolls, pots, pans, and cars. As I grew older, the gifts turned more elaborate; I would unravel gold and silver earrings, necklaces, *bindia*, bracelets, and anklets with dangling bells that tinkled when I walked. Mother told me that he never accepted her contributions, but rather always insisted on buying these gifts with the money that Father would pay him for helping out in the shop.

Manjula would often stand at a distance, both hands behind her back, and watch me tie the *rakhi* on my brother's wrist. But when I opened my gift she would balloon her cheeks, walk away, and start sweeping the floors or shining the windows. Carefully, deliberately, she would keep her back towards Raju and the whole *rakhi* affair.

The seven brothers of my mother and Manjula never made the journey down from Ba, a rural town on the other side of the island. And yet my mother never seemed to care about their absence. Only one time did Uncle Chatur, my mother's oldest brother, came for Raksha Bandhan. My mother did not join the ceremony. She stood glumly in a corner and watched a beaming Manjula tie the *rakhi* on Uncle Chatur's wrist and feed him *gulab jamun* and sugar sticks.

After he left, my mother fell silent and took to bed. She slept curled tightly together, complaining of severe stomach cramps for days. Her eyes appeared swollen and reddened as though from frequent rubbing. Manjula sat at the edge of the mattress and stroked her back. My father told her to end her madness and cook some dhal.

Uncle Chatur never came for Raksha Bandhan again.

4

UNLIKE MANY of the Indians in our village, I had chestnut hair, lightly tanned skin, and light brown eyes. My mother would proudly declare to relatives and guests that I looked just like my father.

"Kalyana looks just like her father," she would say, one hand casually resting on the curve of her hip. The other hand usually bore a tray of fried foods—*bhajiya, saina, dalo,* and *cassava*. My mother was always the perfect hostess.

The relatives would nod their heads in agreement. "Yes, Sister. She looks much like her father." They sat on our sofa, chairs, and even cross-legged on the floor, for frequently the guests would outnumber the available seats.

Sometimes, one mischievous guest would smirk and say, "She looks like the British. Yes. Sumitri?" That one clever individual would pause, gazing around for effect. Some of the guests squirmed, but others boldly snickered or broke out in fits of laughter. My mother would roll her eyes, grasp the tray, and gently place it on the coffee table. She would lower herself onto the sofa and assume a stiff, unforgiving pose. For the rest of the evening, she would merely inject a curt "yes" or "no," into the conversation, giving only the impression that she was still paying attention.

After they left, my mother would take to bed, cursing and complaining about the insensitivities of the relatives. Look how her hard work was rewarded! She had even risen early in the morning to cook them not just two, but four types of fried dishes.

Manjula would stroke her back again, listening, offering advice like a plate of sweets. "Rajdev was born long after the system was abolished. Long after. It is not possible," my mother would complain.

"I know," offered Manjula sympathetically.

"There's no way that his mother suffered the fate of Surya. No way. No way at all."

"I know." Manjula nodded again.

Everyone in the village knew what had happened to Surya. Beautiful, as bright as the sun, and yet cursed, for she attracted the eye of a stranger. Surya, sweet Surya, whose honor was stolen in the looming shade of a sugarcane tree. He unraveled her sari and sliced her petticoat to threads. Surya, whose stomach swelled to the size of a pumpkin, whose ill fate took a physical form. When the child was born, there was little question; the village midwives pronounced her to be of British descent. Surya wrapped her naked baby in a soft white blanket before flinging herself and her newborn into the sea, choosing the bed of the ocean floor and the embrace of the warm waves over the endless scrutiny of the villagers and the words and stares that would follow her and her child all their lives.

"Just don't listen to what they say, Sumitri. You know how people are. They like to gossip about unnecessary things. You know how they like to cause trouble."

But my mother would not let it go. She would frown, speak angrily. How can they not honor Surya? For was it not after her death that they found their freedom from the British rule? Was it not her death that stirred an uproar in Great Britain, America, and India? That caused a movement? How can they forget?

"They have small minds, Sumitri. Just let it go. Do what I do. Go about your own business." Manjula would rub my mother's back, soothing her as though she were the mother and my own mother her unhappy child.

I was caught yet again in the word "movement," and I had questions of my own. A movement must be a powerful, mighty force that could cause such change. Was it like a hurricane that had the strength to raise the ocean waves and topple mighty ships like toys? Or was it more like a fire that started with a small spark and slowly grew in power, spreading over the hills and through the valleys? But then again, perhaps it was cooler in nature, a flood that swept through the towns, slowly sinking homes and fields. After all, my mother had said that the movement had traveled the world, even as far as our small island. And it had brought great change and rebirth, for it abolished all laws and all injustices against the Indian indentured laborers.

I chucked back the single remaining *bhajiya* on the silver tray as I sat contemplating the curiosity of it all.

I had no care in the world that my father looked like a British man. He was good man, and a respected man above all. When I was younger, he would pick me up and swing my legs over his shoulders and we would walk down to the ocean. When I grew older, he would simply take my hand. We would stroll to the sea, basking in the first rays of the morning sun.

Whenever my father strode along the dusty road, young boys looked to the ground or scurried to hide behind the trunk of a large mango tree. Once one of the boys, out of respect, even discreetly shoved his burning cigarette butt in his pants pocket when he spotted my father coming towards him. "Loafers," my father had called them under his breath. "Useless skins." I felt tall, walking beside my father.

As we walked down the dusty path, he would tell me stories of long, long ago. Akbar the Great, the Mogul emperor, had ruled India from 1542 to 1605. My father would tell me tales about Akbar's encounters with a great man, Birbal, who was common and yet was known for his valuable advice, his wit, and his sense of humor. My favorite story was the one about bananas.

My father never told stories with the same color and enthusiasm that my mother would use; he spoke as though he were a historian relaying facts. Yet his tales fascinated me. He had a low, deep voice, and he spoke softly and slowly. Any normal five-year-old would have fallen asleep on his shoulders, but I clung to my father's every word.

The Emperor, he said, had once invited Birbal to the court to share a basket of bananas. The Emperor devoured several of the yellow fruit and threw the peels over to Birbal's side. When all the bananas were eaten, the Emperor laughed at Birbal and said, "Birbal, you are such a greedy person. Look at how many bananas you ate in one sitting!"

Birbal took a minute of silence to gather his thoughts. Then he said, "Maharajah Akbar, unlike you, at least I spared the peels." And Birbal, with a smirk on his face, lowered his head and stared at the ground.

"What did the Emperor do, Father?"

"Nothing!"

"Why nothing?"

"He probably didn't know what to do. Birbal had out-smarted him again."

I wanted to be like Birbal and outsmart the world one day. I would fantasize about this while sitting on top of my father's shoulders, clutching his chestnut-brown hair and lis-tening to him tell story upon story as the sun slowly rose. Unlike my mother's tales, Father's stories would twist my mind in knots, puzzling it. Yet they all made me smile. For this reason, I loved going to the beach with my father in the early-morning hours.

By the waters, sometimes we would encounter the extraordinary. We would glimpse naked Fijians, men and women with light-brown skin and Afro-styled hair, tangled in passionate embraces under the rich coconut trees along the beach. Some would be moving rhythmically, panting and moaning, kissing and biting in a mad frenzy, as the first ray of sunlight flickered off their shiny, tanned skins.

I would feel a strange rush, not describable in ordinary words, possess my immature body. My father would stiffen under my weight as the naked women turned their heads over their shoulders, the small of their backs arched and their hands placed solidly on the ground behind them. They would look directly at us with dark, devilish glints in their eyes and lustful grins spreading across their flushed faces. One woman had a tiny tattoo of a butterfly visible on her naked back. I could not stop staring.

My father would clutch my dangling legs, turn around, and hurriedly walk back home. Yet that same night, as I tried to imitate the Fijians' strange actions in my bed (to Manjula's utter amusement), I would hear my father making the same noises with my silent mother in the next room.

5

MANJULA TOOK me to the ocean, too, when the tide was low. She would grab my arm and limp all the way there, both of us barefoot, ignoring the villagers' stares and even their polite greetings. Manjula never stopped to look at people or even speak to them. "Best to mind your own business," she would say.

I would squat down on the stone wall and stare stubbornly at her. I did not want to mind my own business. And I definitely did not want to help her catch prawns and spear crabs.

"Come, Kalyana," she would say impatiently, forcefully gripping me beneath my arms and dropping me down on the sand. Tiny orange crabs, feeling the vibration of our footsteps, scurried towards their holes. In the distance small fishing boats bobbed up and down on the waves. The breeze would feel warm against my bare skin.

Sometimes, if the sun was still high, Manjula would lean her spear against the seawall. Instead of gathering crabs, she would waste time: limping all over the beach, grinning and inspecting seashells, sometimes even shamelessly slipping one in her brassiere. She would find conch shells and hold them to her ear. "Listen, listen," she would say plastering the shell to my ear, and as though she had made an amazing discovery, a triumphant grin would erupt on her small face.

I would hear the whistle of the winds and the sound of the waves of the ocean trapped in this shell. The sound always filled me with a simple joy. It made me wish that the day with my auntie would not end, that the night would never fall.

Because, when the sun began to disappear in the far horizon, drawing the tide in to the shore, Manjula would bring out her spear and stab the shallow waters, aiming for the little claw marks in the sand. My job was to carry the large burlap bag that would hold the live crabs. If the bag became too heavy, I would have to drag it across the wet sands.

Manjula would tell me to pay attention, but I could only stand still and imagine the crabs clawing and climbing their way out of the bag to crawl all over me, nipping me until I was bloody. Until I was dead. "Are you cold? What's the matter with you, Kalyana?" Manjula would sound frustrated. I could only shake my head, unable to speak, and Manjula would shrug and continue piling crabs on top of each other in the beige sack.

As time stood still, I would picture in the clearest detail my imminent death. When the tide came in, it would surely take my dead body with it to the distant islands. Cannibals must live there, I was certain; my mother had told me stories. When the sea swallowed the sun and darkness wrapped its claws around the tiny island of Fiji, they would emerge from their caves, beating their drums and pounding their feet.

They would shout and yell and light blazing fires, illuminating the night as they danced and sang strange, sacred songs until sunrise.

Manjula would go on spearing prawns and crabs and putting them in the burlap bag.

At home I was no longer afraid of the crabs, but still I was rigid. The crabs, piled on top of one another, would shiver and cry in the sack as Manjula boiled a pot of water on the kerosene stove on the floor. She would squat beside the heating water, take the crabs out of the bag one by one, and place them on a wooden board in front of her. The crabs would hurriedly crawl to get away, snapping their claws, but Manjula's strong hands always reached out and stopped them. She would pull them back and separate their claws from their bodies with a large chopping knife before dropping them in the boiling water. I could see the crabs' round, black eyes blink and peer at me in horror.

Feeling helpless, I would sit at the kitchen table and watch their affliction, and do nothing. What could I do? I was only a child.

Manjula would curry the crabs and make rice. She would wear her best dress for this occasion, though I was never sure why. My brother and father remained dressed in their khaki shorts and torn white T-shirts, and my mother wore her usual petticoat and *kurta*, proudly showing off her slender midriff. Guests didn't line up at the door to celebrate Krishna's birth or Rama's successes or Mother Kali's wrath. There was no such religious ceremony that required Manjula to powder her face, drop *kajal* in her eyes, and rouge the bones of her cheeks or slip into her brightest and loudest frock.

Yet this did not stop Manjula from marking her catch as a celebrated occasion. She would hobble around the table, eagerly serving our family, urging them to "Eat, eat!" as she passed around the bowls.

I would stare at the lifeless pieces floating in the brown juice in my bowl. Despite my mother's offer to crack the shells for me, I could only shake my head and continue staring, solemnly remembering how they scuttled freely across the beach, safe and sound beneath their protective shells. Everyone around the table would crack the shells with their teeth and indulge in the soft, white meat, slurping the juices from the claws and making wet noises of which I was sure the *goras* would disapprove.

Feeling sick to my stomach, I would leave the table and go to my room. Manjula would roll her eyes and shake her head in frustration. She never said anything aloud, but through the transparent white mosquito net that hung from the ceilings above our mattress, I could tell what she was thinking through her grunts. *You ungrateful, spoiled beast. With an attitude like that, no man will ever marry you, Kalyana. You will never own a last name.*

I was to receive my last name much sooner, however. It came through the grace of a balding, fat-bellied headmaster shortly after I had matured to the fine age of six. The headmaster called it a "surname."

I knew this was an auspicious occasion because of the new shoes. Black, open-toed leather sandals constricted my feet and made my toes feel trapped; the silver buckle on the sides dug into my ankles, and the stiff, unfamiliar leather felt hard against my soft skin. I hated those shoes. I wanted to snatch them off my feet and throw them in the ocean, then spread my toes and let the breeze and dirt rush through them. Yet I stood tall in them, with my hair oiled, parted in the middle, pulled back, and braided in two.

My mother had dressed me in a new lemon-yellow dress that buttoned all the way down the front. It had a pocket on the left breast and the middle was cinched with a thick cloth belt made from a darker shade of the same material.

When my mother had asked Manjula to sew me the dress, I had immediately been interested. A brand-new frock, especially for me? But then I saw the lemon-yellow color. I was disappointed; I would have preferred pale blue, the color of my favorite piece in the Ludo board game that my mother, Manjula, Raju, and I would play on dull, rainy afternoons. Blue was the color of tranquility, the color of the skies and the ocean waters. It reminded me of my second old woman, a pillar of calm wisdom and insight.

My mother most appropriately chose the red piece. When she played the game, the air around the square board would crackle with her burning desire to land a six or bump her opponents off the squares. My mother would smile as she sent us home to await the roll of six on the black-and-white die while she, like some victorious goddess, led all of her red pieces to the safety of the circle.

Raju always chose green. Perhaps he thought it resembled the color of money and that choosing it would easily make him a winner in the game of Ludo. I think he forgot to factor in luck, for he usually lost all games, to my distinct enjoyment. Yet Raju never gave up, begging and begging for another chance to play. Finally my mother, Manjula, and I would walk away from the board, smirking. Poor Raju would sit there for a long while afterward, staring sullenly at the abandoned pieces.

Yellow was Manjula's color. I did not want a yellow dress.

I protested silently, sitting on the kitchen mat and refusing to speak. My mother paid me no heed. She matched the hideous yellow material with a similar fabric and smiled. Now Manjula must use her gift and sew the yards of fabric into a high-collared dress, three-quarters of an inch from the knee in length.

Mother and Manjula forced me to stand for measurements. I stretched my arms wide like the wings of an airplane and sullenly watched Manjula measure my chest, waist, hips, and arms. When Manjula measured my mid-section, she shook her head and said, "Too fat." My mother laughed loudly, frightening the lizards. As they disappeared back into their holes, I thought of the third old woman, the one who burned hotter than the fires of the sun itself. I curled my hands into tight fists, fighting the deep surge of black heat that threatened to burst forth and erupt onto Manjula's head. I wanted to run, hit, destroy, but the second old woman stroked me gently until my rage subsided. I bit the insides of my cheeks and glowered.

Manjula wrote the measurements on a flimsy sheet of paper. Her fingers flew and scissors flashed as she cut the material in bits and pieces. The designs did not make sense to me at all, but Manjula always knew what she was doing.

My mother would intently watch Manjula hard at work, but could not keep herself from commenting. "It's such a pity," she would say. "No man notices your skills." I remained quiet and watched her carefully put together an ugly lemon-yellow dress. She called it a uniform.

I would have hated the dress even more if I had realized what it meant, how my life would now change.

I wore this uniform a week later when my mother brought me before the headmaster. He must be important—the most important man I had seen in my lifetime, other than my father—for he sat behind an enormous desk. Black, red, and silver pens stood arrayed in a golden penholder in front of him. Stacks of papers lay beneath his meaty hands.

And his chair! I had never before seen a chair that could turn around and around like the blue globe sitting on the shelf. Fascinated, I watched as it twisted and moved while its owner shifted his ponderous bulk to reach across the desk for a sheaf of papers. My mother, in her straight-backed chair that did not move, fidgeted. She gazed at the floor as she fingered the edge of her green sari, which was wrapped around her shoulders in modest form. Today her taut belly was carefully covered.

The solemn man informed my mother that a late registration presented no difficulty, even though the school had already been in session for two weeks. The headmaster was an Indian man, but unlike my father he used too many English words in his short and direct speech. Rapidly he fired one question after another, and my mother answered them in order. She kept her eyes on the floor.

"Name of the child?"

"Kalyana, Headmaster *ji*."

"Full name?"

"Kalyana Mani, Headmaster *ji*."

"Surname?"

"Surname?"

"What is the child's last name?" My mother raised her face and the headmaster's cold eyes looked directly into hers. His stern face betrayed no warmth.

"She's a girl, Headmaster *ji*. She will not receive her last name until the priest chants the Sanskrit prayers over the open fires and her hand is joined with that of a man." My mother humbly smiled.

The headmaster looked at the papers on his desk, then at us. A glimmer of disgust played around his nostrils. "Mrs. Seth, every child, boy or girl, admitted to the school needs to have a surname. British rules. A middle name won't suffice."

Admitted! The word tumbled around in my brain, twisting and turning like the swivel chair on which the fat headmaster's plump buttocks rested. *Admitted!* A bubble of anxiety rose from the pit of my belly. I struggled to take in life-giving oxygen as I grasped my mother's sari. My palms felt sweaty. I was gasping for breath.

The headmaster threw me a confused glance. My mother patted the top of my head. I clutched her sari still more tightly, pulling it taut around her shoulder and wrapping the edges around my wrist as though to anchor me to safety.

"She's always stricken with worry, Headmaster *ji*." My

mother tilted her head to one side, making an apologetic gesture. "What to do?"

The headmaster rose from his chair and strode to the corner of the room. He picked up the blue globe and set it on the desk in front of us. With his index finger he flicked it into motion, and I almost forgot my fear as it spun wildly, madly, like a ball affixed to a spindle. Then with great suddenness, the headmaster thumped his large hand on one rounded side of the globe. The globe obeyed its owner's command and stopped mid-twirl.

The headmaster took his finger and pointed to a small speck on the globe. "See this, child," he said officiously. "This is Fiji. It sits right above Australia and right below the equator. See here." He pointed to another speck on the globe. "This is Tonga, our nearest neighbor."

I stared at the dots on the globe, wide-eyed. The distraction did not ease my anxiety.

The headmaster stood tall behind his desk, fastening his gaze onto me. "Do you know why Fiji is marked on the globe with a tiny dot?" he asked, pointing to the small speck in the vastness of blue. The blue seemed to be everywhere. I had never given thought to the greatness of the oceans.

I shook my head, unable to speak.

"The legends tell that Fiji is so large that they couldn't put it on the map. So the mapmakers marked it with a tiny dot." Throwing his head back, he laughed loudly at his own joke. Then he eyed me from my head to my toes. "Seth," he said firmly. "From now on your surname is Seth."

He sat back down in his swivel chair and filled out the forms. At the top of the first page, in block letters and in ink, he wrote KALYANA MANI SETH. I knew how to read this much; my mother had taught me how to write my name when she taught my father how to write his. Now Father would no longer have to press his thumb on the ink pad, she said. He could write like a man. I remembered seeing the pen in his fingers, inscribing the words "Rajdev Seth." Now the plump fingers of the headmaster were joining my name with my father's name. *Kalyana Seth*.

The headmaster stopped writing and looked up. "Now it's official," he said.

My mother got up to leave. I tried to follow her out of the office, still desperately gripping the end of her sari. The headmaster reached out his large arm and grabbed the corner of my lemon-yellow dress. I turned around in horror, staring at the large hand grasping the end of my new frock.

My mother tried to break the grip of my hand on her sari, but the fabric was tightly wrapped around my wrist. Her sari began to unravel from her shoulders, exposing the soft skin under her blouse. She gasped and pulled her sari back around her. The headmaster tugged harder.

The headmaster was on one side, my mother on the other, and I, Kalyana Mani, who now had the official last name Seth, stood in the middle, shaking with terror. In the midst of my panic I realized a desperate need to find a place to urinate. I started to scream as tears welled up in my eyes and dropped to the concrete floor.

"Let go!" insisted the headmaster.

I wailed louder. The four old women stood silently, one in each corner of the room, wringing their hands, brows furrowed. They looked worried.

"Now, Kalyana," pleaded my mother.

My wails increased in frequency and pitch. My howls were louder than any conch shell blown by an ancient sage. My breath came in gasps, while the pit of my stomach churned in circles. Without a doubt, I knew that I was being "admitted." Now, more than ever, was I certain of the meaning of this evil word.

I had heard it only twice before in my lifetime. The first was when Uncle Mathur, my mother's third-youngest brother, was shipped from Ba to Suva. I overheard my mother tell Manjula that his condition was serious and that he was being admitted to the Suva City Hospital. "Admitted" was the only *angrezi*, or English, word she used in the whole conversation.

But it stayed with me, because a few days later, a blanket of sadness fell over our whole household. Uncle Mathur slept quietly in a rectangular box, his eyes tightly shut, listless and lifeless. I had lined up behind the adults to get a last look and watched as my mother took a silver teaspoon of crystal-clear water and dropped it into his open mouth. Afterward, family and friends and many people I did not know gathered in a circle, and the wailing began; women and men beat their chests, pulled their hair, and howled. Nobody wore color on that bleak and dreary day, only a single shade of purest white. Through it all, Uncle Mathur slept, frozen in time. It had all begun when he had been admitted to the hospital.

The second time I heard the word "admitted" was when it happened to the daughter of one of my other uncles. The rumor among the aunties was that Shilpa Mani had ripped off all her clothes and run through seven villages, screaming that the seven-headed demons were coming. Amidst her insistence that they had five arms and two horns, she was admitted to the Mental Institute. I heard my mother sadly tell Manjula that poor Shilpa was in a dire state.

We went to visit her there. Because of my age, I wasn't allowed to enter the glass doors of the stark white building. Instead, I sat on a wooden bench outside with Manjula, under the shade of a low-hanging jackfruit tree.

I saw Manjula steal two jackfruits that day. She quickly glanced over her shoulder, then broke them off the hanging branch above us and deftly packed them into the large wicker bag that hung over her shoulder. Winking at me, she said, "We'll cook later. Jackfruit curry for dinner tonight. Okay?"

I sat there with my mouth open, shaking my head at Manjula. Yet before I could speak a word, my mother emerged from the Institute, looking solemn. She paid me no attention, addressing Manjula only.

"I feel a lot of worry for little Shilpa," she said helplessly. "They keep her strapped onto her bed in a locked room. She can't move her hands or feet at all. Every morning, they give her brain an electric shock." My mother rested her hand on her chest as she delivered this grim tale.

She shook her head. "Shilpa's never getting out of there. Her condition is dire."

We never went back to the Mental Institute.

I thought back to Uncle Mathur lying lifeless in his small box and then of Shilpa's ill fate. And here I was, Kalyana Mani Seth, at the tender age of six, being admitted to a concrete building called Mahatma Gandhi Memorial Primary School.

I wrapped my arms around my mother's waist, wailing.

"Let go, Kalyana," she said through gritted teeth, looking briefly up at the headmaster in embarrassment. "Let go."

In the end, she was stronger than I. She firmly grasped my hand, digging her nails into my palm until she could untangle her silk sari from my wrist. She pushed me towards the headmaster, who was still holding onto my dress. I watched her walk through the door, down the concrete stairs, away from the building, and onto the pavement. The further away she walked from me, the smaller she appeared.

I continued to wail. I was to be admitted, and my own mother had abandoned me; and worse, there was no toilet, pit or otherwise, in sight. Desperately I tried to shake free from the headmaster, squeezing my legs together yet knowing that at any minute the yellow liquid would flow from me and spill onto the cold floor. The headmaster ordered silence. "Be still!" he commanded. When I failed to obey, he opened his drawer and took out a long stick, red in color and about half an inch in diameter. He bent me over the edge of his swivel chair, lifted my new lemon-yellow dress, pulled down my underwear, and brought down the stick on my buttocks— once, twice, and thrice.

I could hear the sage blow the conch shell in the distance, and the water wash up against the seawall, and the pundit blow on his *bansuri*, and the frogs croaking in the stillness of night. I heard the strum of an enormous sitar, and the quiet hum of the harmonica, and the howls of the wind, and the echo of a charmer's flute. My father's hands beat on the tabla as my urine flowed down the side of the headmaster's swivel chair and onto my new black flat shoes. The sting of the stick fell on my behind exactly three times that day.

I stopped crying and started gasping for breath. The head-master, with a disgusted expression, gave me a clean cloth and ordered me to wipe his chair. Reluctantly I obeyed, but my heart was black inside. I prayed to God that the stench of my urine might glaze his floors and remain trapped within these walls forever and ever. I wished that the four old women would squat in every corner of his office and urinate fiercely too, creating a warm yellow river in the middle of the cruel headmaster's quarters. My behind still smarted from the pain and indignity of the stick.

News of the red stick and my incontinence reached my mother. She brought clean, white underwear in a plastic bag, along with a new dress. I didn't see her bring these items to me, however; I was shut behind the cement walls with a toilet and a tap that poured water straight into a concrete drain. I had never seen water pour from a tap, and I was fascinated with my ability to turn the faucet on and off and run my fingers through the water. It made me temporarily forget my burning behind.

When I limped home that afternoon, Manjula was quick to chastise me. "Fool," she said, "Ungrateful fool. Now you hate school." Manjula shook her head at my lost future.

The stick had left red welts on my tender brown skin. For a week I had to sleep on my stomach and keep my but-tocks up in the air. School would be out of the question for the duration of the healing, and Manjula was given the duty of fanning me the instant a moan escaped my lips. A burn-ing sensation radiated from my behind throughout my entire being, though not a single drop of blood had been shed.

My father shook with fury as he paced around our small

house. My mother restrained him from going to the school. She knew my father wanted nothing more than to pull the fat, bald headmaster from his swivel chair, drag him onto the concrete stairs of the school, and beat him with his own red stick. Beat him until his own behind smarted and bloodless pain flowed throughout his body.

"Think about Kalyana's future," Mother pleaded. "Without education, the man that marries her will be wearing only a blue collar. What future will she have without education, Rajdev?"

Yet that day I learned that my future was to be one of security and prosperity.

As I stood sniffling and moaning in a corner on the day of my beating, a deafening drum roll and loud chanting and singing stopped all conversation about the headmaster and sent my mother scurrying for the kitchen. She gathered bowls of flour, potatoes, carrots, and onions, as my father gravely watched the procession. A group of Hare Krishna devotees approached: men and women, barefoot and clad in vivid orange and yellow robes.

My mother motioned for me to come forth. I hobbled to her like Manjula, my body aching. Mother put the provisions into a big silver bowl and told me to drop the items into the visitors' sacks. I walked gingerly through the front door, my mother close behind.

The devotees were dancing and singing songs I did not understand. I looked into their eyes. Their faces were frightening: needle piercings from one end to the other. Some heads were shaved entirely, but some boasted hair that grew to their knees. They all smelled like sandalwood and turmeric and had scars and strange piercings that covered their faces, hands, feet, and bodies. I shuddered and willed my feet forward.

An unusually dark-skinned women fixed her protruding eyes upon me as I stood there holding my heart in my hands along with the bowl of offerings. Her companions danced circles around me and my mother, chanting and beating drums. The strange woman held out her empty sack, her eyes never once straying from their keen gaze upon me. I tipped the silver bowl, dropping the rations into it, keeping my own eyes firmly focused on the inside of the canvas sack.

The moment the silver bowl was emptied, the dark-skinned woman closed the sack and flung it over her left shoulder. With her other hand, she grabbed me by the hair and pulled me closer to her. Wild winds of storm rushed through my mind, and I could feel her lift me and drag me into a strange new life. They would pierce my cheeks, lips, and hands with long, thin needles and brand my forehead with strange symbols. My brown locks would fall upon the ground all around me as they shaved my head. I would be clothed in a lemon-yellow Hare Krishna uniform, admitting me to their ashram and sentencing me to a lifetime of godly devotion. As my mother had told me time after time, life was simply unfair.

And yet it was not to be. The dark-skinned woman merely cracked a small smile, exposing a space where she was missing two front teeth. She laid her bony hands on my head and, in a chilling voice, whispered in Hindi, "Bless you, child. You shall prosper."

My mother patted my head happily. I had received the devotees' blessing in return for my selfless giving, and perhaps now my future would be assured.

As for me, I was less interested in future prosperity and more keen to examine the strangeness of our visitors. "Why do they have needles going through their cheeks?"

"Kalyana, they embrace suffering. It's a symbol of their devotion to their Lord Krishna."

"What does suffering have to do with devotion?"

"Kalyana, it is in suffering that we are most connected to God."

I didn't believe my mother. How could pain be the way to immortality?

My mother paused and looked intently at me. "Your mind is greater than your physical being, Kalyana. If you believe there's no pain, then you simply won't feel pain." She stroked my hair. "Later," she said, "these devotees will cross a pit of burning coals barefoot, and the soles of their feet will remain intact and unscarred. There aren't many in the world like them. They are extraordinary—beyond human."

I was feeling the burn on my behind, but in my own agony I had not felt a divine connection or the spark of a godly presence. Yet, in an odd way, I had bonded with Tulsi across the street. I was connected with the memory of Manjula huddled in the corner as my father rained down the beatings on her. I was even somehow linked with my own ancestors, who had crossed the great Pacific Sea and gracefully accepted the lashes that fell on the creases and curves of their hollow backs.

There were two kinds of people in this world: one was the

headmaster, the other the student. The headmaster had the control and the power to bestow the beatings. The student had the task of learning the lessons.

6

I RETURNED TO school, where I learned to spell and write words in the English language, the language of the British people. Every evening after dinner, I would spread my schoolwork in the middle of the mattress I shared with Manjula, and practice writing and spelling big words: "E-l-e-p-h-a-n-t." Manjula, with a curious look on her face, would come into the room and sit on the floor beside me, flipping through my books with wide, eager eyes. Sometimes she would inject words and sounds such as, "Hm. Huh. Hahn." She would look up to me, and I would see question marks in her eyes.

"Manjula, do you know how to spell 'elephant'?"

Manjula pasted a stubborn smirk on her lips and proceeded with pride. "E-l-e-f-a-n-t." And then she raised her eyebrow in a triumphant style.

"It's p-h-a-n-t. Not f-a-n-t."

Manjula would fling my books at me and grunt whenever I corrected her. "How would I know how to spell 'elephant' in *angrezi*, fool?" She would release a string of justifications and explanations: "I was taken out of school at the age of ten, so that I could help my mother care for your mother and our brothers when your mother was a baby!" Now she was hissing with anger. "It wasn't like what it is now. Going to school was a privilege, not a right, back in my day, when I was young." Then, in a higher pitch, shaking her head, she squealed, "How would I know how to spell 'elephant' in English?"

She said the word English strangely. *Ingalish*.

"I wasn't taught to spell in Ingalish," she would snap. "If I went to school like you, then I would know how to spell 'elephant' and five or ten other big words. You think I can't learn?" With that she would stalk out of our room, muttering under her breath. "Now that you go to school, you think I am stupid!"

After several practices alone in my bedroom, I was ready to stand in the middle of the kitchen in front of my mother, hands behind my back, and spell the word "elephant" two times. I was just four feet tall, but I towered over my audience. Raju mocked me, saying that he had been spelling the word "elephant" for years. Manjula pouted in a corner. My father sat by the table, with his head held up high in the air and a proud smile on his gentle face. He said nothing, but reached out to pat my back.

My mother did the usual: she took center stage. She stood up in the middle of the room, flinging her bright blue dupatta over her shoulder and shaking her slim hips, and proceeded to entertain her audience. "Elephants are treasured animals in India, Kalyana. Did I ever tell you the story of how the Lord Ganesha got his head?"

I shook my head, even though I had heard the story before.

My mother tied her long dupatta around the waist of her petticoat and broke out into a soft song. She had long ago claimed to have written the song, on a rainy Sunday morning, when the household was asleep, and Father was puttering mercilessly in the yard. She swayed in the calm of the living room, retelling the famous legend:

It happened a long time ago, in Satyug.
Listen, O devotee, to the story of Ganpati Baba.
Ganpati Baba, Ganpati Baba,
The son of the divine Parvati Ma.

Legends say that Parvati Ma made a statue of clay
In the early, early hours of the morning
When the sun emerged above the Himalayas
And the birds flew to take refuge in their nests.

Legends say that the divine Parvati Ma
Blew the breath of life into the clay
And from it emerged a young boy.
She asked him to guard her temple as she slept.

It happened a long time ago in Satyug.
Listen, O devotee, to the story of Ganpati Baba.
Ganpati Baba, Ganpati Baba,
The son of the divine Parvati Ma.

Legends say along came Shiva ji, her heart, her love.
The young boy denied him entry into the temple.

Infuriated, Shiva ji took his trishul
And beheaded the young boy made from clay.
Legends say that the head of the boy made from clay
Fell on the ground, shaking the earth,
Awakening the divine Parvati Ma.
In anger, she made a final request.

It happened a long time ago in Satyug.
Listen, O devotee, to the story of Ganpati Baba.
Ganpati Baba, Ganpati Baba,
The son of the divine Parvati Ma.

Legends say that said the divine Parvati Ma
To Shiva ji, that if he could find a newborn
That has yet to see his mother's face
He was to bring the child's head to her as a gift.

Legends say that Shiva ji looked and looked
Into all four corners of the world.
And found only a newborn elephant
That slept with his head facing towards the north.

It happened a long time ago in Satyug.
Listen, O devotee, to the story of Ganpati Baba.
Ganpati Baba, Ganpati Baba,
The son of the divine Parvati Ma.

Legends say that Shiva ji beheaded the baby elephant
And brought his head to Parvati Ma,
And she put it on top of the boy created from clay,

Bringing him back to time of being.
Ganpati Baba, Ganpati Baba, Ganpati Baba, Morya.

The song was so lively, my mother's dancing so vivid, that I had to join in; I was bouncing up and down on my seat and tapping my feet on the ground with more enthusiasm than rhythm. With a theatrical bow and a flashing smile on her face, my mother finished her song and dance. "That," she said, "is why we all bow to him and say, 'Jai Hind, glory to him.'"

7

THREE MONTHS after I had started school, I found myself sitting in the middle of the kitchen on a wooden chair, surrounded by newspapers. Manjula took a small, round bowl from a shelf, and upon my mother's instruction she put it on top of my head.

"*Pyala* cut," she said.

Manjula held the bowl in place as my mother cut my hair around it. They talked about things I didn't understand. After ninety-six years in coming, Independence Day was set: October 10 was the final date. Prince Charles himself would be in attendance, representing Queen Elizabeth at this propitious occasion. I did not know what this "Independence" could be, but I knew there would be great festivities. Would there be a bride and a groom? Would the pundit blow the conch shell, a symbol of bliss, celebration, and auspiciousness? Then its reverberation, mirroring the sound of Om, would vibrate through the rivers and sea, and the creeks and valleys of Viti Levu. Their conversation distracted me as snippets of my brown curls fell to the ground, covering the world news.

"Much better, hey, Kalyana! What do you think? It was too much work every morning to wash, oil, part, and braid your hair for school." My mother patted my head. "Much, much better! You'll feel so much cooler now in the hot days when the breeze is still and the salty air is humid." Then with a twisted smile, she said, "Thank goodness the women of America went mad. Now women all over the world can cut their hair as short as a man's. *Jai Hind* to the women of America!"

The four old women danced a fast, rhythmic dance, their arms up in the air and their large behinds creating a hurricane in the middle of our living room. They stood around in a circle and sang songs of the American women going mad.

I did not join in. Like a tree stump I remained lodged in my chair, pouting. My nostrils flared flames. How could my mother think that this was the best style to complement my round, female face? She must have lost her marbles, like Father sometimes said after her elaborate theatrical performances.

"Oh Kalyana, even the Beatles of Great Britain fancied this style." My mother thumped my back lovingly and then walked away, as Manjula swept my chestnut brown locks off the floor and into the rubbish bin.

"Beatles?" So insects fancied this style. I sat with a frown marring my features. The women in America were not the only ones who had gone mad.

There was a triumphant grin on Manjula's face as she disposed of my beloved curls. She showed no compassion as she heartlessly powdered my neck and back with talcum powder, blowing away any remaining brown strands. My neck and back felt itchy.

"Don't scratch!" Manjula hit my hand every time I tried. "Sores will break out!"

She stared into my face, a condescending glint in her eyes. "Do you want to go to school with sores all over your body? What if you meet a boy in school? Do you want him to see?"

I shook my head mutely.

"Then don't scratch! He will reject you for sure, then."

I tried to follow my aunt's direction. But as the tingling sensation overtook my body, I could not stop myself from scratching my neck and my back. Digging my nails into the skin transported me to the heavens above. I thought of the Hare Krishna devotees and their long needles. When no one was watching, I dug my nails deeper into the skin, moving on to the little red bumps on my legs as well. Manjula called them mosquito bites.

As it happened, Manjula was partly right; sores erupted on both my legs, and yellow pus filled the boil-like eruptions. I did not want to go to school with pus-filled sores on both my legs. I complained of stomach cramps, but my mother understood. She soaked my legs in a bucket of warm water mixed into a strange solution that made the bucket of water look like the clouds from the blue skies had fallen into it. My mother then took a rag and cleaned the sores gently. Pus drained out of them and into the warm water. She dried my legs with a clean towel, tossing it into the concrete sink to be beaten on the rocks later. Then she bandaged both of my legs with a white strip of cloth to keep me from digging my nails into the sores, re-infecting them.

A week later, after the sores had healed, I discovered a new hobby. I peeled the scabs and once more found myself hurtling into bliss. My mother smacked my hand every time she caught me.

"Leave it alone, Kalyana! Let it heal!"

But when her back was turned I peeled the scabs all the same. Eventually, despite my efforts, the scabs disappeared and made way for scars. I returned to school with my bowl haircut, my lemon-yellow dress, and my black open-toed sandals. The scars I hid beneath knee-length socks of brightest white, as though the purity of the white socks would miraculously wipe away the bloodless suffering of humiliation.

Each morning I would carefully pull on my dress and socks and shoes and grip the handles of the chocolate-brown suitcase my father had given me. My mother would hand me the lunch she had prepared. She would roll vegetable curry in a roti, a type of Indian flatbread that she made on the kerosene stove. She would wrap the roti in wax paper and then in *The Fiji Times* newspaper that my father had bought for three cents from the corner store. I used to crane my head to find words I could read and recognize. It never occurred to me then, but now I wonder whether my father, who could only write his name, got his daily dose of news merely from looking at the pictures.

My mother would also drop a ten-cent coin into my pocket in case I should get a craving for the popsicles and blood-red sugar candies they sold at recess at the school canteen. I carried the same ten-cent piece every day, too afraid to stand in line and buy a treat from the senior girls who ran the canteen. Then one day, the tallest, heftiest girl in the school asked to borrow it. I watched her stand in line and buy herself a purple popsicle, and though I waited expectantly, she quickly walked away with the treat, smirking.

I returned home with empty pockets that day. I never saw that girl again, even though I looked for her everywhere. My mother, furious, gave me a new ten-cent piece the next day and I spent it in the cafeteria, starting a long-overdue tradition of my own.

School began in the morning and lasted until the long hand of the clock pointed straight north and the short hand, due east. Monday was handkerchief day. Tuesday was lice day. Wednesday was nail day, Thursday was uniform check, and Friday was assembly. Each day was yet another opportunity to avoid the balding headmaster who had made me hear the sound of every kind of musical instrument in my head.

Manjula was responsible for ensuring I carried a handkerchief each Monday. Sometimes, though, her mind was drifting to thoughts of her knight arriving on a black horse, and I arrived at school with an empty side pocket. On the Mondays that Manjula forgot, I would fold a piece of paper in a perfect square and wave it up in the air for the teacher to see as the other students waved their handkerchiefs, a storm of flashing white against the dark building. Later, though, I would scold Manjula for her forgetfulness, claiming she had caused me trouble with my teacher. I liked hearing Manjula's apologetic squeak. The students who didn't fold a piece of paper and wave it in the air on Mondays received their beating in front of the whole class.

I always feared receiving the humiliation of a public beating, but some of the children did not seem to care. On Wednesdays, my teacher would inspect our fingernails for black grime. Rakesh always failed this test, and Mrs. Smith would grab him by the ear, drag him to the front of the class, and snap the square, wooden blackboard duster on his fingers. I would wonder whether he was beyond human suffering, like the Hare Krishna devotees. Week after week, year after year, I saw him receive his beatings and yet never flinch a muscle. He would walk back to his desk with a smirk on his face, as though Mrs. Smith had merely grazed his fingers with a feather. I admired him. Fiercely I wished to be like him: fearless and above the human experience of suffering.

On the final day marking the end of the week, the whole school, boys and girls from classes One through Eight, would become little armies. Each class marched left and right, in a straight column out to the soccer field. We would line up in front of the statue of Gandhi *ji*, while the headmaster stood on top of the concrete steps and barked orders: "Hands out. Hands to the side. March in place." We had to follow his directions no matter the blazing sun or drizzling rain.

Every week followed the same pattern. But on October 10 of that year, we assembled for a new purpose. Fiji had gained independence from British rule, and like little soldiers carrying sky-blue flags, all of the students registered in the school were to go into the town to celebrate. Instead of marching for the soccer fields, we lined up to board brown buses.

I had never ridden in a bus without my mother. I felt both alone and exposed, certain of the penetrating stares of the boys and girls all around me. Their glances burned like fire into my skin. I knew they must be poking fun at my tubby stomach, at how it jiggled when the bus bounced over the potholes on the uneven roads. I knew their nickname for me: Forty-Four-Gallon Drum. When Noora had first yelled that out to the rest of the class that one hideous day, I had wished for the earth to open so that I might fall into the pit and disappear; but instead, upon coming home, hiding in the comfort of my own room, I began, in small sentences and broken words, to try to write away my shame.

I never told my mother that this is what they called me in school, that the other girls giggled and laughed because I was like a forty-four-gallon barrel of lard. I never told her that I ate lunch alone, shut in the toilet behind a closed door. But here, on this field trip, my secret—that I had no friends—was exposed like the emperor in the tale Mother had told me. I was the naked emperor on this bus, but unlike the ruler in the story, I knew I had no clothes.

When we reached the town celebrations, the pundit didn't blow his conch shell. Independence Day was nothing like an Indian wedding, complete with a gleaming bride, vibrantly dressed guests, a tall altar, and a rainfall of confetti. Children from all the other schools, wearing different colors and shades of the same style of uniform, stood in perfect lines, led by their own grim headmasters and stiff teachers.

On a stage, indigenous Fijians, or iTaukei, performed the *meke*. Half-naked, they danced with painted faces and wooden clubs in the blazing sun. They told stories of their past, of wars and surrender. Skilled Fijian women, each with a frangipani tucked behind an ear, shook their grass-skirted hips. People clapped. Children jumped with joy in time with the beating of the drums. Ships pulled into the wharf in the distance. Palm trees swayed in the light breeze. I was horrified to see how little clothing the dancers wore, and yet marveled at how confident they seemed in their movement. What beautiful tales they told through the sway of their hips and the shaking of their chests and the rattle and hum of their clubs.

Mint and vanilla ice cream and cotton candy were there for the taking. I stuffed my face with mint ice cream, and I saw the stout headmaster go for seconds and thirds. The ice cream melted down the side of his face as he wiped the sweat off his brow. He was a ghastly sight.

Ratu Sir Kamisese Mara, our first prime minister, addressed us in a speech. I think he said that we had to strive to be promising youths; that we were Fiji's future, full of opportunity, the privileged ones. His white, curly hair was impossibly frizzy. The burning sun made my scalp itchy and my underarms sweaty, and I was sure I could smell curry chicken cooking in the distance. The aroma made me hungrier than the thought of mother's rice pudding wrapped in grease-layered *puries*, and I wished I was hiding under the shade of her dupatta.

I did not feel privileged.

When the prime minister was done speaking, the whole crowd stood erect, proudly singing the National Anthem:

Blessing grant, oh God of Nations, on the isles of Fiji
As we stand united under noble banner blue
And we honor and defend the cause of freedom ever
Onward march together
God Bless Fiji

For Fiji, ever Fiji, let our voices ring with pride
For Fiji, ever Fiji, her voices hail far and wide
A land of freedom, hope and glory, to endure whatever befall
May God bless Fiji
Forever more!

Blessing grant, oh God of nations, on the isles of Fiji
Shores of golden sand and sunshine, happiness and song
Stand united, we of Fiji, fame and glory ever
Onward march together
God Bless Fiji

When we returned to school the following week, the headmaster proudly announced that we were to sing the National Anthem at all Friday assemblies from then onward. The first day that we stood straight and proud and sang, the rhythm possessed me like the wandering spirits possessed Indian pundits at the yearly *pooja*. I rolled my shoulders back and forth and pounded my left leg on the ground as I bellowed the National Anthem. Now, whenever I hear it play in the corner of my mind, I still feel my classroom teacher's piercing gaze knife through my back as it did that first day, urging me to stand still and sing on key. Later that day, she cornered me and said huskily, "It never fares well to behave unladylike, Kalyana. Keep still when singing the National Anthem next time." Her voice was so low that she sounded like a man. I nodded my head and lowered my gaze to the ground until I heard her footsteps fade away.

At the next assembly, I restrained my burning urge to roll my shoulders and pound my left foot in the dirt. I ignored the rhythm of drums beating through my veins. Yet sometimes I found I must succumb to the music; discreetly I would pound my big toe.

8

A T SCHOOL I learned to put up my hand before asking to go to the toilet. I learned to write "Ana and Tom climbed a tree." I learned to create characters and make up stories. I learned that the dead man after whom our school was named was a great man, full of insight and wisdom. He was a man respected for starting a movement that brought the Indian people freedom from the British rule. So one man of color had stood in front of a crowd of white men and won? It must have been the word "movement" that had possessed him deep in the night as he had slept, for only this word could have the power to cause the submissive to rise. But then, soon after, the great Mahatma Gandhi was shot in a midst of a burning crowd. The teacher said that most great beings go like this.

I learned other stories, stories with happier endings. I read *Cinderella* and compared the char princess to Manjula. Yet Cinderella did not walk with a limp and was blessed with beauty, and in the end had the chance to be rescued by her sweet prince. After that she lived happily ever after.

I wondered what happened to the girls who were Manjulas and not Cinderellas, girls who walked with a limp and stood no chance of being saved by a man. Would they spend an eternity waiting to live happily ever after? Or would their princes emerge one day out of the blue to rescue them from the depths of their suffering? Was every girl, princess or not, promised her prince? These things puzzled me, although at the time I was more interested in begging my father for a pair of glass slippers. I surely liked those shoes!

The story of Rapunzel reminded me of my "pyala cut" hair and my lost locks; the illustrations of Rapunzel's long, golden tresses left me feeling envious. And the image of the gingerbread man sitting on the edge of a wolf's nose as the animal approached the banks of the river made my heart jump out of my skin in anticipation of the cookie's coming end. Was this unpredictability life's only promise? I wondered, but I felt a little sorry for the wolf all the same. A soggy cookie is never fun to eat.

I read that this was the way you went around the mulberry bush, the mulberry bush, the mulberry bush, and this was the way you brushed your teeth, brushed your teeth, brushed your teeth, so early in the morning. I would put a tiny rock on the middle of the floor and stack pillows on top of the stone and pretend to be a princess sleeping on a small pea. I would build my own bridge with cushions in the middle of our living room. I changed my voice from high-pitched to low and gruff, imitating each of the billy goats and then finally the ogre at the bottom of the bridge, as I walked slowly over the cushions.

Raju would say, "If you tried to cross the bridge, it would

break in the middle and you would fall in the river below. But don't worry, sister, you would definitely float!" He would leave the room, laughing loudly.

Manjula did not laugh. She had a new occupation: she became my audience. After dinner she liked to sit at the edge of our mattress and listen intently as I read my fairy tales aloud. Out of the corner of my eye, I would steal glances at my unsuspecting auntie. I could see how she raised her eyebrows with piqued interest or lowered her sad gaze when the prince lost his Cinderella or the beast clutched his heart, falling to the ground as the last rose petal descended into the glass jar. I started raising and lowering my voice to match the action in the story, and took pleasure in capturing her emotions like a fisherman traps the fishes in his net. You could say that, in some odd way I had started to resemble my mother.

At first, Manjula would sit at the edge of the mattress and appear to let her mind wander into a distant world as I read her the children's stories. Then she started sitting closer. She would look over my shoulder and try to see the illustrations, and somehow I began pointing to each of the words I read. Sometimes Manjula would interrupt and say, "Wait, what's that word again?"

Occasionally I noticed her lips moving silently as I read. And gradually, as I saw her eyes roll over the words on the pages, I began to suspect that she was learning and growing in her understanding of "Ingalish," even though I never heard her utter an English word.

To an outsider, it might have appeared that I was the headmaster and Manjula the student. But the truth was that there were no teachers here, only students. For after that,

Manjula began sewing my dresses for a discounted price. I never paid more than three dollars for a new frock or blouse or skirt. She would take me to the seashore more often, and not just to catch crabs; now we lingered in the parks and on the swings. Sometimes she would put me on her lap on the swing and wrap her arms around my waist as we soared to the skies. Or she would stand behind me, her legs parted and steady, and use her strong hands to push me up and up and up. I flew far and away, towards the moving clouds.

I outgrew the fairy tales, but my hunger for books became insatiable. My mother would take me to the Carnegie library every Saturday, right after we stopped for green milkshakes and mutton rolls by the Pacific Harbour. Even now, the memory makes me salivate, for the milkshakes had a flavor that tickled all the taste buds like a million sparklers. I remember my disappointment when I tasted my first Canadian milkshake; it was nothing like the milkshakes of my childhood. In Canada, milkshakes are thick in consistency, but in Fiji they were runny and had their own distinct flavor. I have never tasted anything like it since.

The Suva Public Library had stood there since 1909, making it one of the oldest buildings in all of Fiji. The first time I entered the building, I was in awe. I was like a tiny fish swimming in an ocean of books. I was free to dart through one aisle and come out the other. I could take out one book and shove it back on the shelf and then remove a second, flipping the bent and crisp pages or looking through the illustrations.

"The art of telling stories goes back to the beginning of time, Kalyana," my mother would interrupt my reverie. "And anyone who has this gift is a blessed soul. Read as many stories as your heart desires, my little pumpkin." I blushed when my mother called me such childish names in public.

When I had chosen my stack of children's books, the librarian stamped the return date on a small card glued in the back of each book. I could examine the card at home and know exactly how many times the book had left the ocean with a visiting fish. At first, I only chose the books that were wanted by others, but later I sought out those books that were unwanted and unread. I thought that they also deserved to see the world outside this library.

As I grew older, I discovered Enid Blyton's books. *The Magic Faraway Tree* series became my *Ramayana*. In the hopes of somehow uncovering the thick-trunked tree that housed Moon-Face, Mr. Whatzisname, Silky, and the noisy Saucepan Man, I often went out in our backyard and knocked on the bark and shook the branches of the mandarin, mango, and carambola trees that crowded together there. Manjula would raise her eyebrows, but I did not want to answer any of her unspoken questions.

If I had found such a thick-trunked tree, I would have climbed it and rejoiced when I ended up in the Land of Topsy-Turvy or the Land of Spells or the Land of Take-What-You-Want or the Land of Birthdays. Like the strange folk of the *Magic Faraway Tree*, I wanted to feast on Pop Biscuits and Google Buns and slide down the slippery-slip that spiraled down the tree trunk. I would listen carefully, hoping that deep in the woods I would hear the whisper "Whisha-whisha-whisha"—a sign that the magic faraway tree full of fairies was near. One day I hoped to write stories too, like my favorite author, and hide behind the fantastical heroes and heroines to which I gave birth.

I searched carefully for any fairies who might be buzzing around the thick vegetation in our backyard, but all I ever found were thin-trunked coconut trees and frogs croaking. The only sound would be the coconut leaves rustling in the wind as the spirits of the departed in the nearby cemetery slept peacefully ten feet below ground.

Manjula always confiscated each book I borrowed from the library, and I often found her reading them secretly in the middle of the afternoon when all the clothes were ironed and put away. Eventually she grew tired of my selections and began creating her own library from the Mills and Boon and Harlequin Romance novels she would purchase each week. They had pictures of glistening men and curvaceous, long-haired women embracing in the compromised positions that we Indo-Fijians reserved only for our bedrooms. Manjula kept all her novels shut in a cardboard box. She often burned a kerosene lamp by our bedside in the late evening, reading several short chapters before closing her eyes.

Raju never read books; he spent his time conjuring up useless plans. Once, when I was looking for Mr. Watzisname in our backyard, I saw Raju rise from someone's grave with a white bedsheet covering his head and scrawny body. He had spent the entire morning searching the house for that white sheet. Now the unsuspecting Fijian women who were crossing the cemetery were screaming, "Spirits have risen! Run, sisters! Run! Spirits have risen! Run!" I saw them sprint out of the graveyard, tripping and tumbling on gravestones, clutching their chests.

Unfortunately, Raju did not put the same level of commitment into his studies, and soon he tired of school. As a child I was unhappy that he never had to take his handkerchief and a little suitcase and face the grim headmaster of Mahatma Gandhi Primary School. Years later, I realized the gift he had lost.

While I was engrossed in reading and writing stories or solving mathematical equations, Raju occupied his time with other tasks. He accompanied Father to his shop and helped him with the building of cabinets and chairs and beds, or he strolled to the ocean alongside Manjula. At first, like me, he carried the bags into which Manjula would dump live crabs and prawns. Then he designed his own spear out of metal and wood, sharpening it to perfection and following Manjula's footsteps. He caught prawns and crabs by marking the sea creatures' habitats in the sands and brought home his own bag of live catch. Nonetheless, he still left the cutting and cooking of it to Manjula.

On less-productive occasions, Raju would gather with the neighborhood boys and guzzle large bottles of Fijian beer and smoke Pall Mall cigarettes. Once I even saw him roll tobacco leaves into a rope shape and smoke it. He saw me watching him, winked at me, and said, "*Suki*." He reached out his hand and offered me some. I ran to my mother, screaming that Raju was being bad: He was smoking. My mother told me not to tattle, and that Raju was a boy. "Go and read, Kalyana," Mother said, shutting out my cries.

Raju progressed from smoking suki to sitting in a circle like the native Fijians and drinking *yaqona* or *kava* from a *bilo*, a cup made from a half coconut shell smoothed to perfection. The drink looked like muddy, slushy water. Raju accepted the bilo, clapped once, said *"Bula!"* and drank it in one gulp. He handed the bilo to his friends, clapped three times, and said *"Vinaka vaka levu,"* or "Thank you" in Fijian.

Then he started disappearing for several days at a time. He would come home with disheveled hair and an unkempt shirt, smelling like cigarettes. The talk in the village was that he was educating himself on the physics of the birds and the bees using a permissive older Fijian woman who had borne three children to three different fathers. She lived in a nearby village and grew her own dalo and cassava roots to feed her family.

Sometimes Raju would bring home cassava and dalo leaves. My mother would cook the dalo leaves in creamy coconut milk, calling it *rou-rou*. Soaking the cassava in wet curry spices and deep-frying them, she would seal their softness in the crispy outside. She never asked Raju the source of the food, and she would bat her hands in disdain were anyone to raise the rumor of her dear son embracing a full-blooded Fijian woman.

And so I came to understand at an early age that men had an advantage in this world. They never bled. They need not attend school. And, if they so desired, they might learn certain pleasures without the pundit's matrimonial blessings. No one would blink an eye, though the village women might whisper among themselves. It seemed that all boys might sow their wild oats, while girls must stay home and sew dresses. Women, especially Indian women, embraced the fate that was handed down to them, keeping their mouths sealed as they trudged along and prepared curries and pressed clothes.

I began to wish that I had been born in the land of America, where women were allowed to go mad. Perhaps being under the influence was a good thing after all.

"You read, Kali," Raju would tell me. "That way you can get a better husband—one that doesn't beat you that much, just on the weekends."

Raju was a hopeless case.

9

I HAD A DREAM: I was wearing my yellow school uniform and carrying my little suitcase full of schoolbooks. The sun was sinking in the wide sky, creating a warm orange hue around me. The scent of roses, marigolds, hibiscuses, and frangipani perfumed the air.

I kept my feet firmly pressed on the concrete outside our house. Next to the house, on my right, was a tall lime tree. Or was it my house? We didn't own a lime tree or flowers, nor did we have a concrete driveway. I shook my head in confusion.

The scent of lime hung thickly in the muggy air. A bright light drew me closer to the tree, and it seemed as though a cannon filled with fairy dust had exploded around its thin branches. As I approached, I clutched tightly to the handle of my little suitcase, hoping that I might witness the fairies I had dreamed of for so long.

But when I reached the tree, what I saw quickened the pace of my heart. I dropped my suitcase to the ground. I wanted to run, to scream, to flee, but I could not move.

My body had turned stiff like a cold stone statue, my scream trapped in the hollow of my throat.

A red, hissing snake had mischievously emerged from the light. It slithered down a thin branch and climbed to another. The swiftness and grace of its movement was terrifying. I stood there staring at it with my mouth open, gasping for breath. Large beads of perspiration were forming on my brow.

Then something strange happened. The red snake coiled on top of a thin branch and stared right into my eyes and smiled. It did a little dance and slipped its tail over the branch and hung from it, winking and giggling at me. The scales on the snake's body were made of hundreds of precious stones that shone and glittered brighter than the sun itself. In spite of myself, my heartbeat began to return to its normal rhythm. The burning heat in my body subsided as I felt a strange sensation of peaceful warmth flow through me.

The four old women, giggling like adolescents, emerged from nowhere and flew around the tree, circling it. They chanted a melodious tune which urged me to tap my toes in the dirt and roll my shoulders and shake my hips. Then they all reached out and gently touched my head, giving me their blessing.

By the end of the dream, I knew that I was deeply in love with this snake. It was the most beautiful thing I had ever seen. I woke up and found Manjula sleeping peacefully beside me, one of her legs thrown over a large, fluffy pillow. I wondered if I had been gifted this dream in error. Rightfully, I thought, it belonged to her.

10

THE YEARS following the Independence Day celebrations saw several changes in our home. My father hammered pieces of wood together and raised our mattress from the floor onto a frame. Manjula shoved her little library, her boxes of romance books, under our bed for safekeeping. My father built sturdier chairs and glued a green top onto our dining table.

"It'll be easier to clean the food off now," he told my mother, demonstrating with a wet cloth.

He built cupboards for the cups and plates, and drawers for the big spoons and sharp knives. Then he brought home a stand on which to dangle our cups and screwed hooks into the wall for our towels.

Running water found its way into our home. The big tank of water by the side of the house was taken away in a truck to my cousin's house, where the pipes did not yet bring water. Mother and Manjula no longer had to beat the clothes on the rocks outside; now they could soak them in our new concrete sink.

With running water also came a modern toilet. The old pit toilet outside was covered with dirt. For the first year, my mother had to keep the toilet door bolted, as Manjula and I became frequent guests of that room. She insisted that we were flushing unnecessarily, making the water bills sky-rocket. We had to ask her for the key to visit the toilet, and she became the one who decided whether it was urgent need or just plain curiosity. Sometimes, when it was indeed urgent need and Mother did not believe us, Manjula and I were left squirming in our wooden chairs.

The ceilings were lined with yards of wire in red, green, blue, and yellow, just like the Ludo game. White, square switches were placed on every wall, and with a flick of one of these switches, light flooded every room of our mod-est house. When Father bought our first turntable and a radio, Mother reluctantly retired her transistor set. English and Hindi tunes now vibrated through our home. Manjula began singing out of tune in a shrill voice, while my mother would twist her hips and tap her feet on the wooden floors. She would ask me to come and do "the twist." On most days, I would decline her invitation and remain in bed reading, a stack of condensed-milk sandwiches and a tall glass of Milo handily by my side.

The final big change came when a group of men from the village arrived at our house. Every sunrise, they lined up at our door and helped my father stir concrete powder, sand, gravel, and water in large drums. They dug the dirt in front of our home into a downward slope. Then they laid metal frames on the ground and stacked cement blocks on top of one another along the sides of the slope. A ton of gray concrete mixture was poured into the holes of the cement blocks, creating our new concrete driveway.

I thought of my dream of the laughing red snake.

Raju, as usual, was nowhere to be found, but this time he disappeared for the entire week this transformation was taking place. The four old women whispered amongst themselves. The third old woman, who burned hotter than fire itself, said that the Fijian woman with whom Raju was locking lips was quite large in size. Rumor was that her hips were rounder than a ten-pound watermelon. The fourth old woman disagreed. Her hips weren't like a watermelon, but more like a juicy pineapple, and her breasts were like two small mangoes. The second old woman, who possessed the fluidity and clarity of water, had her own opinion: pineapples had eyes, and a woman's hips could never be compared to this fruit. The woman who was wrapping her plump legs around Raju's scrawny back had hips shaped like an apple. But then the first woman, the one who blew in from the East, spoke. She said it didn't matter whether the woman's hips were shaped like a watermelon or a pineapple or an apple. It made no difference what fruit her breasts resembled. Regardless of what form she took, a woman was a woman.

All four women raised their hands in the air and shouted, "A woman is a woman! God bless Raju's soul! God bless Raju's soul!" I shoved white cotton balls in both my ears to silence the rumors, but the voices of the four old women still echoed in my head.

Every day the men were there working, shirtless and sweating in the burning heat, my mother cooked a large pot of lentil soup and rice. She would taste the lentils several times for salt and tang before she would allow Manjula to take the food out to the men. Manjula would walk with an extra sway of her hips, wearing a kurta that showed a particularly visible amount of cleavage. She would bend low when she handed out bowls of rice and lentil soup.

"No problem. No problem. No problem," Manjula would reply eagerly, brushing away their gratitude. "If you need more salt, more water, more juice, just holler." She would flash her brightest smile.

Some of the men would come closer to her, take her hand in theirs, and say, "You're very kind, Sister. Thank you. Thank you."

Manjula would blush and walk swiftly back into the house, giggling uncontrollably like a school-age girl. My mother would shake her head and grin at Manjula. Unlike Manjula, my mother never came out of the house. These men were not brothers or fathers or husbands, not even uncles or cousins.

It took several weeks before all the work was completed. The final stage came when a tall man leveled the wet cement with a flat tool, leaving our new garage smooth and ready for the car that my father would soon proudly park in our driveway. After that, to Manjula's dismay, I was sure, the strong young men never returned. My aunt was left alone with her library of Mills and Boons.

Yet things were changing for Manjula, too. Word of my father's booming furniture-making business had reached small towns far and wide, bringing Manjula her first suitor. He was a short, plump man with a thick mustache, a full head of black hair, and a large, hideous mole on the right side of his cheek. He did not look like the prince in the fairy tale, but Manjula was enthralled. The meeting was arranged for two o'clock in the afternoon, at a neutral place. The gossip was that he was aware of Manjula's limp, but he still insisted on meeting her in person. He was looking for a wife who came from a prosperous family.

Both families were to meet at the house of my father's older brother. My father had only one brother, Baldev. Even though he carried a name similar to my father's, he looked nothing like him; Uncle Baldev had dark hair and dark eyes and dark skin. His house was in Nausori, a farming town a half-hour's drive from Suva.

Uncle Baldev had been married the same time as my father, but to a girl who was even younger than my mother. I had overheard Mother and Manjula speaking about her in whispered voices. Her eyes had looked like empty sponges and she was praying for her first bleeding when the wedding procession knocked on her door and her hand was joined with my uncle's. The first old woman, the one who blew in from the East, shuddered upon hearing the story. "It is no wonder," she growled like a howling hurricane, "that the girl turned out to be a *banj*."

A *banj*? Indeed, the old woman insisted. Still a child when frangipani was spread on white bedsheets and flowers were hung from the ceilings, the poor soul had yet to soak the cloth rags with her blood. Her nipples were mere buds, not yet open and spread like rose petals.

"What a pity!" the old women cried. "The damage was done. It's no wonder she can never bear children."

Is that why she kept her face half-covered by the fabric of

her cotton sari? My mother called her "Didi." That couldn't be her name, for "Didi" only meant "sister." Did not each woman at least have one name of her own? I realized that I never had heard this woman speak a single word.

Manjula limped around our house in a dither. She went from mirror to mirror, putting her hair up this way and that.

"Bun," said my mother firmly. "It brings out your strong facial features. And it makes you look very Indian." So Manjula soon had a tight bun at the back of her neck, but she was still undecided over the saris.

Mother stepped in again. "Oh, Sister! Why would you wear red? You're not a bride yet. Wear the gold one with the maroon border," she said. "And all the gray hairs," my mother continued. "Men, young and old, only want young, little girls. He will for sure reject you when he sees those gray hairs. Come here. Let me put kajal in your head."

Kajal was only to be dropped in the waterline of one's eyes, yet here was Manjula using it to disguise her appearance! I stared as Mother blended kajal with great expertise into Manjula's hair. Almost miraculously, the gray hairs blended and disappeared.

Manjula rouged her cheeks and colored her lips a bright maroon, matching the border of her sari. She sat at the dining table in the kitchen, listening to the ticking hands of the round clock on the far wall. She didn't eat or drink or even speak, but awkwardly played with the edges of her gold sari. And yet she looked so beautiful, almost like one of those princesses I had read about in the books of fairy tales. Perhaps Manjula was finally to have her prince after all.

At exactly one o' clock, Father summoned my mother,

Manjula, and me. Raju, as usual, was missing, but Father said nothing. The three of us squeezed into our brown car and Father drove us to Nausori. The ride was rough and bumpy, the gravel road dusty. No one in the car spoke.

Half an hour before the meeting, we came to Uncle Baldev's small tin house. It sat alone in the middle of acres of farmland.

Manjula chewed the ends of her sari. "*Are Bhagwan.* What to do?"

"Don't worry, he knows you walk with a limp," said Mother. "Just smile and everything will work out all right."

Uncle Baldev's living-room walls were cluttered with bygone calendars, fake silk roses, old photographs of people, and other knickknacks. I gazed upon a black-and-white photo of my *aji*, my father's mother, a beautiful, plump woman, whose smile reached from ear to ear. She was holding my father in her arms and was standing loosely beside my *aja*. Uncle Baldev, looking miserable, was standing in front of her, holding her pinky. Like Uncle Baldev, my *aji* and *aja* both had darker skin and hair.

"Why is Daddy the only one that looks like a *gora*, Mummy?" I whispered, nudging my mother's arm.

"Shush!" Mother hissed. She threw the picture a nervous glance and turned me away from it. Then she looked around to see if anyone had heard.

To my mother's relief, everyone appeared to be focused on the scheduled guests' arrival and not on my curious inquiries. I was dissatisfied, but then the food arrived and I, too, forgot all about the faded old picture and the untold secrets it held.

My uncle's wife—the auntie without a name—had cooked up a feast. We snacked on *sainas* and *barfies*, drank chai and juice. We indulged in *jalebies* and sugar sticks. All except for Manjula; she sat nervously twitching and listening for the sound of another car driving up the dusty gravel path.

At last the sound of the guests was heard. Footsteps echoed as they approached the stairs.

"Oh, my God. What to do?" gasped Manjula, struggling for breath.

"Shh," whispered Mother. "Sit quietly, ladylike, and look to the floor. Don't smile. They'll think you're too eager."

Manjula moved closer to my mother on the opposite sofa and lowered her eyes, staring firmly at the wooden floorboards. Uncle Baldev, sitting on a small chair placed in the open doorway between the kitchen and the living room, got up and opened the door. His wife, who didn't have a place to sit, disappeared into the kitchen as the guests entered. My father leaned back in a single plush chair placed in the corner of the room. I grabbed onto his legs nervously, glad to be seated on the floor.

"Welcome. Welcome. Welcome," said Uncle Baldev, shaking all the men's hands. Two of the men were tall and slender. It was easy to figure out that the third man, the chubby one with the mustache and the hideous mole, was Manjula's suitor.

All three men were brothers, and the woman was the wife of one of them. She walked pompously, her thin nose stuck high up in the air like the perch of a tree where fan-tailed cuckoos flocked. The two thin men straggled alongside her like frail branches. Manjula's suitor, whose name was Rabir, walked behind sluggishly, a thick tree stump, wearing baby-blue bell-bottom slacks that were a little too tight by the crotch, and a green, flowered shirt that was half-unbuttoned. He seemed proud to show off the grisly sight of his chest hair.

Rabir lit up a cigarette the moment everyone sat down. Instead of taking the seat directly opposite Manjula, as was proper, he sat close to the table that carried the food. The stiff woman sat in between the two other men, opposite Manjula, fixing her penetrating glare onto my aunt's blushing face. As Rabir filled the air with a cloud of cigarette smoke, Manjula crinkled her nose and sneezed. Uncle Baldev yelled to his wife, who had been hovering around the kitchen doorway, to hurry and get an ashtray for the guest.

The high-and-mighty woman rolled her eyes in dissatisfaction at the wall decorations, cheap wood frames, and old calendar pictures that hung all around her. My stomach churned when she momentarily caught me in her stern gaze. Unconsciously, I started thumping the floor with my left toe, evoking a disapproving glance from my mother. For Manjula's sake, I almost wished that they would reject her.

Manjula kept her gaze fixed to the floorboards. She didn't flash her perfect white teeth. Her gold-bordered sari covered her shoulders modestly.

Finally the woman nodded her head and looked at the other three men. "She looks beautiful. Yes." One man smiled. The other hunched his shoulders.

"I don't know," the second man grunted. "Good enough."

Rabir stared at Manjula, taking in her every curve and

movement. He put out a second cigarette butt in the glass ashtray, leaned forward, and started piling food onto a small ceramic plate. The springs in the orange sofa creaked as he shifted his weight. Dipping the deep-fried goodies in mint and mango chutneys, he chewed with his mouth open and made loud, slurping noises. Manjula still remained with her gaze fixed to the floor. Mother and Father exchanged glances.

And then, in between eating noisily and gulping his drink, Rabir said something shocking: He ordered Manjula to stand up and walk across the room. My mother pursed her lips and hugged her sari closer to her shoulders. Father sat quietly, hands placed gently on his lap. Manjula looked up. My mother patted her sister on the shoulder, and Manjula slid out of her chair.

My aunt extended her left leg, then her right one, and then her left again. She limped across the small room. The heat of piercing gazes surrounded her. To my surprise, my eyes welled up with tears for my aunt. I blinked before they could run down my cheeks, soaking my dress.

Rabir grunted. "Not good! Too much of a limp, *Yaar!*" The woman reached out and patted his thigh in consolation. She tousled the hair on his head.

"Sorry, *Bhaiya*," said one of the slender gentlemen to my father, nudging his shoulder regretfully.

Manjula looked defiantly into Rabir's eyes. Her nostrils flared and the blue veins engorged in the crease of her neck. She reached across the table and pushed the bowl of mango chutney onto Rabir's lap, staining his baby-blue bell-bottom pants at the crotch.

Rabir squirmed in his seat. The pompous woman leapt

up, snorted haughtily, and motioned for the men to follow her out the door. Rabir regretfully put down the plate of goodies, noisily chewing what was left in his mouth. Then he took a napkin and patted the front of his pants. The sauce had left a glaring orange stain that I was sure couldn't be scrubbed off even with soapy water.

After a few minutes of futile mopping, Rabir shrugged angrily and stomped out of the house.

Uncle Baldev ran after them, saying, "Sorry. Sorry. Sorry. The woman momentarily lost her mind. All women lose their minds. Sorry. Sorry. I hope there will be no ill feelings. I hope you'll come back."

I heard the car doors slam and the engine putter, then roar to life. They had driven off without saying a word.

Father sat there, leaning back in his chair, his hands interlocked behind his head. Mother sat there with her mouth open. I could almost see the faintest bit of a smile through the transparent yellow sari that covered much of Uncle Baldev's nameless wife's face. I said nothing, but I was certain that, if the four old women had been here, they would have rolled on the floor, laughing and holding onto their sides.

Uncle Baldev stormed back into the house and towered over Manjula, who had repositioned herself on the floor in the corner. "Why did you do that? Now who is going to marry you?"

Manjula started sobbing as Uncle Baldev raised his hand to strike her across the face. She screamed, "No!"

My mother intervened as I sat hunched over on the pillow by my father's feet. "Oh, Brother, let it go. She's a fool. She's a woman. She didn't think."

Baldev lowered his hand. His eyes were protruding with rage. "Now everyone will say that it's not only that you walk with a limp, but that you have a temper, too. You disrespected a guest in my home. Unacceptable!" He slapped her carelessly on her head. Manjula drew further into the corner and squealed.

Uncle Baldev looked towards his wife and shouted, "Why are you still standing there? Go clean the mess on the sofa. It'll stain, and then we'll have to buy a new couch. Do you think money grows on the trees?"

His wife bit the corner of her veil as she scurried around the living room with a bucket of soapy water, urgently trying to clean the mess. She scrubbed the sofa furiously with a wet rag and polished the floors with an old torn towel. Panicking when the stain didn't disappear immediately, she scrubbed still harder under the scrutiny of her husband's eye. Circles of sweat formed under her armpits, exuding a musty smell in the room. She released a low sigh when the orange on the floor and the sofa finally began to fade.

Father quietly leaned back in his chair, as he and my mother watched her work feverishly at the mundane task. Manjula remained huddled in the corner.

My aunt had attracted misfortune from the start. Even her birth had been a difficult one. My mother said that my *nani* had retched by the wooden pole in the backyard for the entire course of her pregnancy with Manjula, turning the green grass brown. Even when the time came, things had been difficult; Manjula stayed in their mother's womb for days too long on end, making her cry out to the goddesses above for mercy. The head midwife had stood around, helpless and confused. Eventually, she had bundled Manjula's ailing mother in a white blanket and taken her to the local hospital, where a doctor took a knife and made a clean slash across my *nani's* belly, scarring it forever. Rumor held that, when the doctor cut her belly, he accidentally sliced off the baby's toes.

Small wonder that Manjula's ill luck had followed her through her life. Now word would spread that even a man like Rabir, one with fat cheeks, a swollen stomach, and a hideous mole, would reject her.

When Uncle Baldev's breathing returned to normal, he sat down, poured himself a glass of whiskey, and lit a cigarette and started to smoke. He noticed me hunched on the floor by my father's feet. I pretended not to notice him. I hated the stench of cigarette smoke and the faint smell of whiskey in the air. After finishing his cigarette, he threw me another quick glance, and then he got up and left through the side door.

"Where's Uncle going?" I whispered to my mother.

"Who knows?" she said. "It's best to not ask questions. Just be quiet."

I looked over to Manjula. She was still seated on the floor, her eyes fixed on the knots covering the wooden floorboards on the ground. I couldn't see the rise and fall of her chest. If she was breathing, it was barely.

After a full fifteen minutes had elapsed, Uncle Baldev came back through the side door. He was carrying sugarcane in one hand and a big knife in the other. He sat back down on the chair, balanced the sugarcane between his legs, and with ease and grace began slicing the purple skin with the big knife. I saw the hard purple shell of the sugarcane fall to the floor around Uncle Baldev's feet. It was a slow, rhythmic motion, almost soothing.

After the shell was peeled from the cane, white flesh remained. My uncle sliced the remains into four equal pieces. He barked an order at his wife, who sprang to her feet and ran to the kitchen. When she returned, she was holding a white-coated steel plate, which she placed on the floor.

"What are you doing?" my uncle said angrily. "Why are you putting it on the floor? We're not feeding dogs." He pointed to the side table. "Put it here."

She obeyed, her hands trembling slightly.

"Not there!" he yelled. "Here, in the middle. If you put it on the side, it will topple over. Ah! Damn women. It's like you all have no brains."

His wife rose to scurry back to the kitchen. "And who's going to clean this mess from the floor?" he demanded. His eyes looked cold and hard.

The wife bent down by his feet, picking up the purple shell. I glanced over to my mother and Manjula. Both of their lips formed a tight, straight line. It felt like watching Manjula chopping live crabs on our kitchen floor, except that here, auntie-without-a-name was the living crab.

Uncle Baldev placed four even pieces of white sugarcane on the plate. He handed it to me.

"There you go. Eat, Kali-yana, eat." He always called me Kali-yana.

"Thank you, Uncle."

He patted the top of my head. "Very pretty," he said. "How old are you, now?"

"Eight and a half."

"Eight and a half. Big girl," he said, smiling at me. He made me feel confident, and superior to the likes of Manjula and the auntie-without-a-name.

Then he turned his attention to my father and talked to him about the falling prices of grain as I chewed the sugar-cane pieces, drinking the sweet juice. I spat the shredded dry fibre back onto the plate. Sugar was always delicious.

11

FOR THE NEXT two weeks Manjula maintained a stern silence. She completed her household chores without a word and then stalked down to the ocean, staying there for hours. The gossip in the village was that she spent her afternoons sitting on the cold, hard seawall, hugging her knees to her chest and staring out to sea. The wind rustled through her dark hair and the waves crashed against the stone wall around her.

The second old woman, who possessed the fluidity and clarity of water, took to the stage in our small living room. With one hand on her hip and the other in midair, she said, "Manjula does not sit hugging her knees to her chest. She sits dangling her feet over the seawall. She sits still, letting the warm ocean waves caress her toes." I told my mother this.

"Who knows how she sits on the seawall!" my mother snapped. "It'll pass. Give it time. Her sun will rise again and she'll come out of the darkness. It's inevitable."

I didn't know how Manjula sat on the seawall, but I did

know that she was reading. Each day, before she would sneak through the back door of the house, Manjula crammed a small book in the waistline of her *lengha*. When she returned from the ocean, she shoved the same small book under our mattress. I was curious. What was she reading as she sat alone?

To my surprise, I discovered that it was a flimsy manual with pictures of roads and cars and turn signals and ignitions. Like the women in America, Manjula had gone mad. She had preoccupied herself with cars.

I didn't tell my mother about Manjula's new obsession. I was afraid my auntie would be shipped off to the Mental Institute like Shilpa, strapped to a stiff bed, and electrocuted for the rest of her living days. Or worse, perhaps Manjula would completely go berserk. I didn't want my aunt to be like the *goras,* shacking up with men like those sweaty Indian workers who poured concrete in our driveway. I didn't want her to find her prince without the circling of the fire or the chanting of the priests. I let my mother go on believing what she wished.

It was in the beginning of the third week that Manjula finally awakened to the reality of our life. She sprang out of her bed and went through the back door like she had been doing, but this time she strode into our overgrown yard. With a large knife in hand, she began slicing branches and trees. She worked hard, and for long hours. My mother, watching from the back window, said that now Manjula had completely lost her marbles.

When the hanging branches and trees were cut and burned in the middle of the backyard, and thick, black smoke floated away to the cemetery nearby, Manjula grabbed a pitchfork and started digging. She dug deep in the ground, overturning earthworms that looked like little snakes. She formed even rows and plots. Then she summoned me and handed me a bag of seeds.

Using her heel to form a perfect hole, she instructed me to drop two bean seeds into it. As soon as I dropped two seeds, she covered the hole. If I dropped in three or four seeds, she snapped, "Two only. I said two only, Kalyana. Listen." She would growl under her breath, bend down, and pick up the extra culprits, handing them back to me as she shook her head.

We planted long beans, green beans, and butter beans. We planted tomatoes and built vine supports. The seeds of potatoes, carrots, herbs, and onions were all placed in the ground, and then we planted flowers around our new driveway. Marigolds, roses, bougainvilleas, hibiscuses, and jasmine bushes created a natural hedge, separating our property from that of our neighbors.

And then, Lord behold, we planted a lime tree at the right side of our house. Manjula dug the earth and planted a tiny tree with beautiful rich, green leaves. She covered the roots with dirt and said, "Lime tree, Kalyana. When it grows we can make sweet lemonade." I smiled at the thought, imagining guzzling a chilled glass of fresh lemonade on a sweltering day. I pictured how it would slide down my throat with ease and smoothness, refreshing my very being.

It took only two months of sunshine and rain to transform our back and front yards into a land of vibrant fertility. Manjula stood over the plots like the Goddess Kali Mata stood over her trembling disciples, tending the plants every evening.

I think even Father had started to become proud of her. He never said so to her face, but one Diwali, when he brought the rest of us gifts from town, he also had a gift for Manjula for the first time in her life: red and plated gold bangles. They couldn't have cost my father more than a few dollars, but it was a gift nonetheless. He gave them to my mother to give to her.

Manjula wailed loudly in the middle of the living room when she received the gift on Diwali evening. All in one breath, she thanked Lord Vishnu and Rama and Brahmin and Shiva. Then she thanked my father, joining her palms together and closing her eyes as tears streamed down her hardened cheeks. Mother smiled and said that they were tears of joy, not sorrow. She said they were tears of love.

Two days after the Diwali festival had passed and the oil in the *diyas* had evaporated into smoke, Manjula, with her head held high, stood in front of her brother-in-law. "*Jija*," she said tentatively. My father didn't look up or acknowledge her in any way. "*Jija*," Manjula repeated. "I was thinking that I could learn how to drive."

At first my father sat there, stunned. Then, as she showed him the driver's manual she had been studying for those weeks spent sitting on the seawall, he burst into a piercing laugh.

"Drive?" he said. "Manjula, have you gone mad? Look outside. Do you see an Indian woman driving out there?" My father laughed again, and shook his head.

My mother rolled her eyes and giggled. "Manjula, how do you come up with all these grand ideas?" she said.

Manjula groaned and escaped to our bedroom. She stayed there for the rest of the day, refusing food and milk, and instead oiling her hair and skin with her precious coconut oil. The next day, however, the scent of the flowers and the budding lime tree drew her out of our room. She grabbed a green hose and tended to her garden in supreme silence, as the fourth old woman, the old Mother herself, hovered over her.

When Father came home from work that day, he casually walked up to her. "I want to see if an Indian woman can learn how to drive," he said. "Besides, if you learn how to drive, then you can take Sumitri for shopping every week, while I sit home and listen to the news on the radio." He nodded his head. "You'll have to pay for your own lessons, Manjula. I won't pay for them."

"No problem. I'll pay myself." She touched the ground he had walked on and raised her fingers to her forehead. She kissed her fingertips. Her eyes were full of light.

"Thank you, *Jija!* Thank you. Thank you." She paused and looked up to the sky. "Ah!" she whispered before she blew a gentle kiss in the air.

The tall, skinny driving instructor arrived the very next evening. He shook his small head when he saw his new student. Mumbling, he said, "A woman driver! And one that hasn't even learned to walk straight. God help this world."

Mother just stood at the window and watched. I could sense her fear in the way she chewed the ends of her blue dupatta.

"Oh, God!" she said under her breath. "Oh, Manjula. Be careful, Manjula," she said, even though my aunt could not hear her. Then she clenched her jaws together and sucked air into her lungs, hissing like a snake. "Oh, God. Let her live!"

Father said nothing. He put his hands behind his head and leaned back in his new chair, listening to the news.

Raju went around the house, making abrupt banging sounds—to scare my mother, I think. Every time he banged the side of a steel pot or dropped a lid into the sink, my mother, stiffening her pose, would breathe in through her mouth and make an even louder gasp. Raju would look at her and break out into fits of laughter.

Manjula strapped on a seatbelt. Taking a deep breath, she turned the key, but then stalled several times as she shifted gears. She clutched the steering wheel desperately, a frown creating deep grooves in her forehead as she leaned forward to peer out the wide window. She worked the windshield wipers frantically, even though the windows were clear and there was no rain; I noticed the instructor leaning forward to turn them off, shaking his head. All this happened before Manjula even left our driveway. It was not promising.

Manjula crawled down the driveway and onto the road. I saw the turning signals flashing randomly as the car made its way precariously down the lane. From the kitchen, my mother muttered, "Good grief." My father shook his head.

Yet Manjula continued her lessons. Eventually, even the villagers, men and women, would come out of their wooden houses every evening with hands interlocked behind their backs to watch Manjula back out of the driveway and cautiously speed away. They would line up at the end of their driveways and gossip about how they had seen Manjula abruptly stop and stall the car in the middle of the street in broad daylight. In the beginning they watched with trepidation, but as Manjula's confidence grew, you could see smirks of amusement begin to spread across their tanned faces.

The older men of the village shook their heads disapprovingly, muttering that Rajdev gave the women of his household too much freedom. They said that his ways were sure to corrupt all the women of the village. Goodness knows, one did not want all women thinking that they, too, could hop behind a monstrous machine and roll away with a turn of the ignition.

The story floating in the village was that Rajdev's *Sali* drove at a tortoise's pace at first, but with a few months' practice she had learned to go faster. She had also learned to back up, park, and even go up and down the hills and screech the tires at red stop signs. Eventually, the signals flickered only at the precise moment that she began to ease into making a turn. The consensus was that an Indian woman could indeed learn how to drive, even if she couldn't learn how to walk straight.

Manjula, as always, ignored the village gossip and remained intent on her goal. She impatiently paced by the driveway ten minutes before the instructor arrived every evening to pick her up for her lessons, and at the end of each lesson she made him verbally promise twice to come back. At first she paid him in Fiji dollar bills, but when she ran out of cash I heard her plead loudly and shamelessly with the instructor to come back anyway. I even heard her offer to sew his wife frocks with frills and pleated skirts for free—something I had never heard her say to anyone before. The instructor shook his head politely; his wife sewed her own clothes. "Too bad," he said, unrolling the collar of his shirt, "I wanted to be the first man to have succeeded in teaching a woman how to drive."

Anxiety, like drifting black clouds, swept over Manjula's small body. Watching from the doorway, I shook my head; running out of money served her well, I thought, since a woman should not have a license to drive. Manjula should not be stomping over traditions and breaking the rules. What kind of a movement was she trying to start?

My father brushed past me, strolling towards the driveway. He took out a roll of cash from his back pocket and offered the money to the instructor. To everyone's surprise, Manjula intervened. She shook her head and said, "No, *Jija*. I can pay on my own. I'll think of something." She promised the instructor that there would be payment when he returned the next week.

The following week, when the instructor returned, Manjula brought out her library. She bent down and pulled out boxes and boxes of dusty romance novels from underneath our bed. There were hundreds of them, all stacked in neat piles. The tall man smiled when he flipped through the collection. "You remembered," he said, "how I told you that my dear wife loves to read romance novels."

Manjula pursed her lips and stood confidently in our small living room, towering over the books. The instructor carried all the boxes out to his car and said, "Let's go driving!"

On the day of her driving test, Manjula awoke before sunrise and knelt down beside our bed. Putting her palms together, she bowed her head and prayed silently. She then powdered her face and put on her best frock.

My mother nudged her. "The worst is over, Manjula. Don't fear. You'll pass. You drive like a man."

Later that day Manjula returned, grinning as she flashed a small card at my mother. I saw that it had her picture on it. She looked like a mongoose caught in the middle of the road in the headlights, but she did not complain. And that evening, when my father came home from work, he quietly dropped a second car key in Manjula's lap. "I don't ever want to see a scratch on my car," he said sternly.

"No problem, no problem, *Jija*. I'll be extra careful." She bent down and touched the ground my father walked on. Kissing her fingertips, she said, "Thank you."

The four old women surrounded our Toyota Corolla as Manjula climbed into the driver's seat, with my mother in the passenger seat and me in the back. The old women cried, "*Jai Hind!*" as my mother clutched the front dashboard and glanced nervously out the window. Yet Manjula rested her palms loosely on the steering wheel and drove just like my father.

As the months passed, my mother eased her grip on the front dash and sat back with her shoulders relaxed. The villagers stopped coming out of their houses to watch Manjula speed away. Rumors floated around the village that Rajdev's sister-in-law, the one who walked with a limp and was unmarried still, was really a man under her *lengha*. Some even said that she had chest hair beneath her brassiere. Perhaps the reason she still wasn't married was that she was really in search of a woman. Lord behold!

"What's next, Manjula?" smirked my mother, a proud look spreading over her joyous face. "Are you going to walk in the door one day wearing khaki pants, like those mad American women?"

Manjula just smiled.

12

THE LIME plant stretched into a tree. Its branches spread to the skies. The tree's leaves were small, green, and glossy, and limes plummeted to the ground in abundance.

Manjula would collect them, wash them, and cut them into even moons. She would squeeze them into a white jug, mix in a half a cup of sugar, and pour in clear, crisp water, right from the tap. Blocks of ice, which made a crackling and popping sound, would instantly chill the lemonade. She would serve the drink to my father when he returned from the shop, and to Uncle Baldev when he came for a visit.

Uncle Baldev had become a regular feature in our home. The four old women would scatter and disappear the moment he set foot inside.

He would come over in the late afternoon and bring sugarcanes, or ripe mangoes, fresh pineapples, or green coconuts. He would lean down, tousle my hair, and kiss me on both of my cheeks. "I wish the gods had gifted me a daughter just like you, Kali-yana."

Mother said that he was yearning to be a father, and it was unfortunate that he had married a *banj*.

The familiar smell of stale tobacco and whiskey would hang in the air when Uncle came around. It still made my stomach curdle like spoiled milk, so that sometimes I could hardly eat the treats he brought. He would sit in our living room and shave the hard shell from the sugarcane, then slice the white fibre into equal pieces—just as he had in his own living room on the day Manjula had met her suitor.

I would sit by his feet, chewing the sugarcane pieces, trying to taste their sweetness. My Uncle Baldev also taught me to squeeze a lush mango, turning its insides into a stream of juice. Making a small hole in the tip of the fruit with a pocket knife he carried in his side pocket, he would hand it back to me and watch me suck the juice. Some would run down my chin, making it feel sticky.

"Is it good?" he would ask. I would nod my head. My mother would tell me to say "Thank you, Uncle," and I would.

My uncle would use the same pocket knife to take the eyes out of a pineapple. He would summon Manjula and instruct her to slice away the skin, cutting the pineapple into round rings and soaking them in salty water. Manjula always obeyed without question.

Sometimes he brought over a green coconut. He always claimed that he had climbed the tree like a monkey, wrapping his legs and arms around the thin, ridged trunk. When he reached the top, he had hung with one arm and used his other to dislodge an unripe green coconut, throwing it to the ground. The coconut made a loud thumping sound when it hit the earth.

I didn't believe that my Uncle Baldev could really climb the coconut tree like a monkey; his bones were too old and would crackle and pop on the way up. I was sure that he had really paid a few dollars to the young village boys, bribing them to climb the coconut tree and drop the coconuts for him.

I never told him this, however. I feared what I had witnessed in his living room, and knew that if I angered him as Manjula had it might be the end of his treats. No longer would he carry sugarcanes, mangoes, pineapples, and coconuts right to my doorstep. I would have to go back to eating the dry scrapings of a mature brown coconut.

"Don't bring any more food, Baldev *ji*," my mother would tell him frequently. She would tap my protruding stomach, sigh, and say, "Too fat."

My uncle would shake his head and smile. "Let her eat, Sister. She's a growing girl. She needs food to grow into a woman. One day she'll run for Miss Hibiscus and win, I am sure."

"Miss Hibiscus, Baldev? If she keeps eating like this, the only thing she'll do at the Hibiscus Festival is line up to eat candy floss and ice cream."

"She would still be able to go on the rides, Sumitri. What are you saying?"

"Rides? The only ride she could fit onto would be the merry-go-round horses! If she went on the swings or the Ferris wheel, the chains would break and she would fall to the ground and crack her head open." My mother shuddered at the thought.

Uncle Baldev rubbed my head in affection and kissed my

cheek as I indulged in the soft coconut meat. I guzzled down the coconut milk in one big gulp. It tasted sweet and delicious. Sometimes my mother's words hurt, but I don't think she ever noticed.

Uncle Baldev grinned and winked at me. "Sister, you are letting your imagination run away. She's a good, solid build. She will be the next Miss Hibiscus, you'll see."

"Whatever you say, Brother," said my mother.

I flashed Uncle Baldev my biggest smile. It was as if he was my only friend.

13

I MET MY first real school friend in Class Four. His name was Kirtan. His face was round, like Moon-Face in my favorite Enid Blyton stories, but his belly was flat as a board. He was an inch taller than me, with shoulders even huskier than mine.

I met him on the same day that I had a brush with the word "movement," except that my teacher called it a "revolution." She had asked me to come forward, to the front of the class.

"What is this, Kalyana?" she asked.

"My essay, Teacher *ji*."

"I can see that. But what is this?" She pointed to my use of "she" in the place of "he." She had circled the word with a bright red pen everywhere it had appeared throughout the three-page essay.

"This is not proper English," she snapped. "When the identity of a speaker or person is not known, proper English demands that you use 'he' or 'him' or 'his.' You never substitute 'she' or 'her' in place of 'him.' Understand?"

I shook my head. The teacher squinted; she looked startled and confused.

"What's there not to understand?"

"I…I don't understand why we…we can't use 'she' sometimes. If…it's not known if it is a boy or a girl…could it not perhaps be a girl?" I stammered.

My heart was already picking up speed. I couldn't understand, but I was terrified that I would be sent to the headmaster's office. I did not want to have the red stick rained down on me again. A few children chuckled under their breaths in the background, but I ignored them.

The teacher stared harder. "No, you can't do that. It's improper. And it's incorrect. You'll be marked wrong."

She flung my essay back at me. I caught two of the pages, while the third fell to the concrete floor. I bent down, picked it up, and walked humbly back to my wooden desk. Out of the corner of my eye, I saw my teacher shake her head.

"Today's children," she mumbled. "Give an inch; they take a mile. And young girls everywhere think that they can start a revolution! Good grace!"

Revolution? That was a new word.

That lunch period, a boy followed me outside. Gone were those days when I hid in the toilet to eat lunch, for I had made peace with my shame. Time, it seemed, could make one embrace the unacceptable things: the constant leering, the ceaseless teasing. Still, sometimes I wished that I could be more like the women of America or like the man behind the stone-cold statue gracing our school's front steps. I would start my own movement and forever banish Ashita and Noora from the playground. Like Mother Kali, I would stand upon their heads with my two small feet.

Although now I embraced the daylight outside, I still hung my head low and ate alone. That day, I took my curry and roti roll and an Enid Blyton book to the shade of an over-grown bougainvillea hedge by the netball field, sitting on the green grass and watching grasshoppers skipping around me as butterflies floated on colorful wings.

I was sitting there when the boy approached me. "You are the girl who was starting a revolution in class," he said, and then plunged down and sat beside me. "Do you know what 'Revolution' means?" he asked.

I was silent; this was a new experience, as welcome as it was. How should I respond? I didn't know what to say, what to think, or even how to move. Should I shake my head and tell him "no"? Or should I lie?

He was new in my class. The gossip was that Kirtan's family had moved to Suva from Nadi, the land where airplanes raced down concrete strips illuminated by white lights, bringing with them people who were not Indians. I wanted to ask Kirtan if he had seen a true *gora*, with hair the color of buttercups and skin lighter than cream.

But I remained quiet, for I was seized with a sudden fear that he would break into shattering laughter and leave me sitting alone. He might join hands with Ashita or Noora, the class queens, who had every boy buzzing like crazed bees around their fat, ugly heads. I hated them and the way they fell into fits of giggles every time I walked by them in the open hallways.

"There goes the forty-four-gallon lonely drum," they

would whisper loud enough for everyone—even me—to hear. Their words were like the bite of a poisonous plant. Kirtan's laugh would be much worse, like the sting of a bee; it would swell, infecting my body and wounding my heart. So I said nothing. I looked ahead and let the breeze blow through my short brown hair.

Kirtan broke the silence. "I agree," he said. "I think we should be able to write 'she' if we don't know whether the person is a boy or a girl. The teacher doesn't make sense. I think it's good to start a movement sometimes." He started unrolling his lunch, still sitting beside me.

"Movement?"

"Yes," he said. "It's just like a revolution. A change! That's what my father told me, anyway."

"My mother told me all about American women going mad and starting a movement while being under the influence," I offered. "What did you get?" I added in a low voice.

"Pardon me?" he said.

"Your lunch," I said, leaning over. "What did you get?"

"Potato, onion, and masala. And you?" He leaned over to see what my mother had packed.

"Green cabbage and roti." I scrunched up my nose. "I hate cabbage. I like potatoes better."

"Here," he said. "You eat my lunch, and I'll eat yours. I don't mind cabbage."

And that was the beginning of Kirtan and me, our story. We traded lunch under the shade of a bougainvillea hedge and talked about being revolutionary. The sun shone and the grasshoppers skipped, the flowers smiled and butterflies rose all around us. I was no longer alone.

14

TO MY DISAPPOINTMENT, the next time Uncle Baldev came over he didn't bring ripe mangoes or raw sugarcanes. I pouted in a corner and blamed my mother for opening her mouth and telling him that I was too fat.

Instead, he brought a small, brown cardboard box that was covered with a translucent blue material. It smelled like dung. My mother was horrified when she came out to greet Uncle Baldev. Manjula followed close behind her, looking curious.

"Go on," said Uncle Baldev. "Look inside, Kali-yana."

I did, and a thrilling sensation soared through me the moment my eyes rested on six yellow, fuzzy creatures. They looked up to me with piercing black eyes and then wobbled around the box, using their tiny beaks to peck at grains of food or drink water from a pink plastic bowl. I picked one little chick up and caressed it, bringing it close to my cheek. Its down felt soft against my skin.

"Baby chickens? Oh, Baldev *ji*!" My mother waved her

hands, upset. "What did you do now? Kalyana can't take care of them. The task of looking after them will fall only on my head."

I tugged the end of her sari, begging to keep them. "Please, Mummy. Please."

It was Uncle Baldev who persuaded her. "Sumitri, I am sure Manjula would help," he said pointedly. My mother remained unconvinced. "It's not like Manjula is getting married tomorrow." He winked and smiled mischievously. My mother nodded her head hesitantly and sighed, but dropped the subject.

Uncle Baldev looked over to me and smiled again. Since the last time I had seen him, he had lost one of his front teeth. He looked even more homely than before, but I ran over and hugged him tightly. I was getting used to the whiskey breath and the stale stench of cigarettes on his clothes. Even the feel of his whiskers brushing against my cheeks was becoming less repulsive.

Uncle Baldev went back outside to the front porch and moved a sack of shavings and a bag of chicken feed into the living room. My mother shrugged and put her hand on her head. Manjula stood by the doorway, expressionless. Was she offended by the careless words? Perhaps she was simply remembering what she had done in Uncle Baldev's living room, all that time ago. Nonetheless, I was happy. I had two friends, Kirtan and my uncle, and now six baby chickens of my own.

I was in love with my new pets. I took turns patting all of the baby chicks, stroking their heads, rubbing their backs, and tickling their bellies.

"Every day, Kali-yana," said Uncle Baldev in Hindi, "you have to take them out of the box and change the newspaper lining the bottom. Use fresh, clean newspaper and a few handfuls of shavings. Put water in this bowl and food in this one." He always spoke Hindi, like my father. I think that, like my father, he also read the newspapers by looking at the pictures.

"No problem, Uncle," I said.

Manjula rolled her eyes.

"How about that?" said my Uncle Baldev.

How about that!

I did change the newspaper lining and give the baby chickens food and water as Uncle Baldev had instructed me—for the first few weeks, at least. After that, I left the care mostly to Manjula, although I continued to pet them and cuddle them every afternoon when I came home from school. Two months later, the chickens were too big to stay in a cardboard box, so Manjula went to the far corner of our backyard, close to the cemetery, and with Father's help, built a small wooden shed, surrounded by a metal fence. She called it the "Chicken House."

"The Chicken House is far away enough from our house that we won't be able to smell their poop," she declared confidently.

The Chicken House stood less than five feet in height and was only six feet wide and seven feet long. My father covered the ground with hay and put a round tire in the middle of the wooden shed.

"The little house will keep the chickens warm and dry in a rainstorm," he said. "They can jump on and off the tire and keep themselves amused, Kalyana."

I told Kirtan about my new pet chickens. He wanted to see them, so I invited him down to our house. "Kirtan?" said my mother, right before his father dropped him off on the front porch steps of our house. "What kind of name is that?"

I shrugged my shoulders and looked up to the ceiling. "That's what he says his name is. So that's what it is."

"Kirtan is not a name. It's a song of devotion." Manjula limped into the living room. "You haven't even finished primary school and you've got a boyfriend already," she said, smirking.

I stopped smiling. I didn't want Manjula to tell him that he was my boyfriend; Kirtan might never come to visit me again. "He's not my boyfriend. He is my friend," I said forcefully.

"Whatever you say," said Manjula. She turned abruptly and walked away, and thankfully my mother also stopped questioning me.

Yet when Kirtan stood at my door, looking sharp in khaki shorts, a crisp white shirt, and a red striped tie, my mother still smirked. "Is Kirtan hungry?" she asked.

"No thank you, Mrs. Seth. I already ate."

"Thirsty?"

"No thank you, Mrs. Seth. My mother gave me a glass of almond milk before I came."

My mother shook her head, smiled, and told me to go and play outside with my little friend.

I took him out to the backyard, to the Chicken House. We squatted side by side and watched the chickens graze and peck on seeds. They made noises that neither of us could understand, but they looked peaceful and content.

When we got tired of visiting the chickens, we went and sat underneath the lime tree and played house. I brought out my most treasured possession, the stainless-steel stove, and shared it with Kirtan. We stirred rose petals and lime leaves in plastic toy pots. We decorated mud pies with scrunched-up marigold flowers and jasmine petals. He never complained once, but happily went along with all the games I created for us.

When the make-believe dinners were eaten and the dishes rinsed in water, we sprawled under the lime tree on a thin blanket and pretended to sleep side by side like real husbands and wives. I knew then that one day I would grow up and ask the pundit to chant Sanskrit over the open fires, joining Kirtan's hand with mine. But I would wear pink, not red like most brides, and I would look ahead instead of down to the ground, disobeying my mother's well-meaning advice. Should I change my last name to Singh? I had come to like being called Seth.

Perhaps even after all those years, Manjula would still be waiting for the arrival of her groom. Would she plant a joyous smile on her face and carry on with my wedding chores, as if it were her true calling? Perhaps she would take to bed and nurse her bleeding heart and count her sorrows one by one. Manjula or not, on the day I married my Kirtan, the four old women would beat the drums with their bare hands and bellow songs out of tune. I knew they would dance like hurricanes under the giant yellow moon, and I couldn't wait for this day, my day, to come.

15

UNEXPECTEDLY, Manjula's day arrived more quickly than mine.

A gentle Christian man, a lonely widower who was only forty-five years old, was seeking a good wife to care for his two teenage sons. We knew very little about them, but my mother said that Peter was an Anglo-Indian: half-British and half-Indian. She called him an effect of colonization. Mother also said that he was from the land where maple leaves grew bright red, like the color of blood. It was a place where buffalo used to roam wild, where buildings now scraped the skies.

Buffalo?

Mother didn't know exactly what they were. "He's from overseas," she explained. "From Canada. A big Canadian city called Toronto."

This intrigued me, for this place called Toronto was close to America. Some even said that, in actuality, it sat right on top of America itself. To think that Manjula could marry a half-*gora* and make her way to America! Who knew what might happen then.

The gossip was that Peter had moved there from the Fiji Islands with his entire family when he was only five years old, soon after the Great Depression had ended. Since he grew up in Canada, he was Western in his thoughts and values, the villagers said, some disapprovingly. Most importantly, though, he was forgiving of small flaws such as limps and gray hairs and slight wrinkles. The word in the village was that he was already impressed that Manjula knew how to drive and read in English, as these skills would create one less headache for him.

For one month before their meeting, Manjula religiously arose before dawn and started pacing the house. Over and over, she practiced walking slowly and gracefully. After a few hours of pacing, she would stop and ask my mother, "How's the limp looking? How am I doing?"

My mother would shake her head and say, "Just keep practicing, Manjula. It's looking a little better. But keep practicing."

So Manjula would go back to the slow, controlled pacing. She concentrated on every step, every sway of her hips. On the weekends, I watched her go up and down the living room for hours on end. I couldn't tell whether she was walking better; at least from where I was sitting, it didn't appear that she was limping any less. The limp was part of Manjula, after all. It was the life of her, like the milk of the coconut or the juice of the mango. Or as Manjula might have to say now, the sap of a maple.

This time the meeting was to take place in the comfort of our own living room. When the day arrived, my mother came to Manjula and dropped *kajal* in her hair again. Manjula wore the same gold sari with the maroon border that she had worn for Rabir. She rouged her cheekbones and once again put maroon lipstick on the curve of her lips. She looked beautiful as she sat stiffly, awaiting her second suitor.

He arrived right on time, in a beaten-up car. Unlike Rabir, however, he didn't have a pregnant belly or a mole on his cheek. Instead, he had a square face, similar to Manjula's but with masculine features. Covering his graying hair was the most charming black hat, one that he took off the moment he entered our home. Later, I learned that it was called a fedora.

I thought he was such an attractive gentleman that Manjula would be no match for him. Surely he would turn my aunt down, destroying her dreams once more. And yet he smiled at Manjula when he sat down in front of her. All this I observed from my perch on the chair across the room.

This Peter came with his older sister, who was nothing like Rabir's sister-in-law. She was humbly dressed and had gray hair oiled and tied back in a ponytail. She said little, choosing to sit silently through the process. She did not look down her nose at Manjula or my parents.

My mother served Indian sweets and deep-fried goodies, with ginger chai in real china cups. She only brought these out on special occasions. "Have some more *bhajiya*, Peter *ji*. Manjula woke up before dawn to prepare all of this for you. Come on, have some more."

After a few casual exchanges with my father, Peter looked directly at Manjula. I think she believed that humiliation was imminent. Sitting at the edge of her seat, she clutched the armrests in nervous anticipation.

But her suitor didn't ask her to show him how she walked. Instead, he reached in his pocket and bought out a pamphlet. Leaning over, he handed it to her and said, "I hear you are learned in English. I couldn't believe it. Could you, please?"

"Sure. Sure," said Manjula, shocked into speech. "No problem." After a small pause, she read slowly, careful not to make a mistake. "For God so loved the world that He gave his only begotten Son, that whosoever believeth in him should not perish, but have everlasting life."

Peter clapped his hands together and smiled, brightening up the entire room. "Fabulous! Fabulous!"

I nudged my mother's sari and whispered, "What does that mean, Mummy?"

"Shh!" warned my mother.

"Do you drive as well as you read?" Peter paused, and then answered his own question. "You probably do. Very progressive! Fiji has come a long way since my family and I left. Good to see!"

He clapped his hands again, looked at his sister, and said, "Shall we?"

She shrugged her shoulders and said, "Sure. Why not? She's very pretty."

Peter put his palms together, looked to my father, and said, "I am leaving in two weeks. But I'll be coming back to Fiji in three months. I would like to take my wife with me at that time." He looked over to Manjula and said, "If she agrees to have me as her husband."

Manjula looked at the ground shyly, batted her eyes, and

smiled. It sickened me to see my aunt flaunting herself so shamelessly in front of these strangers. I pouted unnoticed in a corner.

"Three months?" said my mother. "How can that be possible? Indian weddings can't be put together in three months. There's saris to be bought, henna to be painted, food to be planned, decorations to be hung, halls to be rented, sheds to be built, invitations to be sent. Oh, my God! Three months!"

"Don't worry, Sister. We were hoping for a small wedding. And we are more than willing to help with any costs…"

"We're a prosperous family, Peter. Cost is not an issue," my father interrupted. He sounded mildly insulted. "We can put it together in three months, if you so wish."

"Sure, sure," said Peter. He leaned closer to my father and said, gently and softly, "We were also hoping for a Christian wedding in a proper church, if it's not too much to ask."

"Christian wedding?" said my father sternly. "No woman from my home will leave without a proper Hindu ceremony."

Manjula flared her nostrils. My mother tilted her head and pursed her lips, sealing them tightly. I wondered whether Manjula would leap out of her seat, saying the wrong thing or defying my father in front of these foreign guests who wore hats and came from a land where leaves turned red. She certainly looked mutinous.

Manjula's suitor leaned back in his chair, frowning. I was sure that he would stride out of the room, leaving Manjula to wait another five years for an offer to come. I sat gripping the arms of my chair, envying Raju for not being present.

Peter hemmed and hawed. Then, looking at Manjula sitting calmly, he smiled and said to my father, "Tell you what,

Mr. Seth. You put on an Indian wedding. When I go back to Canada, we'll do a small church ceremony."

Manjula looked to the floor and smiled more brightly than the small bulb on the ceiling. My mother relaxed in her seat; I heard her sigh under her breath.

So it was settled. But I felt like as though I had been struck with a hammer, a blow that blurred the thoughts stirring in my head. Perhaps I had truly gone mad, like Shilpa, for I must be hearing things that weren't being said and seeing things in different shades. Manjula, our Manjula, was going to get married! And not just once, but twice! Could that really be?

And yet it was. The final date was set for December 15, in the heat of the blazing Fiji sun.

As Peter and his sister were walking out the door, my mother whispered to him, "You are aware that she walks with a limp, Peter *ji*?"

He looked at my mother's concerned face. "God made her as she is, Sister. Why should I think that He went wrong? I am sure she is as He intended her to be. I hear she's a virtuous woman—still untouched. In Canada, you can never be sure if a woman is virtuous or not."

Taking my mother's small hand in his, he tilted his head. "She is all that I am looking for, Sister." Then he bowed and tipped his charming hat. "Good day to you, Sumitri *ji*," he said. "I am sure we'll be in touch!"

Winking at me, he put his hat back on his head and went out the door and out of sight, his sister following close on his heels.

As soon as he was gone, Manjula sprang up from the chair and screamed at the top of her lungs. I sat frozen in time, still and silent. Manjula, our Manjula, the Manjula who walked with a limp and had a temper that rose and fell like the ocean tides, the Manjula whom Rabir had rejected those many years ago, was getting married at last!

Father put his hands behind his head and leaned back in his chair. My mother shook her head and exclaimed, "We all find our princes one day! It's fate! Destiny! What else would it be? My beloved sister is getting married!"

Manjula was getting married.

Oh, my God!

16

PETER RETURNED unexpectedly right before he left to return to Canada. He sat and talked with Manjula under the lime tree. They looked charming together, and I suddenly thought of Cinderella in the fairy tale. Manjula glanced at the ground often and blushed, as her suitor sat there staring at his bride-to-be under the tree. Once, I even saw her whisper something that made him chuckle loudly.

I wished I knew what they were speaking about.

When he left, Manjula disappeared into a dream world. She sat in silence for hours, staring at the ceilings and her bedroom walls, smiling the whole time. My mother said that she was madly in love, that's all.

I started singing romantic songs every time Manjula passed by. I would sing one song in particular: "*My heart is beating. It keeps on repeating. I am waiting for you...*" The Hindi movie *Julie* had not even been released, but the radio was already playing its theme song. Just like Manjula was not yet married, but I was singing of her love.

Manjula did not take offence. She would just look at me out of the corner of her eye and smile. It was as though she had left her anger on the shore the last time she visited the ocean. There was no penetrating her happiness.

An aura of light would envelop her wherever she went, and she began to act foolishly. She would forget to feed the chickens or wash the clothes or pound the masala or scrub the cement. My mother would cringe and say things such as, "Future Mrs. Peter Simmons, please come back to this world. Chores still need to be done." Then she would shake her head and say, "I swear love ruins everyone's brains—even a grown woman's! Go figure. Huh!"

Days passed and the wedding plans started to take form. I was afraid that this must be all a hoax: the wedding day would arrive, the procession would come with a loud bang, and everyone would be there except for the groom. Manjula would sob in front of her laughing guests. Her red sari would be thrown into the wedding fire and turned to ashes. Her jewelry would be sold to young girls awaiting their lovers, and her henna would be scrubbed clean. My mother would rub her back to bring light back into her eyes, all to no avail. She would spend her days sitting alone on the seawall, sobbing, and her tears would mix with the ocean waters.

And yet my worries were for naught. Just as he had promised, Peter returned from Toronto in exactly three months. He bore a bottle of Canadian rum for my father, chocolates for my mother, and a wrapped present for Manjula.

"Just as you asked—a twenty-six-inch waist and light blue in color. I hope it fits well and you like it," Peter said with a smile. He presented the bottle of rum to my father, who put it away in the top cupboard.

In all my life, I don't think I had ever seen Manjula receive a gift that was as beautifully wrapped as this one. It was covered in silver paper and even had a red bow. I was left open-mouthed, and a deep burn spread across my heart. Manjula glowed and said in English, "Thank you. Thank you. I'll open it later."

Peter sat and had chai with Manjula under the lime tree. Then he left.

She wouldn't tell anyone what he had bought her, although we were brimming with curiosity. "I'll show you later, Sumitri, I promise." She winked and shoved the gift under our mattress.

When Father went to work the next day, Manjula came out of the room. She had hoisted blue bell-bottom pants high up to her torso and put on a plain white top. She limped through the house, giggling uncontrollably. I still couldn't tell if she was missing any toes, as she had put on my father's big striped socks to hide her feet.

"Sister," she said to my mother, "when I fly away to Canada, I'll have to wear pants like all the other women. So I thought I should get in some practice before I go. Yes."

Shocked, I left the two women giggling in the living room. And that wasn't the only law Manjula broke that day, for she persuaded my mother to put red and green straws in Peter's red-labeled bottle and guzzle the golden liquid! Even though my mother made the excuse that their teeth were hurting and they had to numb their gums, I didn't believe her.

They both giggled all the more, acting like foolish school-aged girls right in the center of our living room. They danced around in a mad frenzy to English songs blaring on the radio. I felt a rush of anger buzz through my body, seeing my grown mother and auntie acting like such fools in the middle of a bright, sunny day. I left the room in a huff and went and wrote down my feelings in a blue-lined notebook.

I don't think Manjula or my mother noticed my departure or disapproval, but, if they did, they didn't seem to care. They continued their senseless charade until my father and Raju came home. Then they quickly scurried away to put food on the fire and chai on the stove.

Since the adults were busy with the wedding preparations, Kirtan and I could venture a little further than before. We crept across the street to Tulsi's house undetected; we were spies from a film, waiting and watching. We hid behind the jasmine bushes and peeked in the bedroom window.

Tulsi sat still at the edge of her bed, unaware of our presence. I had never seen Tulsi in a dress before. When she walked about the village, she was always wrapped up tightly in a plain sari, head and all. She would walk a few feet behind her husband, her head bent and eyes lowered.

Tulsi was studying her palms. Kirtan thought that perhaps she was observing the cuts and bruises, stamps and evidence of hard work, but I wondered if she was desperately looking to see if the markings on her palms foretold a better future. We heard her mother-in-law's bellowing voice resound through the walls. "Tulsi, dishes won't wash them-selves, you know!" Tulsi got up from the edge of the bed and slowly walked away.

Kirtan and I moved towards another window and saw that she had assumed her position in front of a stack of dirty pots and pans. She squatted on a mat on the hard cement floor, scrubbing a blackened pot with steel wool. Her mother-in-law, a large woman with white hair, sat on the middle of her bed and stared intently at her. She wore a widow's white gown.

From what I could see, there were only two rooms in this house: one room where Tulsi, her husband, and their three sons slept, and the other, to which the mother-in-law had laid claim. I knew the boys slept in the same room as their parents, because a separate mattress was laid out on the floor in the room where Tulsi had rested so briefly.

Tulsi was working hard; she had moved on to the second blackened pot. The mother-in-law still sat. Unlike our home, where everything was tucked away in drawers, these rooms were clean but chaotic and disarrayed. They had a cuckoo clock that ticked noisily in a corner. The drapes were bright orange and seemed gaudily out of place. Stacks of paper had been untidily shuffled across the coffee table, and an old glass vase of dusty silk flowers sat by the mother-in-law's unmade bed.

We had bouquets of fresh flowers in our house; they stood submerged in clear water, in real china vases with blue drawings of children playing by the ocean.

What shocked me most wasn't the vase, though: it was noon and the mother-in-law's bed was still unmade, something that would have been unheard of in our home. My own mother would have thrown a tantrum right in the middle of our house if Manjula had forgotten to make the beds in such a tardy manner.

Kirtan tugged at my dress and tried to pull me down to the ground. He signaled for us to go, like a chief detective, but I did not want to listen. Greedily I watched, staring like a thief in the window, stealing details of Tulsi's life, hoping to put it in a story I was writing secretly. I might never get a chance like this again.

Tulsi scrubbed the dirty pots and pans hard and fast; her soapy hands were blackened to the elbows. When she turned on the tap and washed away the soap suds, I noticed that, on the back of her right arm, from her wrist to her elbow, stretched a tattoo of her husband's full name. It was as if a young child had scribbled his name on her arm in uneven thick black letters. The image made me gasp and dig my toes into the soft dirt. Tulsi looked up to the window, as though she sensed our presence.

Kirtan and I ducked down quickly, and I stepped sideways to avoid being seen through the window. But I did not see the small hole by my feet, and my left foot became tightly wedged inside. A terrible thought crossed my mind. What if Tulsi's husband emerged and found Kirtan and I examining the bits and pieces of his life? What if he picked up a stick, like the headmaster, and beat us with it?

As tears started to well up in my eyes, I thought about calling out to my mother. But Kirtan grabbed my ankle and pulled my foot out of the hole. We scurried away, now like lizards instead of spies—quickly and quietly. We crawled out of the yard, hiding behind hedges and trees. My heart was beating at a fierce pace. Kirtan's hair looked disheveled and his expression troubled. We ran home like wild dogs and collapsed by the Chicken House.

Later that night, as my mother sat in the dim light and painted henna on Manjula's palms, I asked her why she didn't have my father's name tattooed on her arm.

"I don't have his name burned on my arm because I was given the choice not to. Besides, they did that in the olden days. That's how they marked which woman belonged to which man. They don't do that anymore, Kalyana." She looked closely at me and said, "How would you know about such things?"

My eyes flitted away and rested on the floor. "Oh, Kirtan told me!"

My mother nodded her head. "Of course. Kirtan!" She looked at me mischievously and said, "Does Kirtan want you to get his name branded on your arm?"

She and Manjula burst into laughter. I pouted and stalked out of the room. "Sensitive," I overheard her whispering to Manjula. I just rolled my eyes and hid myself in bed, under the mosquito net.

Before, Manjula had been my ally against Mother. But now she was a proper woman about to be married; in a few days, she would become just like my mother, a lioness ruling over her small clan, in a vast land. This wedding fuss would be over and she would be gone. She would not be there to laugh at me with Mother, and she could no longer kick me or punch me in the middle of her sleep. I would get to spread my body across the mattress at last.

That night when I fell asleep, I had another dream.

I was sitting under a jasmine hedge, just like the one in Tulsi's yard, except that this one grew in the wooden shack in the Chicken House. There were cobras tattooed on the front of my hands, and the serpents were weeping tears of blood. My hands rested on my plump thighs, palms facing the dark night. The air was still and calm. The sky was empty of moon and stars, yet light still reflected off the jasmine flowers. I sat alone. Blood soaked through my maroon dress and moistened the ground all around me. I knew that the jasmine tree was drinking my blood, for, as I sat there, howling in pain, I saw the white flowers change colors. I called to my mother, but she never came. The white flowers withered and turned red as blood.

I woke up soaking my pillows with tears. I cried for myself and for the flowers, but mostly I cried for Tulsi, I think. I couldn't fall back asleep, so I closed my eyes and prayed to the mighty Goddess Kali. I prayed that she would touch Tulsi's arm and make her hideous mark disperse into smoke. I prayed that someday she might give Tulsi the courage to run through the meadows, alone.

17

DECEMBER 15, 1974. Manjula's wedding.

The flowers—frangipani, hibiscus, marigold, bougainvillea, and jasmine—were in full bloom during the weeks leading up to my auntie's wedding. So was my mother; I had never seen her so distracted. I missed Kirtan, but when I asked my mother if my friend could come too, she always brushed me away. Kirtan wasn't family, she would say firmly.

Now, when I voiced my request yet again, she sent me away to see what my father was doing. "Go be useful, Kalyana. See if the men helping your father build sheds outside need a cold drink or a warm cup of chai."

With a long face, I stomped outside and slumped on the porch steps. I was wearing my printed yellow dress, but even though it was a bright and sunny day, I had a halo of black clouds upon my head. I sat there, silently sulking and watching Raju and the men help my father thump wooden posts into the ground and slide slabs of tin onto them to create roofs. Watching the preparations, I forgot all about my own troubles. I also forgot about asking the men whether they preferred hot tea or a cool glass of juice.

A casually dressed man brought branches of fresh coconut leaves, and after the shed was built, he tied them around it with special knots. "To keep the rain, wind, and sunshine out, Kalyana *ji*," he said. I watched the men stack three concrete blocks in perfectly straight rows, making a border around the center. They dropped wooden boards over the blocks, and my mother came out of the house with a roll of white paper to cover the seats. I helped secure the paper on the boards by putting clear tape on the edges, as my mother instructed.

With the shed and seats in place, aunties young and old piled into our front yard. The uncles and cousins were set to work stirring giant pots of jackfruit curry and vegetable *pilau* with fat wooden spoons. Tonight the women did not stir food or make fires. They sat around the altar in the center, tucking the edges of their saris in their *lenghas,* and sang songs and beat drums. Their rhythmic songs pushed away the black clouds that had hung over me. I found myself rolling my shoulders, thumping my toes, and even shaking my hips, and other children were doing the same. No one here told us to stand up straight or to keep still. We danced late into the night, until we heard the yellow moon roar, the black clouds fading away into the disappearing sky.

As custom dictated, for the entire week before the wedding, Manjula sat alone in her room while we danced and sang. She was wearing a bright yellow sari, like my school uniform, but it was a color of celebration for her; yellow was always Manjula's color. Seven times a day, for seven days before the wedding, she would come out of that room. She was always smiling, even grinning. She would limp to a wooden chair in the center of the room, but no one spoke about her limp now. The only thing the villagers could whisper of was how Manjula, like a slick fisherwoman, had laid out her bait and charmed and trapped a foreign man in her net.

When Manjula was seated, I joined other young girls who rubbed turmeric paste on her arms, legs, and face. Mother said it was to prepare Manjula for her wedding night; her skin must be soft, supple, and glowing. I didn't really know what she meant, but I masterfully dabbed handfuls of yellow paste onto Manjula's forehead, spilling some on the ground. She wrinkled her nose. "Too much, Kalyana. Too much! Only a little bit, Baby!" she said.

I ignored her protests and continued with the turmeric paste. She did not wash it off, even the gobs. It crusted over her dark skin, turning it as yellow as the insides of a ripe papaya.

On the night before the wedding, women and girls lined up in a circle in the middle of our living room to cook stacks upon stacks of *puries* for the auspicious day. My mother instructed me to sit cross-legged. A new white sheet was spread before us and covered with dry flour. My mother showed me how to use the rolling pin to flatten the dough into a perfect round shape. After a few tries, I got it right, good enough for it to be submerged into pure ghee. I glowed as I sat back and watched mine puff up and rise.

We made dozens and dozens of *puries* and stacked them in tall piles for the holy day. We cut and washed banana leaves and stacked them along with the *puries*; in Fiji, wedding guests ate on banana leaves rather than on china or paper plates. Eating on banana leaves was a rare treat, and I was certain that it made the food taste better.

I thought that surely, after this task, I would have no more chores to complete, but I was misguided. When the blessed day arrived, my mother handed me a red bucket and ordered me to go and pick fresh flowers. This was a pleasant task, for I liked breaking off the flowers and gently dropping them in my bucket. The delicate scents blended like the auras of my four old women, teasing and embracing.

Mother spread the flowers onto pieces of newspaper in the middle of her bedroom floor. She showed me how to sew them together with a thread and needle, making garlands for both the bride and the groom. This time there were no patterns to be followed, no order to adhere to. I joyfully linked the flowers together on a red thread, adding colors and varieties to my personal preference. My mother would occasionally glance at my progress and, to my surprise, compliment my work. Manjula would be so happy, she said.

As I sewed the flowers together with my small fingers, Manjula, behind closed doors, poured warm water over her head. She bathed for the first time in seven days and scrubbed the dried turmeric paste off her skin. I went into the room after her and saw the yellow water still flowing down the drain.

Afterwards, cousins—all of them young girls—decorated Manjula's forehead and painted her nails and spread red lipstick on her lips. They wrapped her in a glittering red-and-gold sari, the one my mother had bought her especially for this occasion. A ruby-studded *bindia* lay across the top of her head, falling beautifully at the crease of her brows. Manjula seemed strange, not like the Manjula I had known. She did not fuss or even grin, but sat quietly in the middle of the room as women buzzed around her. There was no impatient sighing as she waited for her groom. Her legs were crossed and her eyes fixed on the far mirror hanging on the wall.

There was a beauty I had never seen in her, and it was not merely from the sparkly sari that was loosely covering her head and shoulders. Looking at her made me dream of my wedding day. I, too, would sit like a queen. A glittering bright pink sari with an oversized silver border would be draped over my shoulders, and my feet would be encased in glass slippers like a fairy princess.

My mother had painted my nails a bright reddish-purple, but the dress laid out on my bed did not make me feel like a fairy princess at all. I threw my hands up in the air and tossed my new black sandals onto the bed.

I hated the dress, I told my mother. It was too tight and made me look fat, like a big maroon pumpkin. "Kalyana, stop being difficult," Mother grunted impatiently. She brushed away my excuses the way she would brush away a flyaway hair, as if even the annoyance was nothing.

I was unhappy, but I squeezed myself into the new dress. It was only a little bit snug. I had not been telling the truth; the real reason I did not want to wear that dress was that it looked exactly like the one I had seen in my dream.

The pundit, a young man with jet-black hair, arrived early in the morning to bless the altar and prepare the fire for the wedding. There was not the slightest crease or stain on the cotton pants and the white kurta he wore. Even his nails were short and clean. He mumbled holy verses and chanted hymns that no one but priests could understand. Ignoring the pundit's chants, my mother joined my father at the entrance of the shed, greeting the guests and shaking hands. I stood by them, holding onto my father's free hand. I couldn't decide whom to watch, so I kept one eye on the pundit's activities and the other on the arriving guests.

The guests: There were so many, and they sat where they pleased. Some sat on the wooden benches we had prepared, and a few took the chairs that had been set in far corners of the shed. Others sat on the mat on the ground, and still more found their places on the porch steps. Our front yard was overflowing with vibrancies: bright saris, printed dresses, and colorful suits.

Manjula was led out of her room by a group of young girls. She came out slowly, with her eyes cast down and a red and gold dupatta covering her head. When she was seated next to Peter, his hand was placed underneath hers and a red ribbon was pinned at the ends of her sari and joined with Peter's kurta. We sat around the bride and the groom as they adorned each other with the garlands I had made. The pundit was chanting prayers I could not understand.

Now that the great event was finally happening, I was suddenly bored. I sat in a corner, on the wooden seat that my father and Raju had erected, and watched the smoke of the small fire escape into the humid air. A traditional Hindu ceremony went on for hours, it seemed, and I fidgeted on the bench. I wished that Kirtan were there. He could make the time pass like a swift, cool breeze.

Out of the corner of my eye, I saw Uncle Baldev standing at the side of our house. He took something yellow and small out of his pocket. Winking, he flashed it quickly towards me, making me smile. He discreetly put it back in his pocket, and I suddenly became curious. What was it that he was hiding? Another baby chicken, or perhaps a baby duck this time? I had never owned a duck before. It could be a yellow toy. Or perhaps *barfi*—my favorite Indian sweet? He motioned for me to come to him.

Nobody cared what I did. This was Manjula's day, like my mother had said; all eyes were on her alone. I was not used to being ignored, and I really wanted to know what was in my uncle's right jacket pocket. I nudged my mother. "I got to go *soo soo*, Mummy."

"Ssh!" she hissed.

"I *really* have to go, Mummy." I looked back at the house. Uncle Baldev had disappeared.

My mother glanced at the house briefly. "Fine, fine, go, Kalyana," she hissed. The pundit, still chanting, reached over and placed sandalwood paste on the foreheads of both bride and groom. Then Manjula bent her head forward and Peter lifted her *bindia* and dropped a pinch of vermilion powder in the part of her hair.

I got up from the bench in the shed and walked slowly to the main door. Then I ran through the house and slipped out the back door. I ran straight to my Uncle Baldev, who was loitering among the tall vines and swaying trees.

"My big girl," he said, gently grabbing my hand. He rubbed my fingers. "Was the wedding boring?"

I nodded my head. My Uncle Baldev understood me

better than my mother, I thought, and I snuffled a little. I kept eyeing his right jacket pocket, but I didn't want to ask him what he had hidden there. He might think I was forward and rude and choose to give me nothing.

"Kali-yana!" He sang my name as he led me away, holding onto my pinkie. "Let's go see the chickens."

We walked towards the Chicken House. The pundit's chants grew fainter and fainter as we moved further from my father's house. Soon all I could hear was the clucking of the chickens and the rustling of the coconut leaves in the distant cemetery. Hot air blew through my hair and the blazing afternoon sun beat down on my skin. I fixed my eyes on Uncle Baldev's jacket pocket.

"Oh, I almost forgot," he said in Hindi. He laughed, dipping his hand in his pocket, and brought out a fat, ripe mango. His big fingers squeezed the fruit as he handed it to me. Reluctantly, I took it from him. I loved fruit, but I had hoped for a different treat: some fuzzy, living creature, perhaps.

Holding the mango in my hand, I stirred the saliva in my mouth. I gingerly bit the top of the fruit, and then sucked the juice vigorously. Rivulets of juice streamed down the sides of my cheeks, making them moist and sticky. Uncle Baldev stood there silently, watching.

When I finished eating the mango, I threw the skin in the Chicken House. The chickens flocked to it the moment it landed on the ground. I noticed Uncle Baldev quickly look back over his shoulder, towards the back of our house. I turned around and followed his gaze. The curtains in the back windows were drawn and the backyard was bare. The house stood alone, silent and still.

"Come," said Uncle Baldev, motioning for me to enter the wooden shack of the Chicken House. I felt a knot building in the pit of my stomach.

I shook my head. "I don't want to miss the rest of Manjula's wedding. I better go back, Uncle. Mummy's probably looking for me."

"Your mother knows you're with me," he said smoothly. "She told me to take you to the Chicken House."

I looked up at him, confused. Why would my mother tell my uncle to take me to the shack? I told her I was going to the toilet, didn't I? It made no sense.

"Come on," he urged. "Let's go." He grabbed my hand and led me inside the shack. I didn't want to disobey my mother or my uncle, so I meekly followed his lead.

The chickens scurried away as we entered. Uncle Baldev sat at the edge of the tire and placed me on his lap. The smell of whiskey on his breath and the stale cigarette stench on his clothes seemed more pronounced in this small space. He kissed my cheek and rubbed my head. "Very pretty," he said. "Very pretty."

My stomach felt hollow and sick. I couldn't understand why my mother had wanted me to come to the Chicken House with Uncle Baldev.

"Your mother told me that you have a boyfriend," he said, stroking my back.

My spine tingled strangely, but I shook my head. "He's not my boyfriend!"

"He's a boy and a friend, so he has to be your boyfriend." His smile was strange, twisted. Chills shot through my plump body, making the hair on my arms rise.

The strong stench of the chickens' dung filled my nostrils. Uncle Baldev's hands slipped under my red dress, up my thighs. His hand burned a hole in my skin and yet turned my body to ice.

I started to cry.

"Don't cry," he ordered. His sweet tone had turned curt and cold, like the ugly ogre who sat below the bridge. "Sit still or else I will beat you like I was going to beat Manjula that day in my house. You remember, Kali-yana?"

I hated being called Kali-yana. I had always hated it. I nodded my head but could not stop crying.

"See this?" he said. He showed me his pocket knife. It had a red handle and a pointed blade that flashed in the dim light. He twisted the knife in his hand. "If you tell anyone, I'll take your eyes out like I take the eyes out of a pineapple." My uncle's face was cold and hard.

I shuddered in his tight embrace. The shack became blurry. I couldn't breathe, couldn't think. It was so hot, yet I shivered constantly. I could feel his breath in the hollow of my neck. The mango juice churned and bubbled like acid in my stomach, leaving a pungent taste in my mouth.

His weight on top of my small body muffled my cries. Snot and tears ran down my face. I closed my eyes and clenched my fists, but I did not make a single sound for fear of having my eyes taken out like a pineapple's. I was quieter than a dead snake as the first burst of pain exploded in my small body.

In the hollow darkness of my mind, I saw roses turn to ash and fall to the ground. I saw the four old women rise from the earth and circle the shack, like dead spirits circling the grave. The first one blew in like a mighty hurricane. The walls shuddered with the force of her wind. The second one, like a fierce rain, fell upon the shack with a violent might, making the ground flood and the chickens drown. The third woman brought fires, like lightning that struck from the skies. My father's shack was enveloped in choking black smoke. Then the last old woman, the Mother, appeared. She was the mightiest of them all. The earth shook and trembled as she stood over it like Goddess Kali stood over Lord Shiva. The shack, like a stack of playing cards, crumbled to the ground, and the fourth old woman swallowed us whole.

I opened my eyes.

In the distance, I heard my mother's voice calling my name. Uncle Baldev grunted, "Pull up your undies, Kali-yana. What's your mother going to think?" I did as he asked, without question or arguments. He carried me out of the shack in his arms, that same horrid smell of whiskey on his breath. The stale cigarette stench on his clothes was now on mine.

"I found her sleeping in the shack, Sumitri," he said smoothly. He smiled then, a horrible grin that exposed his missing front tooth. His skin smelled like dog's urine.

Squinting, my mother snatched me from his embrace and pulled me close. "What was she doing in the Chicken House?" Her voice hid a tiny shiver.

"No idea, Sister." Uncle Baldev's face was smooth, expressionless. He shrugged his shoulders and turned away. I buried my face in my mother's chest, smelling the lavender scent on her clothes and jasmine in her hair. I could hear the same coconut leaves rustling in the warm breeze. The clouds floated away, taking foreign shapes and forms in the pale blue sky. I never wanted to leave the warmth of my mother's bosom.

My mother carried me, I do not know how, across the backyard, through the door, and into her bedroom. She set me gently on her bed and stood back a moment.

I had seen the look of horror flit across her face and then the odd chill, a forced casualness, that followed it. Her tight face and lips insisted wordlessly that nothing out of the ordinary had taken place. Everything else was the same in her room: The dresser stood in a corner, the bed was made without a wrinkle, and the nailpolishes stood in a straight row on the dresser. My reddish-purple color was a little off from the center.

My mother took my bloody underwear and discreetly shoved it underneath her mattress. She looked over her shoulder once. The room was still empty; the guests, along with my brother and father, were outside, celebrating the propitious occasion.

My mother said that she would burn my panties in the fire later. They would turn to ashes and become part of the earth, burying my secret. Nobody could know.

"Later?" I croaked. It was as though my voice had disappeared, although I was sure I hadn't screamed.

"Yes, later. When the guests are gone, Kalyana. When the guests are gone." She was busying herself around the room, not looking at me.

I could hear the pundit chant Sanskrit prayers as he rang the bell. "*Svaha*," he said over and over again. I could hear the fire crackling as he dropped the offerings on the burning wood. Was that the smoke of incense I could smell from far off? I hid my body underneath my mother's blanket.

"There are some stories in this world that should never be told, Kalyana." My mother said this calmly, as if someone had just burned milk and it had overflowed, staining the stove. I didn't say anything.

"You hear me, Kalyana?" she said. "You hear me?" I nodded my head weakly. "I feel shame. I feel a tremendous amount of shame," she sighed, shaking her head. Her eyes were empty vessels. I retreated further under the covers.

I had shamed my mother.

"You can't tell it to Daddy."

Then I would shame my beloved father.

"Daddy will kill him, and then the police will come and take him to jail. How would we survive without a man? Do you want your daddy to go to jail?"

Then I would shame my entire family, cousins and all.

"Promise me that you won't ever tell him. Promise?" She took my hand and placed it on her head. It was a symbol of a true word given—a promise that couldn't be broken. She smiled faintly. "You can't even tell it to Raju or Manjula or your teachers. You can't tell this to anyone."

"Kirtan?" I broke my silence.

"You especially can't tell it to Kirtan."

"Why?"

"Because he wouldn't want you if he knew."

She paused. "Listen carefully," she said. "This is the curse of being a woman, Kalyana. We are blamed for everything that goes wrong. For every child that dies in birth or in the womb. For every child that loses his way. For every time a

154

man lies with a woman, we are blamed. For every heart that breaks. For every unfaithful man who strays. It is not the man who carries the blame."

I began to cry, and my mother sighed and stroked my hair and kissed my forehead. "You can cry," she said. "Maybe in secret."

One day my mother had cried alone; but it was not in secret, for I had heard her. I cried now, sobbing helplessly until I had fallen asleep in my mother's bed.

I did not awaken until all the guests had departed and my blood-soaked panties had become part of the earth.

18

I TRIED TO transform my feelings into characters, and my pain into words. But the paper before me, remained blank; the black chalkboard in front of me remained bare. Days passed. Nights turned chilly. Flowers died and then bloomed again. Rain splattered on the tin roofs. Coconut leaves continued to rustle in the wind. But then the sun's rays emerged from behind the clouds again. Yet I remained unchanged. I remained cold.

On my first day back to school, I took a tensor bandage and wrapped it tightly around my right arm. I frantically covered the blood, the pain, and the cuts that were not there.

Kirtan was horrified to see me with this injury. During lunch, when he was sitting by my side under the bougainvillea hedge, he asked me about it outright. "What happened to your arm?"

"Cut it, Kirtan. That's all."

"Let me see."

"No."

"How did you cut it, Kalyana? You have to be careful."

"My uncle cut it."

"Your uncle cut it?"

"Yes." I looked to the ground. Kirtan noticed. I looked away to the side.

"Does your Mummy know?"

I could not tell Kirtan that Mummy knew. Kirtan would wonder why Mummy did not beat Uncle Baldev for hurting me. He would think that she did not love me. I could not let him think that, so I shook my head. Quickly, I invented an excuse. "Uncle Baldev said not to tell anyone."

"Why?"

I shrugged my shoulders. "I don't know." I paused. "He did it on purpose, that's why." I blurted out forcefully, suddenly angry.

Anger seeped into Kirtan's eyes, too. He stood up abruptly and kicked and punched the tree, hurting his knuckles. "I'll kill him!" he yelled.

I smiled contentedly.

"Where does he live? Tell me." He was full of energy and passion.

"Nausori."

"Nausori? I don't know how I'll get there. My father will have to drive me there. I'll cut his arm first before I kill him."

"I love you, Kirtan."

He sat back down and relaxed. We rested there, basking in the sublime quietness of the warm afternoon, and I wondered whether Kirtan indeed would have his revenge. I hoped that he would keep entertaining such thoughts. It gave me tremendous pleasure to picture it in my mind's eye.

19

MANJULA REMAINED in Fiji with Peter for a full six weeks before flying away to Toronto. During her final week, she stayed with us.

My mother never left her side. They spent the afternoons talking in my mother's bedroom, eating Kit Kat chocolate bars and mint ice cream and oiling each other's hair. I had heard my mother tell Manjula that, on the night of her own wedding, she sat sobbing at the foot of the bed as my father soundly slept. She was sure that Manjula, a hungry tigress without any fear or womanly shame, had pounced on her groom. Manjula had smirked while my mother's laugh rattled the windows and shook the curtains.

I sat in my room, staring at the bare walls. I had longed for Manjula's departure, for life to resume its normal course. I had anxiously awaited the day when our bedroom belonged solely to me. But now, I dreaded having to sleep alone.

On the final night, Manjula went out to the sea and collected crabs for the last time. Peter also came for the feast. As always, my aunt wore her best frock, but this time, the whole family dressed finely. All except me. I sat and watched as the strangers around me laughed and gabbed well into the night.

While usually I abhorred Manjula's crab feasts, this time I devoured four bowls of crab curry and three platefuls of rice. Every breath was a struggle and every movement difficult. I lay in a corner on the floor with my legs apart and my stomach swollen.

My mother sat shaking her head. My father ignored the whole matter, and Raju just laughed like an underaged child. But I said nothing.

Peter and Manjula sat side by side, holding hands. They gleamed in the evening light. I had never seen my mother and father sit so close or look even half as happy as they did.

"Newlyweds!" said my mother. "That's what they are. The glow fades with time."

I was hunched in the corner when Manjula came to bid her farewell. Kneeling down beside me, she said, "Kalyana, my baby. Always keep your head up high. Whatever you do and wherever you go, remember this. Okay?"

I heard what Raju whispered in Manjula's ear before she left. He said, "Bring me back some Canadian cigarettes and beer, okay Auntie Manju!"

She winked at him and kissed his cheek and forehead. She then thanked my father for his generosity, for keeping her in his house and making her part of his family. My father leaned back in his chair and, putting his hands behind his head, he watched her say her departing prayers. I thought his manner cold. He could have at least said, "Good luck, Manjula," before she left.

Perhaps my mother said "goodbye" for both of them. She broke into a fit of tears first, soaking the ends of her sari as she cried shamelessly. The neighbors, hearing her loud wails, came out of their houses to see.

Manjula pulled her close to her heart and squeezed her back. They stood there holding tightly to each other, filling buckets with their tears. Then Manjula finally broke away from my mother. My aunt and her husband walked out of the door and out of our lives.

With Manjula gone, I feared Uncle Baldev even more. But thankfully, he came to our house only five more times after the wedding. As usual, he bore gifts for me: fruits and sugarcane and Indian sweets. My mother asked him to sit outside and swat flies on the porch. She made excuses: "Brother, I just swept and washed the floors. Mud will come in and I'll have to do it all over again. It's better if you stay outside."

He always said, "No problem," and stayed outside, smiling without a reason.

My mother would hover over me every time he was near. Sometimes he would boldly ask her to let me go to the oceanside with him. I would tremble with fear at the thought of being alone with him on those same shores where the naked woman with the butterfly tattoo spread her wings. A tinny taste would fill my throat as I waited shivering, certain she would approve his request this time. But my mother always shook her head. "Not today, Baldev *ji*. She has homework." Or she would say, "Not today, Baldev *ji*. She has to help me with chores."

Her excuses always prevailed. He would soon leave quietly, without saying goodbye. The yellow swatter would sit abandoned on the chair on the porch.

Strangely, it was my mother who always developed stomachaches after visits from Uncle Baldev. She would vomit what she had eaten that day, right into the kitchen sink. Then she would run the tap and let it slip quietly down the drain, far into the depths, where no one would ever see.

Doctor Sudhir Singh, a slender man with graying hair, came to the house once. He carried a black briefcase and wore a stethoscope around his neck. He tut-tutted away as he examined my mother. Then he took out a bottle of large brown pills. These must be taken for thirty days, or she would not be able to cure the sores that had erupted in the lining of her stomach.

"Manage your stress better, Mrs. Seth," he told her with an air of authority. "And keep away from spicy food. It does your stomach no good."

My mother would lower her eyes to the floor and mutter, "No problem, Doctor. No problem." But after he left she would shrug her shoulders. Bland food would never please my father or console him on troubled days.

My mother twisted and twirled each pill between her fingers for a few minutes before plopping it into her mouth. Sometimes she would choke and cough and spit the soggy pill back in the sink before immediately popping another one into her mouth and trying again.

Eventually the pills were finished, and so, it seemed, were visits from Uncle Baldev. Whenever my aging father insisted on taking us to his home, my mother would take to her bed. She would say things like, "Maybe next month, Rajdev.

Maybe next month we can go. Today, I don't know why, but I feel sick. I might even be coming down with a fever." She would crinkle her nose and rub her forehead, looking pitiful.

Once, my father objected. "Always you are making excuses!" he complained. "Next month, we will go." His voice was firm and scolding, flat and angry. I thought my father would strike my mother, like he had once struck Manjula, ending all arguments. We would then find ourselves once again sitting in Uncle Baldev's gaudy living room, eating bitter sugarcane, staring at black-and-white photos of my *aji* and *aja* as the auntie-without-a-name ran like a squirrel, scrubbing stained sofas and sweeping clean floors.

I stood in the corner, choking on my tears.

But Father merely stared as my mother's face crumpled and she began to weep. He dropped the matter immediately, and soon afterward he stopped making requests to see his brother. Over the years, he had grown in his devotion to my mother. Pleasing her had become his primary focus.

My stomach was not fragile like my mother's. I never developed sores in the lining or had to take brown pills, but my eyes burned and my joints ached. Like my mother, I would take to my bed.

Some nights were worse. Then my sleeping mind would paint pictures of Uncle Baldev slicing the purple skin off the sugarcanes, chopping them to pieces. I would see him using his pocket knife expertly, with a swift motion gouging the eyes out of pineapples. He scattered pineapple pieces and sugarcane skin across our living-room floor and smiled a horrible smile. I would awaken in the dead of night, shuddering with the memory, but I never screamed.

I had not screamed in the shack, either. Why? Thoughts tortured me constantly. I should have stayed among the guests, where it was safe. Why had I not refused the mango, the sugarcane, and the pineapple? I could have chosen not to go to the Chicken House. I might have known better than to trust my uncle and his oily voice. Most of all, I should have listened to my mother and refused the baby chickens when they came to our door in that small cardboard box.

I never blamed Raju or my father for what had happened on that cursed day, even though they had not been there when I most needed a man's protection. But I did blame my mother. She was the one who had told me that Kirtan wasn't family, who refused to allow him to attend the wedding. Her attempt at rescue was minutes too late for me; minutes that marked the end of everything I had once known. I hated her for this, but even more, I hated her because of what she had done in the bedroom afterward. She had burned my past and crumbled my present.

When I woke from my nightmares, I would shake with relief to find myself in my own room. The shadows of branches and trees were quivering on the dim walls, the windows rattling in the wind. To be alone was both a blessing and a curse. I would stare at the layers of mosquito net draped around my bed, trying to sense protection around me. Sometimes in the quiet night, I would wish for Manjula's soft grunts and snores. I would wish for the warmth and security of her arms around my waist.

When she left, Manjula had taken down the picture of the birds and bees, leaving behind an empty space on my far bedroom wall. With the picture stuffed in her bag, she had flown away to the land of maple trees, where she would live a different life than the one she lived here. Instead of catching crabs and sitting on the seawall, she would run amidst the buffalo. She would pick strawberries and cherries and make jam. She would wear a badge saying "Mrs. Simmons," and with Peter she would trap beavers. She would believe in a bearded old man called Santa Claus.

Sometimes in the quiet, lonely nights, I wished that Manjula had been my mother. For surely, wedding or no wedding, *she* would have gathered her sari, limped directly to the burning altar, and taken a hatchet to my uncle's head. With Kali's vengeance strapped across her chest, my auntie would have stood in the middle of that wedding and shouted to all the guests what my uncle had done. She would have arranged them in lines, sewn a bright yellow flag, and taken charge. She would have begun a movement, a movement that would have made Uncle Baldev quake with fear, stammering through his whiskey-soaked breath. And then, after she was done, she would have clutched me under her arm, and she and I would have grown beautiful wings and flown away to America—a land where women carried less of a curse, a land where a woman could perhaps forget.

20

NOW THAT I could not transform my feelings into words and put them on paper, I developed a new obsession: I sat on the steps by the back porch and, for hours on end, stared out at the dead resting under the ground. In the cemetery I had found the answer: My mother had been right, for every woman's life, regardless of the circumstances of her past and present, was entwined with pain and suffering. It was only in death that true freedom could be found.

Sometimes my reverie would be interrupted when I noticed the Chicken House in the far distance. I wished that a lightning bolt would strike the shack and burn it to the ground, taking all the chickens with it. The very sight of the building deadened my spirit.

My mother seemed to agree, if in an unspoken manner. She constantly complained about having to feed the chickens. "I don't have enough hours in the day to feed the chickens along with all my other chores, Rajdev. Then there's the garden that needs tending."

"Kill the chickens!" I shrieked across the kitchen, one quiet Sunday afternoon when my father was resting.

"Kalyana, there's no need to raise your voice!" My father always raised his when I raised mine.

Nevertheless, the first chicken was slaughtered the next weekend. It ran frantically around the backyard, headless but spilling blood, until it fell lifeless. I devoured three bowls of chicken curry that day, despite my mother's disapproving glares.

"No more," she said, when I headed for the fourth bowl.

"Let her eat, Sumitri. She's a growing girl." My father still rose to my defense.

"Rajdev. She's getting out of control," said my mother. She sighed when she saw the stack of dirty dishes in the sink. "Now there are bloody dishes to do, too," she said. "It never ends." She paused, and then made a unique request. "Kalyana, come and help me do the dishes."

"Why doesn't Raju help?"

My mother shot me a glance. "Men don't do dishes, Kalyana. But it's time for you to learn how to do them properly."

"My stomach hurts, Mummy. I ate too much chicken," I lied, shifting my gaze away from her questioning eyes. I feared that she might catch me in the middle of my fib, so I slouched on the sofa, a pained expression on my face as I looked at the bare wall. Mother looked away.

Later that night, I heard pots and pans banging loudly in the kitchen. It made it difficult for all of us, especially my father, to fall asleep peacefully.

To ease my mother's load, my father invited Auntie Shami to come and live with us. She was the unmarried sister of Uncle Baldev's wife. Word was that she immediately accepted my father's offer, for in her current situation she had only a thin mat on the floor on which to sleep and was surviving on one small meal a day.

"Does she walk with a limp?" I muttered, rolling my eyes when I heard the news that Auntie Shami was to arrive the next day.

"Why would you say something like that, Kalyana?" said my mother. She sounded hurt. I remembered how, when Manjula left, my mother and Manjula had stood there holding tightly to each other, in full sight of the neighbors. Their tears, like blood, could have filled buckets from deep wells of pain within.

But all I said to Mother was, "Well, she's not married, so she must have something wrong with her. Why is she not married?"

"Her head shakes."

"Her head shakes! What do you mean, 'Her head shakes'?"

"She has some kind of a condition. Her head doesn't stop shaking. Sometimes her hands shake, too. You'll see."

"What's a condition? What causes it? Did she eat something bad?"

"Nobody knows. The doctors don't even know. Maybe it's too much activity in the brain."

I stood up, arms folded across my chest. "I am not sharing my bed with a stranger whose whole body shakes," I said defiantly. "Does she shake in her sleep, too?"

"She will sleep on the floor, Kalyana. Father will buy a mattress and put it on the floor. At her own home she only has a thin mat to sleep on. That's what I heard, anyhow. She'll love a thick mattress."

"Does she shake in her sleep?" I persisted.

But my mother didn't know.

Auntie Shami, a rather large woman, arrived on a rainy Sunday. She carried two small bags. I stared at her balefully as she entered the house, willing for her to leave and Manjula, shining happily, to come back through that door instead. But she was not Manjula, of this we all became sure. Auntie Shami lasted only six weeks in our house.

First, even though she may not have shaken in her sleep, she certainly snored. Her snores from the mattress were loud enough to split a coconut tree in half. The noise kept all of us, even my father, awake every night.

Second, she was of no help to my mother, as we all came to know. For every time my mother asked her to help with the chores, Auntie Shami's head and hands shook with greater intensity, making it necessary for her to rest her back on my bed. She plopped her large frame on my bed often: in the middle of the noon hour, when lunch had to be prepared; after breakfast, when dishes had to be done; in the middle of the afternoon, when clothes had to be taken off the lines outside and brought into the house; and especially in the evenings, when the clothes had to be ironed and put away or dinner prepared and dirty dishes soaped and rinsed. I had to help Mother fold wrinkled clothes into heaps and piles. Even Raju had to start rinsing dishes.

Even worse than her snoring and her laziness were her tales. Auntie Shami, too exhausted to help Mother, would shake all the way to the neighbors' houses and entertain them with her own kind of storytelling. She started distasteful rumors about the horrors she had to endure in our home, horrors that included sleeping on the floor on a thin mat without blankets to keep her shivering and aging body warm. She insisted that we fed her just one small meal a day in return for completing all the household chores.

My mother very quickly realized that Shami was not Manjula. She wasn't pretty like Manjula, for Manjula had been pretty despite her limp. Shami had a weathered look to her face and a rather large nose. Unlike Manjula, she didn't wear a traditional *lengha*; instead, she chose knee-length dresses with polka-dots in all different colors and sizes. Sometimes, on special occasions, she put polka-dot ribbons in her hair or wore silk polka-dot scarves.

My mother frequently wiped the dust off the empty wall where Manjula's birds-and-bees picture had hung. She would curse in Hindi as she slaved around the house and in the kitchen, completing other necessary tasks. She would ramble on for hours: "I never had to ask Manjula to get the clothes from outside. I never had to ask Manjula to help me with the dinner. I never had to ask Manjula to feed the chickens, water the gardens, or sweep the floors. I never had to wait for Rajdev to drive me to the store. I never..."

At first, Auntie Shami sat quietly in the living room as she watched my mother charge like lightning from one room to another. She listened without comment as my mother complained. Then Auntie Shami's nostrils began to flare, and her head started shaking at an even fiercer speed. She would glare as though she might spit red dragon fire from her eyes, scorching my mother to a miserable heap. She stopped eating with us and took to her mattress and slept with her face to the wall.

On her fifth week in our house, Auntie Shami stopped glaring and took to yelling. "I am not Manjula!" she would shriek every time my mother made a comment.

"Manjula planted the whole garden in the back all by herself."

"I am not Manjula!"

"Manjula even knew how to catch crabs."

"I am not Manjula!"

"Manjula sewed."

"I am not Manjula!"

On Auntie Shami's final day in our house, it was my mother who screamed at the top of her voice, "I know! I know! I know! You're not Manjula!"

The next day, under skies as mournful as those on the Sunday on which she had arrived, Auntie Shami packed her two bags and left without a word. After her departure, we followed a trail of ants to the scone and bread crumbs hidden underneath her mattress. Of course, Mother had to clean that too, along with the butter-crusted bedsheets, late into the gloom-filled night. She did not complain, though, for I think her relief was greater than her anger.

That night we all slept soundly for the first time in six weeks.

21

MY MOTHER began nagging Raju to settle down and get married to a nice Indian girl, one with long hair and large eyes. "Bring a bride into this house, Raju," she said. "My bones are getting old. Who will take care of this house after I am gone?"

"Mummy, I've barely turned eighteen. It's not 1950 anymore."

She told him that she didn't approve of him lying on top of the Fijian girl, the one who had already borne three children to three different men. Neighbors were talking, she said, and relatives snickered when she passed. Her son, mingling casually with a native Fijian woman! Did Raju only want to be a father to someone else's children? Did he not want to bear his own blood, his own flesh? She couldn't go to the town or the temple without feeling shame or hiding her face in the shade of her dupatta.

Raju would embrace her and smirk. "Okay, Mummy, anything for you. Anything. Even marriage." And then he would walk out of the house, smiling like he had won the Fiji Six lottery, but all the same disregarding my mother's tearful pleas.

When Raju went to his lover's house, he wouldn't return for three or four days. Word was that she fed him well. She fried dalo and cassava and made coconut rice and sweet tapioca. Sometimes she boiled potatoes and made fish soup.

My mother would shake her head and sit on the edge of her bed, mumbling and staring at the wooden boards on the floor. "What will I do, oh God?" she would moan. "What will I do?"

Sometimes she would sigh loudly and bite her nails, making them bleed. "I have to feed the damn chickens! And water the damn gardens. Manjula, you left me with a big headache!"

But then she would rise from the edge of her bed and go outside to hose the gardens. Still with hunched shoulders and a morose face, she would mix grain with water in the red bucket and feed the chickens. The chickens would noisily flutter around her at the sight of their dinner, but my mother would pay them no attention.

At least in this respect my mother and I were together: We both hated the poor birds. And whether it was my angry wishes or my mother's negative thoughts, a few weeks later a roaring storm came and shredded the Chicken House into a pile of rubble. The newspapers and the radio called it Cyclone Elsa.

The night of the cyclone, we huddled in our living room to wait for the storm to pass. Mother had bought enough oil for the lamps and had cooked all the food for the day. She had forbidden Raju from leaving the house, and together he and

Father had hammered shutters over our windows to keep out the storm. The noise of the rain on our tin roof was deafening. All through the night we listened to it beating upon our home, pounding even louder than the howling of the winds and the crackling of trees. It was almost sunrise before the raging winds subsided and the ocean ceased to rise and swell.

When the winds had stilled and sunlight finally pushed through the cracks in the shutters, we went outside to assess the damage. Power lines had fallen on the ground, and my mother instructed me not to touch anything, especially the fallen wires. I nervously watched my step, staying safely behind her and Father. The neighbors came out of their houses and walked the streets. Some carried gossip, but some brought furrowed brows and creased foreheads.

"Did you hear that the wind snatched the roof right off Kalwant Singh's house and took it to sea?"

"They ran out of their house in the pelting rain and stayed at Kunti's house. Nobody got hurt. They are all okay, surviving."

"Thank God they are safe! But their belongings, not so good—the wind took everything out to the sea."

The villagers, all Indians, gathered together to collect money, clothing, and furniture to replace Kalwant Singh's possessions. Each person in the village worked to pick up broken branches and fallen trees and to clear paths. Everyone had assigned duties.

My task was to collect the limes that had showered to the ground beneath our lime tree, which was still miraculously standing. This was a good assignment, much better than picking up pieces of wood, my father said. He took the limes and sold them for three dollars a dozen to the Guajarati ladies who lived close to his shop. Then he took me to the bank, where we deposited the money in a savings account under my own name. We—or I, rather—made over $80.

Our house and the lime tree had been spared by the grace of God; except for the fallen limes, both stood strong through the storm, unscathed and untouched. But Cyclone Elsa had ripped the roof and walls of the Chicken House right from the ground and carried them off into the blackened skies. The fence surrounding the coop remained where it had toppled to the earth. The remaining two chickens were never found.

Raju helped my father clear what was left of the Chicken House, as my mother cleaned the back gardens, salvaging any undamaged produce and throwing the rest away to feed the birds. When I had finished gathering the limes, I sat and looked out upon the backyard. How strange it seemed without the looming structure that had housed my dark and painful secret, the vision that seared my mind each time I had looked outdoors.

But although the Chicken House had disappeared, the winds of Cyclone Elsa had failed to sweep away the memory of my uncle. A mark had been made, and even though the visible reminders had been burned to ashes or swept into the wild winds, the effects of what had happened in that shack was to follow me though the rest of my days.

22

IT WAS THROUGH these neighbors who worked together after Cyclone Elsa that my mother first learned of Roni. Roni, it was said, cleaned the house for Kathir. She finished her chores in Kathir's house at exactly two o'clock in the afternoon, and she only charged a small price for her housekeeping services. My mother's eyes had bulged when she heard that, for ten to fifteen dollars a week, Roni could wash and iron the clothes, do the dishes, clean the windows, sweep the floors, and, on brighter days, shine the brass.

Fifteen dollars a week was of no concern to my mother, for Father's furniture-store business was booming. Everyone wanted a bed to sleep on and a chair to sit on. Cabinets were required, and school-aged sons and daughters now must have whole desks on which to complete their lessons. In fact, my father had been obliged put an ad in the local newspaper, seeking two employees to keep up with the customers' demands.

My mother, with me by her side, stood at the side of the road at a quarter to two the following Monday. We both

craned our necks as a curvaceous Fijian woman emerged from
Kathir's house. She wore a flower-print wrap-around skirt
and a light orange shirt: a traditional Fijian woman's outfit. I
stared at her vigorous afro that swept up to the sky. She had a
bright red hibiscus flower behind her right ear.

My mother waved her hand and signaled to her to come
closer.

"*Bula*," the strange woman said warmly, flashing her
bright set of perfect white teeth. While we Indians greeted
each other with "*Namaste*" or "*Ram Ram*," Fijian folk used
"*Bula*" as a similar salutation.

"*Bula, bula*," my mother said, shaking Roni's hand. I
wrapped my mother's petticoat strings around my fingers and
stood there nervously, open-mouthed as I observed the business deal in progress.

Roni tapped my head lightly. "Ah, big girl," she said,
smiling broadly.

My mother and Roni had an instant chemistry, a har-
monious chord seeming to pass between them. Even though
Roni didn't speak Hindi and my mother didn't speak Fijian,
both found common ground in simple English.

"Wash clothes?"

"Yes."

"Iron, too?"

"Yes."

"How much?"

Roni put her palms up in the air and gazed at my mother,
waiting for her to suggest the wage.

"Ten okay?"

"Okay, Sister, okay."

"Five hours every day, three days a week?"

"Okay, no problem."

"Maybe more hours?"

"No problem."

Roni was agreeable to anything my mother proposed or suggested. She took my mother's hand in both of hers and shook it lightly. She spoke with a humble gentleness and walked with charming grace. When the details of the arrangement were explained and agreed upon, my mother invited her inside our house to explain the household chores.

I plopped myself on the living-room chair with a plateful of arrowroot biscuits. Even though I chomped noisily on my cookies and deliberately avoided the sight of Mother guiding Roni around our small house, my grim face displayed my shock. A Fijian woman, with skin the color of caramel, standing in the middle of our house in broad daylight!

In Fiji at that time, the Indian and Fijian communities remained segregated. Fijian children attended only the Methodist schools in their villages, while Indian children studied in schools led by Hindu believers in larger towns. Yet here was my mother, bending all the rules to suit her personal selfish pursuits.

When Roni left that day, I confronted her. "What will Father say about Roni ironing our clothes in the middle of our living room? She's Fijian."

"She's a woman first, Kalyana."

"I don't understand."

"How do I explain this?" My mother thought for a while then said, "There's not a woman in this world whom I wouldn't welcome into my home. We're all bonded to each other in one way or another, Kalyana. We all help one another in different ways, even in ways we cannot see."

I thought about what my mother had done on the day of Manjula's wedding. I didn't say anything.

"Look at the American women," my mother continued. "If they hadn't caused a stir far away, none of us would have a chance. We would still be burning widows and killing brides at altars. And we would still be letting men decide on our future. We wouldn't even be able to stand in line and vote, Kalyana." She paused with a triumphant smirk, and I sighed a little, rolling my eyes.

But my mother spoke gently. "A woman—regardless of her age, race, hair, skin color, or the rhythm of her heart-beat—will always be welcome in my home. It's just the men who will have to stay out on the veranda."

The slightest smile creased the corners of my eyes.

For a few dollars a week, Roni soon filled the empty hole Manjula had left behind in my mother's life. Housework was no longer my mother's biggest concern, and gradually she eased her nagging of Raju. He was no longer expected to bring home a bride, and Mother even stopped complaining when he continued his sexual misadventures with the older Fijian woman.

"Boys sow their wild oats," she declared once again. "That's the way it is in this world. Raju is no different than any other boy. He's not ready for marriage."

Roni filled another unspoken emptiness as well. As the

days passed, it became common for me to come home from school and find my mother sitting with Roni on our small veranda, laughing as they drank hot masala chai and ate Indian sweets. Soon my mother began to talk about Roni as though she were a distant member of our family.

"I wanted to cook *saina*," she would say, "but Roni prefers to eat sweet sticks. I should make some sweet sticks for chai tomorrow."

Or she would say, "Roni had the misfortune of being chased by wild dogs with long ears last week. The poor girl is so frightened of them now. People should tie up their animals when they know that they have raised them to be vicious. Poor Roni. She says her heart goes thump-thump-thump when she sees a dog of any color or size approaching."

On occasions when I stayed home from school, I witnessed my mother presiding over Roni like the Queen of England reigned over her country. She stood in the middle of the room, watching closely, giving precise orders on how to fold shirts or iron creases in pants. She hovered behind Roni as the Fijian woman soaped and rinsed the dishes in the metal sink. My mother was never shy to point out spots and stains missed.

She let Roni know her preferences. She liked the dishes done twice; she took her chai sweeter than the other Indian ladies she knew; she didn't like her panties ironed, a normal custom of Indo-Fijian households; and she liked the handkerchiefs folded in quarters, unlike Manjula, who had preferred to fold them in half. My mother would roll her eyes and shake her head as she pointed out this minor detail. The list of requirements she relayed to Roni went on for miles, it seemed, but Roni never challenged her or questioned her. She simply smiled and nodded her head, diligently following my mother's instructions.

Occasionally, Roni brought my mother produce from her communal garden. Dalo, cassava, tapioca, fresh bananas, papayas: "For you, Sister. I pick for you. All fresh. Fry banana. Kalyana like," she would say.

It was obvious from my mother's expression that this gesture always touched her heart. She would hold Roni's hands in hers. Tears flooded her eyes as she said simply, "*Dhanewaad.*"

"*Dhunwad?*"

"Means thank you."

"Aww. *Dhunwad*, Sister. *Dhunwad.*" Roni gave the Hindi word her own twist of iTaukei flavor.

Roni's mastery of the Hindi language quickly blossomed; and so did her friendship with my mother, buds opening their petals, drinking the light of the sun. Roni started telling my mother about the drama occurring in her own village, as my mother listened attentively, chuckling and laughing loudly. Lela's son Vacemaca was found lying in bed naked with a neighboring girl, and her father chased him around the village with a dog-beating broom. Like a first-class coward he ran, shivering and crying, completely naked. "He was quite a sight," Roni said, joining my mother in hysterical laughter. And then, just today, as she was walking to our home, Roni had spotted that same boy peeping through the young girl's window. He must have known her father was at the market, selling fresh produce.

Over the months that followed, Roni became an equal collaborator with my mother, telling stories and gossip like any Indian friend might have done. But occasionally she would also report matters that were more serious than the love troubles of the neighbors. Roni was the first one who delivered the news to my mother that a young girl from her village had flown to Australia to study in their university and become a world-class journalist.

"What's a journalist?" My mother was a little miffed that Roni would know an English word that she did not know or understand, and use it in her own house.

Roni glowing with pride, now being given an opportunity to teach my mother a new English word, eagerly offered a definition. "A news reporter, Sister. A news reporter."

My mother had at first shifted her eyes, then looking far away, into the horizon, she had smiled then sighed. I remember now the delight in my mother's eyes, delight at the thought that women everywhere were capturing opportunities, making waves, taking stands.

23

RONI ALMOST never gave advice to my mother. In their conversations it was Roni who listened, nodded, and sympathized when my mother complained or gave voice to her concerns. And yet, as it happened, it was Roni who first suggested that my mother take me to a spiritual healer to cure me of the chronic breathlessness that had slowly started to take over my life.

The sky would be soft blue, the air moist. I would be listening to the radio and transcribing Hindi duets, or finishing my homework, when without warning I would find myself clutching my chest. In the kitchen or the living room I would sit, gasping and squirming for even one full breath. The tight embrace of an invisible boa constrictor would wrap itself around my neck and my chest, slowly and determinedly squeezing the life from me like Manjula had squeezed the life out of the limes when she made lemonade.

My throat would stiffen and close. Panting and struggling, I would whimper, "I can't breathe, Mummy! I can't breathe! I can't breathe!" As I struggled to fill my lungs with air, I would find myself falling, dropping to the ground like a lime breaking free from the branches.

Doctor Sudhir Singh was frequently summoned. He always arrived at a confident trot, a stethoscope around his neck and a black briefcase in his left hand. He would listen to my heartbeat and lungs and then shine a light down my throat. He never failed to tap my knees and press on my stomach, though I could not understand how these things would help my breathing.

Staring into my pupils, he would speak coolly and professionally. "Well, her eyes look normal. Her whites are clear and the pupils are steady." He would plaster the cold stethoscope on my chest and ask me to take in deep breaths. Then he would shake his head and roll his eyes. "She's not asthmatic. I can't hear any wheezing in her lungs. Not even faintly."

"Nothing," he would say to my mother, a tone of disgust creeping into his voice. "Absolutely nothing wrong. I can't find anything wrong at all. I think she's looking for attention, Mrs. Seth."

The doctor always seemed annoyed that he had been summoned in the middle of a scorching afternoon and yet could find no ailment that he could name. His shoulders would sag as he left the house. My mother would sigh and go back to stirring the pot of curry.

One day, Dr. Singh had had enough; he took out his writing pad and prescribed small green pills. He didn't look at me once while he scrawled vigorously on the white pad. "Here, give her these. She'll sleep it off." He snapped his briefcase shut abruptly and left in a huff.

The pills made me fall asleep and momentarily forget my pain, but they hardly eased my affliction. Whenever their effects wore off, I would awake to find the four walls of my body closing around me once again. The color would drain from my face as I gasped for air. During my good times, I would lie in terror and await the next attack, horrified at the prospect of approaching my end at the mere age of twelve.

Gradually, I found I could no longer swallow solid foods. The doctor still was convinced that nothing was wrong with me. "It's all in her head," he insisted. My mother had to prepare potato or carrot soups alongside the usual roti and curries she cooked for Raju and my father. She would sit by my bedside in the dimly lit room and feed me warm, buttery soup. Her lips were smiling, as always, but her eyes were pools of worry.

Father and Raju were worried, too. Father would bring home red, blue, and green balloons, tying the bright globes above my bed. Perhaps he hoped that the sight of them floating above me might snap me out of the darkness that had overtaken my body.

Raju, of course, would make jokes to ease the tension that had gripped our home. "Kali, get better soon because I have no one to punch!" he would laugh. Sometimes he would bellow "Kaaaaaali...Ka Ka Ka Ka...Ka...Kaaaali," as though my name were a musical piece and he was a conductor.

I missed months and months of school, and Kirtan surpassed me by two classes, or grades. He faithfully came to visit me each and every every month while I was confined to bed (and to the mercy of my mother's care). Sometimes he brought me *Archie* comics, thinking that they might cheer me up. He looked pale and distressed, as if absorbing my condition.

I would drift in and out of consciousness, like the ocean waves that rose and fell.

Upon Doctor Singh's orders, my mother took me to the hospital for chest and stomach X-rays. Blood was drawn from my veins and put in hollow tubes. Doctors listened to my heartbeat with intense curiosity. A crowd of men and women wearing white hospital gowns and stethoscope necklaces discussed me dispassionately, as though I was not even present. I was a caterpillar caught in a jar and placed on a windowsill for examination, but even these white-robed saviors could not help me change into a butterfly.

My frailty became more and more obvious as my body began to wither away. My once-round belly flattened like a mattress. Dark circles appeared under my eyes, and my short hair grew thin and limp.

A thought grew in my mind: *admitted*. Was that not what befell those people with ailments like mine? I began to wonder whether one day I would emerge from a deep sleep and find myself strapped to a hard metal bed in an empty room where the walls were white as ghosts and the windows covered with iron bars. A place where time moved, yet stayed still. The climax to my fears would come when, lying beside me, I would find my hysterical and laughing cousin Shilpa.

"She's only looking for attention, Mr. and Mrs. Seth," Doctor Singh insisted to my parents again and again. According to the test results, I was healthy; there were no problems that could be found. "There's nothing wrong with her. Nothing at all." Doctor Singh, as always, would roll his eyes as though he had been terribly inconvenienced.

The day after my hospital visit, my mother told Roni what the doctor had said. They both turned and looked at me as I slept on the living-room sofa. Exhaustion was written across my slumbering face.

"Doctor said nothing wrong," said my mother. "What to do, Sister? What to do?"

The friendship between my mother and the Fijian woman was unusual enough for the time. Certainly, regardless of race, a hired woman did not give advice to the people for whom she worked. Yet this time, Roni looked at my pallid face with transparent care and said, "Sister, problem is spiritual, I think."

"Meaning?" My mother looked confused.

"Kalyana need prayer. I know a good healer, Sister. Take to him. What harm?"

That night, as my mother rinsed dishes in the sink full of soapy water, she asked my father for permission to take me to a spiritual healer. My father protested as fiercely as he had contested Manjula's Christian wedding.

"Sumi, why are you now taking advice from a Fijian woman—and a housekeeper?"

My mother sighed as she watched the soap suds slide off the clean plates. Her back was still turned away from my father, but her shoulders slumped in defeat.

My father, after a long moment of silence, spoke quietly, declaring his wish. He knew he had exhausted all medical avenues. What other choice was left?

"I have heard of an Indian healer that cures all ailments," he said, in his usual soft, quiet voice. "Why don't we go and see him instead?" He sat down at the edge of the dining table and watched my mother as she rinsed the evening dishes. His eyes were full of worry.

The ride to the healer's house was a bumpy one, as the road was poorly maintained and full of potholes. I lay under a blanket in the back seat, with my mother sitting nervously beside me. Raju sat in the front. I noticed my father's tense shoulders as he drove up the steep hill, clutching the steering wheel. My breathing was slow and ragged.

The healer's house seemed in dire need of a fresh coat of pale blue paint. My father would never approve of our home looking like this one, with age and hard use marking the outer walls. The healer himself stood on his front porch, smiling as we started to make our way to his doorstep.

I raised my eyes and stared at the healer. He was an old, long-haired Indian man, who spoke both Fijian and Hindi fluently. My first thought was that he must be an ancient sage, a yogi who had spent decades meditating on divine revelation. I had heard about such wise men, who in their meditative state kept their bodies alive with neither breath nor food, merely with thought and dew. They sat on the top of a mountain or in the middle of a desolate forest, thinking only of the divine.

But with his long hair and shabby clothes, he more resembled the city beggars who sat at the side of the dusty roads and streets, their legs tucked beneath them and a large hanky spread in front of them. Whenever women out shopping paused with pitying eyes and dropped coins in their laps, they raised both their hands and mumbled a quiet prayer: "May God be good to you and your family! May God make your husband prosperous and see that your children are mindful!" Then they would quickly reach out, grab the money, and put it in the locked tin can that they kept hidden beneath their thin, bony legs.

The healer did not shake our hands or put his palms together and say, "*Namaste.*" He threw me a quick glance, and his eyes widened. Then, as if the world must be about to end, he hastily turned around and began striding towards the temple behind his house, silently motioning for us to follow. Father and Raju kept up with his brisk pace, as my mother and I struggled behind them. Mother kept glancing at me with concern. What if I were to stop breathing here, on the top of the hill?

As the temple came into view, I clutched my mother's hand. The sight of its yellow curtains reminded me of the long-robed and sandalwood-scented Hare Krishna devotees who had come to our home so many years before. I wanted to go back down the hill and bury myself in the safety of my own bed.

The healer had not spoken, but his sudden movement cut through my thoughts as we stopped at the entrance of the temple. The smile on his face lit up the space between us. When we got closer, he motioned for us to take off our shoes and wash our feet before entering.

The temple was small and cluttered with statuary: numerous Indian gods and goddesses, seated or standing on red velvet thrones. The walls were hung with paintings and images of divine symbols, forces, and wise words. Incense sticks smoked in all four corners, filling the room with an earthy aroma. I liked that the smell of sandalwood seemed to permeate my fragile lungs.

In the middle of the floor lay a red velvet mat. As the healer took his place there, another man entered the room. This man was short and plump, wearing a printed blue shirt and gray slacks.

"Interpreter." The healer spoke for the first time. His voice was extraordinarily low, but gentle. He motioned for us to take a seat on the floor, directly opposite him. Unlike the doctor in our village, he rarely spoke, and he never looked at my mother or my father once.

Interpreter? If the healer spoke both Fijian and Hindi, what was the use of the interpreter? Even my father squinted with confusion, but out of respect we did as we were told and asked for no explanations or justifications.

After we were all seated, the healer closed his eyes and bowed his head in prayer. The interpreter lowered himself gently onto a stool close to the healer's feet. I stared at a large conch shell that faced the sun streaming across the small windowsill in the far corner. When light flooded its creases, the shell sparkled like a jewel.

The healer opened his eyes and focused all his attention on my ravaged face. His eyes were dark and piercing. He pulled me close to him by my hair and sniffed the top of my head. I clutched onto my mother's sari with one hand and my father's hand with the other. I was twelve years old, but I closed my eyes and shivered.

After a few sniffs, the healer roughly pushed me back to my mother and father. Then I thought that the man must be possessed, for he took a deep, long breath and began loudly babbling in a frightening tongue that was neither Fijian nor Hindi. Yet it seemed as though this was a language that the interpreter could understand. The healer did not speak to us, but directly to the interpreter, who nodded his head fearlessly and listened with care to every detail he conveyed.

Finally he finished speaking, but the healer had one more thing to do. Shifting on his mat, he reached over and placed a small charm in the middle of my open palm. A chill went up my spine when I saw that he had given me a tiny gold snake. But the healer, perceiving my pain, took my hand in both of his and closed my palm over the small metal creature that sat harmlessly in its center. Bowing his head and looking meditatively to the floor, he indicated that his brief interaction with me was finished.

It was only then that the interpreter turned to my parents and spoke. "Mr. and Mrs. Seth, the healer could not smell the presence of any evil spirits. Your daughter is clean of their influence. That is not the problem." He spoke like an ordinary person, in the quiet and polite voice of a gentle messenger. He did not interpret the anger that the healer had placed into the strange words he had spoken. "Mr. and Mrs. Seth, the healer did say that your child sat under a jasmine tree in a wooden shack. The night was still and the air calm. Cobras shed tears of blood and soaked the ground: that is the problem."

My father squinted again, but remained silent.

The interpreter continued in his gentle voice: "The healer said not to worry, Mr. and Mrs. Seth. Wipe away all your fear. No harm can touch your child when she's holding the charm in the center of her hands."

The healer, smiling, reached over and touched the top of my head.

"He blesses you," said the interpreter enthusiastically. He nodded his head and rose from the stool to go.

"That's it?" said my father, throwing a quick glance to my mother. He still looked confused.

"That's it. As long as she keeps this charm close to her heart, she will get better. She'll no longer have anything to fear. It will ease the silent suffering." The interpreter looked deep into my eyes with sincerity and gentleness. "The healer has blessed it."

Doubt clouded my father's eyes, but he paid the healer for his services and his gold charm. The interpreter silently left the room in the same manner that he had come in. I leaned on my mother as we walked back to the car, my father and Raju walking slowly a few steps ahead of us. We drove home in silence and did not discuss what we had heard or seen.

But my health did start improving after that day. Every time panic threatened to tighten its grip around my throat, I would squeeze the gold snake charm and pray intently, envisioning the healer's glowing face. The breathlessness would pass and I would no longer tumble to the living-room floor, losing all consciousness. Gradually, I stopped taking the green pills, and soon I was even able to eat full meals again.

Raju started punching my arm again, calling me "Kali," and I did not complain. Roni, smiling brightly, frequently raised her hands over her head and praised the gods above. My father breathed a sigh of relief and stopped coming home with balloons. My mother did not comment on what the interpreter had said, although I knew she had understood better than any of us had. Instead, she bundled me into a brand new yellow uniform and took me back to school.

At first I carried the golden charm with me everywhere I went, for I never knew when my throat might constrict. I kept it hidden in my pocket, and sometimes I placed it for safekeeping in my pencil case or my new school bag or rolled up in a hanky or in the middle of a book. At nights, I kept it under my pillow or in my hand. I touched it frequently and obsessively. But with time, as my strength increased, I started forgetting the charm at home. I would come home to find that I had left it on the dresser, in the drawer, or on my bed. Eventually I placed it under my mattress and forgot about it completely.

My father, elated over my recovery yet still doubtful of the healer's powers, shrugged away the cure as nothing more than a placebo. I overheard him say to Mother that I had been cured because of my unyielding belief in a charm that had the potential to keep away fear and the power to give me limitless and uninterrupted breath. "Blind faith," he had said. "Blind faith."

After a while I began to bond with my father's logic,

though occasionally my mind would wander, and I would begin to question the healer's knowledge of my dream. For that, I still had no explanation.

24

TIME PASSED swiftly.

I retired my hideous yellow uniform as I entered secondary school, instead choosing a purple one with a light-pink belt. My mother had to hire a professional seamstress to sew me my new dress. Of course, she complained; Manjula would have instinctively known the correct measurements, the correct patterns. Manjula's fingers would have moved swiftly among fabrics, wielding scissors and slicing fearlessly. Manjula would not, of course, have charged such a fee.

Raju was no longer rumored to be seen coming in and out of the older Fijian woman's house. For this my mother was thankful, but now she had something new to worry about. Three sisters, who had no father or brothers to protect them, had boldly moved to an empty house at the end of our street. To survive, these women openly exchanged sexual favors for money. Several men, young and old, had been seen leaving their shack at strange hours of the night or day, looking joyful and happy. Women like my mother worried about

losing their sons and their husbands to these three wild-spir-
ited sisters.

But I knew that Raju was not among those men who
came in and out of the sisters' shack. Raju spent his weekends
and nights dancing at the clubs. He would come home late
with traces of lipstick on his clothes, and during the day he
might secretly frolic with a particular Indian girl. She was a
rather large young woman of a similar age. My mother and
father remained blissfully—or, in the case of my mother,
fearfully—unaware.

Raju would leave the house, his black hair gelled close
to his scalp, wearing snug blue jeans and smelling of strong
cologne. In those days it seemed as though the scent of Raju
entered a room before he himself did. I would have to seal my
nose shut whenever my brother strode in and out through the
living-room doors.

If I ever commented on his fascination with large women,
alluding to his secret new love interest, he quickly and swiftly
would retort, smiling. "Curves, Kali, curves. I am a lover
of curves." But he would never be careless, as he had been
with the Fijian woman, and openly flaunt his new interest
or admit his affair. She was, after all, an Indian woman, and
even a boy who sowed his wild oats knew that he must protect her honor.

In those days I, too, would be subject to the worried,
watchful gaze of my mother. She knew I had begun reading
Manjula's collection of romance novels, which she had left
behind. Manjula had, of course, replenished her library after
she had traded the original stack for driving lessons so long
ago, but she had not taken them with her after her marriage.

My mother knew that I had started noticing boys, and, perhaps worse in her mind, was losing interest in school. Some days she even worried aloud about a boy impregnating me; then she would have to sweep away my shame, bundling me up and shipping me to a distant island. She would have to insist to all the relatives that I had been sent abroad for further studies, but on that distant island, behind secluded concrete walls, my baby would be born and left. This, it was rumored, was what had happened to our loud-mouthed cousin Nisha, who lived in the town of Lautoka.

For this reason my mother and father forbade me to see Kirtan any more. Mother said that I was a growing girl. That it would not appear proper. Neighbors, relatives, oh, even the frogs and lizards, would all talk. Mother wanted me to put all my energies into attaining higher learning.

Yet my heart was not in my studies, to my mother's dismay, and I wholeheartedly resented the assumption that university must be my calling. Although I finished high school, I did not earn marks good enough for entry into the prestigious University of the South Pacific, an institution that was only a twenty-minute walk from my house.

Fijian schools used a system of class positions, where each individual's success was compared to another person's in the same class. I came in twenty-seventh, which meant that there were twenty-six people in a class of fifty-two who did considerably better than me. I had passed, but it wasn't a score to boast about; anything over fifteen was considered a low ranking.

I took this opportunity to tell Mother to her face that I was not going to university, because I wasn't meant for it—even though at her insistence, I had attended grade thirteen, after completing grade twelve.

My mother looked disappointed, devastated even, as though I had suffocated all her dreams. "Manjula and I cried when we got taken out of school," she said angrily. "And here you are, with opportunities to go as far as you possibly can in your life, and you just throw it all away. Just throw it all away. Even Roni tells me a Fijian girl went to Australia to study and become a news reporter." She shook her head and turned to the wall. Then, after a brief moment, she whipped around again and snapped, "Don't you realize, Kalyana, education alone is the key to a woman's freedom. Without it, you won't have a chance in this world."

I looked back at her coldly, straight in the eyes, and said, "No. The key is marriage."

My mother was stunned that I had risen to challenge her. I folded my hands across my chest and leaned back on the kitchen wall. My mother was standing at the counter, flipping rotis on a portable kerosene stove, as Roni hovered nearby, completing dinner tasks.

"Marriage is the key to a woman's freedom." My tone was fiercely assertive. "Manjula found freedom when she married Peter. Manjula flew away."

My mother kept stirring dhal and buttering steaming rotis. She stacked the rotis on a stainless-steel plate.

"I will fly away too, one day, like Manjula," I said coldly, thinking about Kirtan's round, soft face. I walked away with my chin up in the air and head held high.

As I left the kitchen, I heard her mumble to Roni, half in Hindi and half in English. "She's gotten so spoiled!" my mother hissed. "I told Rajdev not to coddle her like he did. He didn't listen to me. Look at her now. She walks around like she owns this bloody place." She wrung her hands and gritted her teeth. "It makes me want to rip all the hair off my head and scream." My mother looked expectantly at Roni.

Roni, a red hibiscus in her hair, was sitting astride a wooden coconut grater, shredding dried coconut for *rou-rou*. She shrugged as she laughed at my mother's discomfiture. "She's a young woman, not matured yet, Sister. Still a child. She'll come around. Don't worry."

My mother worried anyway. She would furrow her eyebrows and push out her chin, her lips forming a grim line. She did not speak to anyone other than Roni about my future, after I disclosed that I had no intention of pursuing a career. Looking defeated, she moved around the house as slowly as an old woman. As passing seasons, gone were her days of standing in the middle of the living room, her bright blue dupatta flowing around her. No longer did she sing songs and tell tales. Gone were some of her ways, but it was not only due to her disappointment in my choice.

There were other changes. Over the recent years I had noticed that she no longer wore the tiny blouses that revealed her slender waist, something that seemed unnecessary to me. Even during those turbulent days, I could recognize that she still looked stunning despite the passing of time. Her weight had stayed the same, her skin supple—perhaps the result of the creams and the exercise regimen she was always urging me to follow.

My mother now moved around the house in long, loose dresses that hung from her neck to her toes. Perhaps she had imposed a personal restriction on herself as she got older, thinking that small blouses and low-riding petticoats were no longer suitable for a woman of her age. Neighbors surely would talk: "Look at Rajdev's wife, parading around in garments that were made for a budding woman!" they would say. And although I knew in my heart that I was not the cause, these changes in my mother's life formed just one more wedge among the many that had lately seemed driven between us.

I plopped in a Betamax video of Princess Diana and Prince Charles's wedding. By that time, in addition to a gray rotary phone that allowed my mother to occasionally hear Manjula's distant voice, my father had invested in a color television set. Usually it sat silently in the middle of our living room or played Hindi films with big stars like Amitabh Bachchan, Mithun Chakraborty, Hema Malini, Rekha, and Anil Kapoor. The royal wedding, however, was one of my favorite English videos to watch. I never tired of seeing Prince Charles and Princess Diana in their regal splendor. Their grand royal occasion made me dream of my wedding day, much like Manjula used to dream of hers.

Although I would never have admitted this to my mother, staying at home with no school or trade to prepare for was a somewhat unsettling experience. I was also starting to get a hint of the torment that Manjula's unmarried life had caused her. Whenever I watched this video, instead of Princess Diana walking down the red velvet carpet towards her shining prince, I would see myself striding confidently towards my own prince, the one who could take me away.

The one difficulty was that my father would never permit a Christian wedding, so a white dress and a long aisle were nothing more than a young woman's fantasy. I was sure of my prince, though. Even though I was forbidden to see Kirtan alone, my childhood friendship with him had still managed to survive and slowly built to something deeper and ever stronger. He and I talked on the telephone, under our parents' noses, and we met secretly under the cover of carefully constructed lies. While I was still at school, I would tell my parents that I was going to a study session with a cousin—and, like other Indo-Fijian girls not allowed to meet with boys, we would abandon each other immediately, her to frolic with her boyfriend and I with mine.

Kirtan and I met behind the rose bushes at the University of the South Pacific, where Kirtan was completing his second year of accounting. Sometimes we met in parks, in abandoned *bure* houses, in theaters, in restaurants. From time to time he would drive me to the Suva Point in his father's car; there we could join lovers of all ages, shapes, and statuses, who were parked in rows, locking lips, holding hands, and watching the sun set over the ocean waves. Listening to romantic songs play over and over again on the radio, we would remain oblivious to the disapproving glares of passing fishermen.

Sometimes instead, Kirtan took me for picnics on the sandy beaches or in dense forests. Once we went to a Chinese restaurant, where we ate chicken chop suey with forks, like the *goras*.

Kirtan promised to marry me in two years, when he would be finished his accounting degree. And in 1985, a few months after I turned twenty-two, he came to my house unannounced.

It was a sweaty Saturday. I was hiding up in my room, perspiring fiercely in an agony of expectancy. Kirtan, his mother and father by his side, strode to our front door and asked my father for my hand in marriage.

My mother was shifting plates and cups alone in the kitchen when this happened. Roni was not with her, as she seldom came over during the weekends when my father was home. I craned my head, anxiously awaiting my father's decision. Manjula had been allowed to marry a Christian man. Raju was able to sow his wild oats with an older Fijian woman, one who had already borne three children to three different men. Why should I not be allowed to marry my Kirtan?

Yet still I feared. I worried that my father—or worse, my mother—would bring out excuses, such as "Kalyana is too young to get married. She's practically still a child." Or "Kalyana might still want to go to university."

But my father smiled at Kirtan's modest proposal. After all, he was a Hindu boy studying to be a chartered accountant at the University of the South Pacific. His parents owned their own jewelry store and were well off, and Kirtan was their only son, their only heir. It was a good alliance from any viewpoint, especially as I was, to my mother's eternal regret, not planning to pursue a career. The date was set for us to marry the following November, during the school holidays.

My mother may have initially insisted that marriage was not my best path, but that did not stop her from plunging into wedding planning with a trace of her old enthusiasm.

She was in her element, and I began to understand and sympathize with what Manjula must have gone through. Mother's demands often sent me storming out of the room and heading for the ocean seawalls, much like Manjula had done. *Don't slouch. Stand tall. Sit straight. Don't sleep in until noon; it's best to awaken before seven in the morning. Put coconut oil in the hair to strengthen it. Amla oil to darken it.* On and on she went.

Why would I do any of that? Kirtan knew I had brown locks and that I liked to sleep in, and he had seen that sometimes I slouched or sat crooked. He didn't require me to change anything, so why should my mother be so concerned?

Mother's biggest worry was fitness. She gave me a Jane Fonda videotape and told me to squeeze my buttocks hard and slow. I felt like a fool as I jumped up and down in the middle of our living room.

"You need to start exercising, Kalyana," she would say. "You're too fat to be a bride. Your stomach will hang over the petticoat. What are your in-laws going to think? Do it for at least twenty minutes a day."

When she wasn't commenting on my weight, she was nagging me about my inability to stir dhal or flip rotis. "Kalyana, come here and learn how to flip rotis properly. If you can't make them perfectly round, your mother-in-law is going to say that your mother never taught you properly. She'll tell everyone that you make crooked rotis. Is that what you want? Come and learn. Do you even know how to cook cabbage, cauliflower, potato curry?"

"I've watched you all this time," I would snap. "It's not hard. You throw bloody onions in oil, fry cumin and spices all together, stir it up, and put whatever vegetables you want in it."

"What about salt? When do you put salt in? How much do you put in? Do you know?"

I would turn up the volume of my Walkman, plastering the spongy earphones to both my ears. "Kalyana, put away that music and go help your mother in the kitchen." Father took her side more and more often those days.

So, to please my father, I would snatch the earphones off my head and throw the Walkman on my unmade bed. I would gather my long, brown hair and put it in a bun—gone were the days of bowl cuts—and with grim lips and a cantankerous face, I would help my mother prepare meals in the kitchen.

In the same way, I begrudgingly took out the Jane Fonda tapes every morning. Summoning up every ounce of energy within me, I hopped around in the middle of the living room in front of the small television set. I hated the way my white T-shirt and purple leotard became stained with sweat.

I recalled how, many years ago, my father had begun each morning with vigor. He would punch the air with great enthusiasm, breaking sweat, and then run for miles. Yet now he started the day more slowly, leaning back on the sofa with his hands interlocked behind his head. Age had crept up on him more severely than on my mother. Harsh lines creased his face and forehead, and sometimes I thought he seemed frail and old.

And so, partly because of this, I did the exercises my mother thrust upon me. But Fonda or no, during the course of the months before the wedding my weight was highly variable. The intense scrutiny of my mother's watchful eyes was like a scale tied to my back. Worse, relatives and neighbors soon made it their business to comment on my frequent fluctuations.

"Rajdev's girl is looking good now. She's slimmed up quite a bit."

My mother would proudly tell them it was Jane Fonda. It was the miracle of *aerobics*.

But then, when my waist ballooned up again like a pregnant woman's belly, they said, "What a pity! Rajdev's girl was looking good when she slimmed down."

My mother looked defeated then. She had no good answer to give. She would whisper to Roni, "She cheats on her diet. That's why she can't keep it off. Just last week she didn't exercise at all, and I saw her stuffing herself with a bowl of dried coconut shredding mixed with brown sugar. I don't know what to do with that girl. Maybe God will kick some sense into her head one day."

Roni would tap my mother lightly on her back and nod her head. I would simmer with rage, believing she was on my mother's side. But now I wonder whether her understanding was greater than my mother's ever could have been.

25

NOVEMBER 23, 1985. My Wedding Day.

Unlike Manjula's wedding, when frangipani, hibiscus, marigold, bougainvillea, and jasmine exuded the most beautiful scents for the entire week my auntie sat preparing for her day, the week leading to my own auspicious day was different. We were in the midst of a bout of miserable weather; rain fell constantly, blotting out the sun, and the flowers, leaves, and trees were limp as they trembled and shivered in the wind. For this reason, my father rented a big hall in which to safely celebrate my wedding. I would not be joined to Kirtan in the yard, under the gentle skies, with the soft lull of the ocean for accompaniment.

Naturally, my mother was not pleased. She complained about the rain, the noise, the sun—or the lack of it, that is. The wind and the tin rattling sent her nervously twitching. She did not want to move all arrangements to the hall. She complained about the inconvenience. And to make matters worse, my fitness was worse than ever; on my wedding day, I tipped the scale at exactly 182 pounds.

Yet, despite it all, I could still be married. I wore the traditional red sari with gold jewelry, not a pink one like I had imagined as a child, and my blouse slipped over my petticoat and covered my wide stomach. The sari draped around me in a flattering manner, thank God. My hands, like Manjula's, were painted with henna, and like her I wore a ruby-studded gold bindia.

The priest began chanting his mantras. Initiating *Vara Satkaarah*, he lit a fire in a small concrete box, as my mother welcomed Kirtan and his guests at the entrance gate of the wedding hall. The rice rained gently on Kirtan's head as my mother reached over and put a long streak of vermilion powder on his forehead. She took his face in her hands, planting a kiss on both of his cheeks. It warmed my being to see this, though I could only observe at a distance from a small room at the end of the hall.

Then it was my turn to step forward. Young girls led me to the altar, initiating *Madhuparka*. I could feel the guests' gazes penetrating my skin, even though I kept my eyes lowered, as was proper for an Indian bride. As I walked towards the altar, my surroundings seemed to blur for a moment. I remembered how Manjula had limped to her groom as I had sat back on a wooden stool, watching and yearning for my own day to come. I was filled with an understanding of how time could at once pass so quickly and yet stand still.

As I approached the altar, my father humbly took charge. With tears in his eyes, he came bearing gifts of pots and pans, of long-sleeved shirts and silk pajamas, and of rings and chains and gold coins on silver trays. He placed them at Kirtan's feet, asking in return for the gift of his daughter's well-being, my happiness. Perhaps that was all my parents had truly wanted for me after all.

The pundit continued chanting prayers as the smoke from the fire filled the altar. My father took my hand and placed it onto Kirtan's, initiating *Kanya Dan*: the giving away of a bride, a daughter, a woman.

The pundit dropped a small silver spoon of water on the sacred fire. This was *Vivah-Homa*, the blessing of the altar and the purification of the air. He said, "Let this auspicious occasion begin with purity, with love, and with joy, with goodness." Then Kirtan took my right hand in his left, accepting me as his lawfully wedded wife. *Pani-Grahan* had begun, and, following the pundit's orders, I led Kirtan around the fire. Together we took vows of loyalty, steadfast love, and lifelong fidelity to each other: *Pratigna-Karan*.

My mother gently placed my foot on a cold slab of stone, initiating *Shila Arohan*, and counseled me to prepare for my new life. I could not hear what she said, for in that moment I saw among the guests a small girl with a round face and innocent dark eyes, sitting close to her mother. The girl fidgeted and played with the ends of her mother's pale-blue sari, whispering something in her ear. My heart stopped as the girl rose to leave, and it seemed I must leap to follow her. But then I saw her mother also rise and take her hand.

The pundit, with one hand in the air, softly asked us to complete *Laja-Homah*. He instructed me to put my hand on top of Kirtan's. Together we offered the sacred fire a teaspoon of ghee-soaked rice each time he uttered the gentle benediction "*Om Bhur Bhuva Svaha*."

The fire blazed louder and brighter, consuming the mixture. The pundit continued chanting Sanskrit verses, saying ancient prayers that neither of us could understand. Yet we knew that the gods and goddesses were gathering up above, hearing the chants of these prayers and raining blessings like confetti on Kirtan and me, sanctifying our new spiritual union.

Then, following the pundit's instructions for *Pradakshina*, we both stood up, Kirtan and I, our pinky fingers linked. Together we walked around the fire seven times, making seven promises:

May we be blessed with an abundance of resources and comforts, and be helpful to one another in all ways. *"Om Bhur Bhuva Svaha."*

May we be strong, steady, and healthy in our minds and our bodies and our spirits. *"Om Bhur Bhuva Svaha."*

May we be blessed with prosperity and riches; may we share happiness and pain together, and may we work and live together. *"Om Bhur Bhuva Svaha."*

May we be eternally joyful, and smile in each other's embrace, and forever be faithful to each other and to our love for one another and to our respective families. *"Om Bhur Bhuva Svaha."*

May we bear fruits and multiply plentifully; may God give us noble and heroic children. *"Om Bhur Bhuva Svaha."*

May we live in harmony and peace, true to our values, true to our promises. May we always be the best of friends. *"Om Bhur Bhuva Svaha."*

For the final time, the pundit called upon the triple worlds: the earth, the sky, and the atmosphere in between.

"*Om Bhur Bhuva Svaha,*" he said softly, as I looked into the eyes of the love of my life.

The marriage knot, the *Saptapadi*, was tied between Kirtan and me. We were connected with a long, red piece of ribbon and instructed by the gentle priest to take seven steps together as husband and wife. Seven steps for nourishment, strength, prosperity, happiness, progeny, long life, and harmony and understanding. Kirtan stared into my eyes, not even glancing once at the flabby arms or protruding stomach that had caused my mother and me so much distress. He put his hand upon mine, and in perfection we walked.

We completed *Abhishek* and *Anna Praashan*. We sprinkled water and meditated on the sun and pole star. We made food offerings, first to the fire, then to each other. We bent down and touched the feet of our parents for *Aashirvadah*, touching our fingers to our heads. We received their blessings, their good wishes, and their benediction.

Smiling confidently, Kirtan dropped vermilion powder in the part of my hair, marking my status as a married woman. The pundit blew the conch shell loudly and clearly. We were united, Kirtan and I, like princesses with their princes, like Juliets with their Romeos, and like Mumtaz with her Shah Jahan.

Now I understood why Indian marriages took so long to celebrate. The joining of two families and a lifetime of promises can never be made in mere minutes.

During the reception, my father supervised the hired men who had cooked goat *pilau* and an array of vegetarian curries for the four hundred guests. Instead of banana leaves, as there were at Manjula's wedding, we used paper plates and paper cups. My mother and father, Kirtan's parents, and Raju all stood together in the receiving line and accepted mountains of presents on our behalf: from bedspreads to drinking glasses and spoons and knives to wall hangings. These gifts would help Kirtan and I start our new household, away from both of our families.

As I was leaving the reception that evening, out of the corner of my eye, I noticed Uncle Baldev standing silently by a far wall, watching the proceedings. These days, he carried a walking stick and wore round caps to hide his recent baldness. I glanced at him briefly, then swiftly turned my head back to Kirtan, who had noticed nothing.

Though Uncle Baldev was at a distance, I was sure I could still smell the faint whiskey on his breath and the stale stench of cigarette on his clothes, and my stomach churned. But I gripped Kirtan's hand tightly and stepped forward. Together we walked out of my old life forever.

Svaha.

The sting of that word.

The crackling fire.

The pundit's gentle voice, so far and so long ago.

It plays like a haunting melody—over and over—ceaselessly repeating—in my mind.

Kirtan, hovering above me.

Then the song—the love song.

Kabhi kabhi…

Sometimes, sometimes…

Mere dil mein khayal ata hai...
A thought flickers across my heart...
Ke jaise tujhko banaya gaya ho sirf mere liye...
Like you have been made only for me...
The sound of a conch shell blowing through the wind.
Kali-yana.
I hate the sound of that word.
Suhaag raat hai, gunghat utha raha hoo mei...
It's our wedding night, as I lift up your veil...
The smell of whiskey on his breath. Though Kirtan did not drink tonight, I am sure.
I close my eyes. I disappear, even for a moment.
Tu ab se pahele, sitaro mein bas rahi thi kahi...
Before today, you were among the stars up above.
Tujhe zamin pei, bulaya gaya hai mere liye...
You were called to the earth for me alone...
The love song still ringing in my head.

Mango juice, running down my face. Sweet, bitter taste on my lips. Is that the scent of sandalwood smoke that I smell? My heart is all tied up in knots. My chest is feverish and cold, at once alight with fire and frozen with fear. My body is tense, closed, ungiving, unforgiving.

I lie in the warm glow of the starlit night, listening to the wild dogs howling outside. I wonder if, in time, I will become accustomed to Kirtan's hands grazing my skin, his lips finding mine, in the quiet shadows of the long, sweltering nights. I wonder if, in time, I will learn to trust and to succumb to my husband's tender touch. If, in time, I will learn to slowly open, to allow him fully inside. But even then, I wonder, will I ever erase Uncle Baldev's scent completely from my mind?

Then I see in the far distance of my mind shadows of four women. Shadows only, but they are dancing and thumping their feet, shaking the ground. I succumb to Kirtan's embrace. His gentle kisses rain over my back. But they touch my soul.

Traditionally, after marriage a young couple moves into the home of the groom's parents, so that the wife might take on many of the household duties and ease her mother-in-law's burden. But Kirtan's mother and father had moved back to Nadi, their original home. Kirtan and I could not go with them, as Kirtan was now employed as an accountant in a prestigious Australian bank located in the middle of Suva. His office sat in the downtown area, overlooking both sides of the capital city: the deep blue ocean and the hustle and bustle of a growing town.

Moving in with my own family was out of the question for Kirtan. Like my father, my husband was a proud man. He did not wish for his first actions as a married man to raise curious eyes or tickle ears. "Men must be able to support their wives, Kalyana. It is simply not right for a man to move into the home of his wife's parents." Then, chuckling, he said, "Besides, a household can't have two masters." Two masters? Perhaps he meant to say a household can't have two womanly heads. Together, we set up our new home, a rented flat on the outskirts of Suva.

One thing that did not change with marriage was my name. For a woman in Fiji, the object of taking a surname was to finally have a last name; if I already had one, what point was there in pushing the matter further? Kirtan had tried, weakly though, to make a case. "How will people know that we are a family if you go around with a different last name than me?" he said gruffly.

"You take on my last name, then," I said calmly. The headmaster's big stick had forever burned my new surname into my mind and body, but it was no longer a painful memory. I had grown up a woman with her own full name, and through the years I had proudly clung to it. It was a possession all my own, much like the treasured stove of my childhood.

"Kalyana, men don't take women's last names," my husband persisted.

"Well, you be the first then. Be progressive, Kirtan." I smirked, but I could sense that he was still unconvinced; and so I spoke in a language that I knew he could understand.

"You know when a man looks at his wife, years later, and says, 'You're not the person I married?'" I said. "It's because your life path and the person who you are meant to be is tied to your name. When a woman changes her name after marriage, she does not just change who she is. She also changes who she becomes."

Kirtan perked up slightly, eyes open and bright. "It's like she changes her destiny."

I smiled.

He was smiling, too. "Everything is tied to numbers and the stars up above." He paused. "Besides, you'll do whatever you want to do anyway, Kalyana," he mumbled before dropping the subject.

Perhaps he still harbored a secret fantasy that, in due time, I would soften my resolve and discard my father's name and take his, just as a snake sheds its old skin and reveals a new one. But I never did take his last name, and eventually he became accustomed to marriage to Kalyana Seth.

26

QUICKLY WE settled into the routine of married life. And a full year passed.

Kirtan worked from nine until five, Monday to Friday, a typical office worker's hours. I had expected this, of course, but what I had never anticipated was the haunting loneliness that Kirtan's daily absence left behind. And yet in a way I relished being alone for what I believe may have been the first time in my life.

Being alone brought its own kind of pleasures. I, the lover of late risings, now slept in until ten in the morning most weekdays. My mother was not there to criticize me, awaken me, scrutinize me. No one breathed a word about aerobics or mouthed wise proverbs about early risers. If I chose, I could spend a few hours watching videos and movies, then rush through the mundane housewifely chores: make the bed, throw the clothes in the washer, hang them in the sun to dry, cook a big pot of curry, potato, or beans, or chicken or rice *pilau*. I would have some of that meal for lunch and save the rest for dinner. Why did my mother always prepare two meals when one would have sufficed?

In the late afternoon I would drop *kajal* in my eyes, paint my nails and lips, and rouge my cheeks. Then, like Manjula waiting for her groom so many years ago, I would await Kirtan's return.

Although I enjoyed the quiet of an empty house, Kirtan's homecoming was a source of great pleasure every evening. Sometimes we would go to the cinema, hand in hand. On weekends we might walk in companionable silence, through parks, along shores. Occasionally, we would pay calls on Kirtan's friends, cousins, uncles, and aunts, for his family was much larger than mine. We often visited the temple, where he would sing *bhajans* and beat tablas.

Kirtan was a good man, and he offered me a life that was full of predictability and certainty. In many ways, it was the life that my father had given my mother. In many ways, it was the life I had not realized how much I wanted.

My mother often telephoned me to talk about this and that. Some days I just ignored the calls by pretending not to be at home. I would listen to the telephone ring twenty times, my face turned away. Half an hour later, it would ring again.

I knew what she wanted to talk about these days: the newly formed Labour Party, the Indian people's own political party. She was rooting for them to win the election.

Since 1970, when Fiji gained independence from British rule, the predominantly Fijian Alliance Party had run the nation's political affairs. But in recent days, with trade union support, a new party had arisen. This so-called Labour Party would allow the Indo-Fijians to gain political power by filling a majority of the seats. To my mother's intense pleasure, the new party was sweeping through the Fijian towns and villages and growing in popularity every day.

Yet as the Labour Party emerged out of obscurity, another political group was stirring on Fiji shores amidst the beating of drums: the iTaukei Movement.

As a child, I had firmly believed that a movement was mighty, powerful, and a necessary good: a fight for equality, a struggle for the submissive to rise and take the reins. But my mother insisted that this new movement was born out of a greed for more power. It arose, she insisted, to stop equality from truly blossoming.

And yet I understood differently, for I saw beyond the iTaukeis' long speeches in the burning sun. The iTaukei Movement had arisen because of fear: fear of uprisings, fear of losing the way of the past, fear of change itself. I thought of how fear of my mother had paralyzed me and kept me in silence, and how my mother's fear of shame had caused her to deny the present and dictate my future. If the subservient grasped the reins and gained power, throwing tradition on its head, the uncertainty of the future could be overwhelming. For this reason I did not believe that the iTaukei Movement arose from greed.

But I did not express these or any other political ideas to my mother. If I did allow the subject to wander to such things, my mother would quickly make her political fervor personal. She would implore me to ensure that Kirtan and his family voted for the Labour Party in the elections. And her interest was not limited to family alone; she even set up her own mock poll in the village, teaching aging Indians who couldn't read properly how to recognize the Labour Party symbol on the ballot and cross it off with a blue pen. Carefully she instructed them to avoid going over the lines, which she feared might spoil the ballot. In other villages, women like my mother, whose children had grown and left home, who now had idle time with nothing to fill, followed suit. They trained the illiterate to vote for the Labour Party.

When she wasn't gathering support out in the village, Mother was glued to the radio. On election day, she must barely have breathed as she awaited the final count.

I wonder whether she screamed with joy when the Labour Party won the elections, and by twenty-eight seats, too. On April 13, 1987, Dr. Timoci Bavadra took office as the prime minister to head the nation's first government of mainly ethnic Indian origin. He announced his cabinet members the next day.

My mother celebrated. Kirtan and I were invited to my old home for a feast: duck curry and goat *pilau*, eggplant and potatoes, *puries* and rotis, and *raita* and tomato chutney. For dessert, Mother cooked rice pudding and even bought a can of pears and a carton of vanilla ice cream. She glowed in her pale-blue printed dress.

"For more than a century, Indians have bled and sweated in this country!" Her enthusiasm was like a benediction, her confidence unwavering. "We've built roads, hotels, and buildings that reach to the sky. Finally, we get some recognition! Finally, we gain more political power! Praise God!"

Kirtan chatted with my father and Raju, but I sat quietly, taking in my mother in all her glory. I wondered when

I had last seen her this way. Her political chatter rarely held my interest, but tonight I could not keep my eyes off my mother. The illuminated woman of my childhood had long disappeared into the shadows. How had I not realized it until this night, when I saw her once again shine as brightly as the moon?

My mother's joy, however, was to topple as quickly as the newly elected government. Just a month and a day later, ten soldiers, all wearing masks and carrying ammunition, led by Sitiveni Rabuka, the head of the military, took Dr. Bavadra and all his ministers to some unknown place. And just as years ago, in one instant, my world as I knew it lay on the floor, crumbled to pieces, the great nation of Fiji, peaceful and kind, as its people knew it, fell into chaos. Though there were some things that did not change: Ratu Sir Kamisese Mara, who had been ousted from his seat of prime minister at the election earlier that year, was reinstated, leading people to suspect that the defeated Alliance Party was behind all of this.

After that terrible day the political situation rapidly got worse. Another coup quickly followed. Martial law was declared, and all commerce on Sundays was banned. Separation of state and religion ceased to exist: Fiji was declared a Christian state. I think that there was no one more baffled by this than my mother. She frequently said, "We follow the Hindu faith. So why should we be forced to obey the Sabbath? It doesn't make sense, Kalyana. Before the missionaries came, *they* weren't Christians, either. Have they forgotten?" Her voice sounded wrung with a new kind of sorrow.

Further changes on the people of Fiji were imposed. A curfew of eight in the evening was set. Soldiers with large guns strutting along village streets became commonplace. Senseless violence erupted in every corner of Fiji, whether town or village, and no residents were immune. Poor and rich, young and old, healthy and feeble—everyone moved in wide-eyed terror of what might happen. As the months passed, the separation between the indigenous Fijians and Fiji-born Indians grew increasingly wider.

Fiji-born Indian women were beaten and disrobed in the middle of the towns. Pitifully, Lord Krishna was not there to elongate their unraveling saris; the women could only run naked or in torn brassieres and panties, screaming with shame and pain as they took cover in deserted buildings and empty stores.

There were threats of bombs in every Indian-dominated school, even minor explosions. It became a common sight to see Indian mothers and fathers rushing from their daytime jobs and commitments to rescue their sons and daughters from elementary or secondary schools. Fear, like the black clouds billowing from schools and buildings, darkened the villages and city streets. All of Fiji lay under its choking hold.

This sent a chain of reactions through other parts of the world. Fiji, for the first time in its century-old history with the British, was expelled from the Commonwealth. Britain, America, Australia, and New Zealand suspended aid.

My mother telephoned me to tell me that Kunti had been scrubbing green mildew off her concrete steps on a Sunday, when the military came and took her by the hair. They cleaned the concrete with her face, leaving splatters of blood. A tall soldier stood on a wooden platform and said, "Let this be a warning to all of you. No work is to be done on Sundays. It's the new law for a new Fiji."

My mother had always worried enough for everyone in the family. And yet now, a different mood had overtaken her, eclipsing every part of the woman I had once known. For now she was without hope, hope for her children and grandchildren. What life could her children's children have when the world we had always known had been turned upside down?

"For more than a century, Kalyana, for more than a century we have labored for this country. We have built houses and bridges and businesses and schools. We have rooted for this country in soccer and rugby games played around the world. When do we get to call this our home? When?" And then she wept, crushed. It was something I had only seen when Manjula stood on her doorstep, for that last time, and said her final goodbye.

My mother had always been one to exaggerate and magnify grief, yet I came to understand that, this time, perhaps she spoke with truth. And so it was that, just as a fleet of hard-working Indians boarded British ships and came to Fiji more than a century ago, so in 1989 a crowd of their defeated descendants boarded airplanes and fled Fiji with suitcases full of dreams, seeking hope for the future. Kirtan and I were among them.

As I packed the few belongings we were taking with us to this new life, I pondered Fiji, the forgotten paradise. What had Pope John Paul said about our country once? "It's the way the world should be." As I carefully folded Kirtan's shirts and pants and stacked them upon my dresses, I came to realize that we had become a part of history, a pattern that had been repeated for centuries upon centuries. For this was no different than a British Sergeant-Superintendent standing over the Indians with a whip in his hand; it was no different than men towering over women for centuries, denying them the right to vote or own property. It was the same story as the punishment Tulsi's husband continually gave her; and most significantly, to me at least, it was no different than the torture Uncle Baldev had inflicted upon me or the silence my mother had imposed on me afterwards. For the first exercised dominance and power over the latter.

Nor were pain and suffering, loss and sacrifice, merely the lot of a woman, as my mother had told me that terrible afternoon. For there was a greater truth: every life, regardless of skin color, place of origin, birth rights, status, and, yes, gender, was entwined with pain and suffering. There was no escaping it. But if we tried to stand tall amidst the chaos and to contemplate, looking inward, we could perhaps learn the lessons and look beyond into a brighter future.

As Kirtan's family drifted in and out of our flat to bid their goodbyes over the course of our last week in Fiji, I cleaned the walls, swept the floors, and prepared for our departure. I could not allow myself to walk outdoors and see the flowers: marigolds, buttercups, frangipani, bougainvillea, and hibiscus in bloom. I must not see the coconut trees swaying in the breeze or the butterflies circling the rose bushes. I stopped my ears so that I did not hear the sound of the ocean waves crashing against the eroded seawall. For if I did, I was sure I would convince Kirtan to stay. I was sure I would then be unable to leave the only home I had known.

My mother helped me to close up the flat, and that evening my family came to bid Kirtan and me our final farewell. My mother had chattered throughout the day, but when my father came he did not say a word. Quietly he sat in a corner, back against the bare walls, until it was time to leave. I had never seen a grown man cry buckets of tears until that day. He held me close and long, and wept shamelessly for the loss of his child. I knew I was taking a piece of his heart.

Raju stood back and watched our father weep. Then, to clear the air or perhaps to come to his own understanding of my upcoming departure, he did the usual: He punched me for the last time on each arm, calling me "Kali." "Take care," he said, laughing as always. "Be careful how much you eat in Canada. I hear some people over there eat so much that they have to be carried out of their flats with cranes. I don't want to have to cut the doors when you come back to visit, so that you can fit through them." His loud chortling made the lizards on the walls perk up their heads.

I would miss Raju and his foolishness. I told him to find a wife and settle down before he turned into a flabby, flaccid old man who wasn't desired by anyone. My brother flexed his biceps and said, "See, Sis—strong and young. That's what I'll always be." He grinned. "Kaaaaaali! Ka Ka Ka Ka Ka Ka Ka Kaaaaali." I heard his voice echo long after he had walked out into the night.

When the shelves were packed into boxes and the floors swept and wiped clean of dirt, my mother took me aside. She gently touched my forehead, moving a stray hair. Her eyes found mine, just for a moment. How long had it been? She took my hands in hers and put the small gold snake charm in the center of my palm. "I found this under your mattress, in your old room" she said. "Take it with you. Just in case you need it there."

She studied every inch of my face as though she could burn it into her memory. I waited for her to speak, to say something to obliterate the years of pain. I wanted her to talk about the silent moments and the untold tales. I wanted her to hang her head out of a window and scream, scream loudly so that the world could hear, to cry for my silent suffering, and to weep for the years lost and the years gained. To tell me that she loved me, if not more than Raju, then at least an equal amount. I wanted her to tell me that she was proud of who I was and who I was becoming.

I wanted her to tell me that a woman's strength is hidden, yet encompassing. That just as a movement is only as good as its leader, so is a household only as good as its mother. This was the power that had been bequeathed to a mother, to a woman, for generations upon generations past, and that would stand for centuries to come.

But my mother did none of these things. Instead, she spoke in a slow, self-assured manner, like an actor delivering a monologue on the Broadway stage, and she imparted what seemed like others' wisdom, telling another woman's tale. She whispered what I already knew: "Everyone in this world is granted one beginning and one ending, Kalyana. Life is made up of what is in between: the connections, the discoveries, the triumphs, and the losses. Some of these inspire us, some mold us, and some destroy us. But remember that no experience leaves our spirits untouched. Remember that, Kalyana. Remember that wherever you go." She forced a faint smile, kissed my forehead and, following my father and Raju, she hurried out of the room.

I left the gold snake charm on the windowsill in the empty flat.

The wind blows me away
Away to another home
As the clouds keep drifting above me
The mountains cry out to tell me something
But all I can hear is the melody the stream creates,
Close by me
The smell of spring fills my soul with dreams
Dreams of another exciting adventure
I open my heart and hug the new life before me
And I see the rainbow
Making sweet and sour promises to me again
Just like yesterday

CANADA

27

A FAT MAN with a fluffy white beard and a red-and-white suit walked up and down the corridors of the airport, screaming "*Ho-Ho-Ho*" and jingling golden bells. Another one dressed just like him sat in a busy open restaurant, eating fries smothered in cheese curds, gravy, and ketchup. I wrinkled my nose at the sight. Kirtan said it was called *poutine*.

"Father Christmas," I said, nudging Kirtan on the arm. This was the first time I had seen one in person.

"I think they call them Santa Clauses here," Kirtan whispered back. The sound of airplanes landing and taking off filled the air, and my heart lurched a little as I thought of the tiny strip in Nadi, now left far behind. I noticed that Kirtan's hands were trembling as he sorted out our passports and documents. He had seemed so strong, so sure, back in Fiji, but for the first time I realized that the anxiety of starting a new life in a foreign country must have drained him, too. He seemed to have aged a few years in the past week.

Kirtan's sister and brother-in-law, who had emigrated to

Canada already, met us outside the glass doors. They moved fluidly through the chaos of Vancouver International Airport, not batting an eye once at the serious security guards who were running baggage through scanners and frowning over the arriving passengers. They did not seem to notice eager relatives standing behind the glass doors, hoping to see familiar faces. Nor did they stare at a young couple who embraced passionately and flooded each other's faces and necks with soft kisses, leaving behind red patches where lips had grazed upon skin. My mother would have stared at them. Kirtan and I tried not to.

Young people locking hands and lips in broad daylight was something that we had never seen on the streets of Suva, Lautoka, Nausori, or Labasa. Even if such a thing had happened, it would have ended quickly. The brothers and cousins of the young girl would have beaten the boyfriend until his white T-shirt was soaked in his blood.

Kirtan's sister and brother-in-law put our bags in their car and drove us to their home, leaving the airport and its strange people behind.

If I had known the significance of the month of December for Canadians, I would have urged Kirtan to select another month to move here. I found the hustle and bustle of the Christmas season overwhelming; from morning to night, the streets were congested with strangers rushing in and out of stores with shopping bags over their shoulders or wound around their fingers. Some wore designer jackets in bright, vibrant colors, while others walked the streets in plain coats. Women sported perms that made their hair dry and frizzy. Some wore electric-blue eyeshadow.

One man wore a skirt, with fishnet stockings and high heels. People snickered and stared at him as if he was a foreign animal trapped in a zoo. He reminded me of the young boy who lived a few apartments down from Kirtan and me back in Suva. He went to the clubs every weekend, dressed in ladies' clothes and heels. Strangely, in Fiji, nobody had stared at him disapprovingly, the way they would have glared at the passionately kissing teenagers. I wondered if I would ever become used to this place.

Women were different here, too, in the way they carried themselves and in the way they dressed. They trotted the streets quickly and confidently, wrapped in cardigans and wool coats. I saw women wearing pants, and I thought of Manjula strutting in our living room. For a moment, I wished I had thought to practice wearing pants before coming to Canada.

Some young boys shaved the sides of their heads and dyed the small remaining strip of hair on the top of their heads red and blue. It stood upright like a strange flag. Beggars— "bums," they called them here—lined the city streets, asking for money and cigarettes.

One day, in the drizzling rain, I bought a cup of hot chocolate for a bum with a straggly gray beard. He reminded me of the healer whose strange words had lifted the cloud of breathlessness from me long ago. Unlike the healer, however, he didn't smile; his eyes were full of suspicion as he grabbed the hot chocolate from my hand. I felt an unpleasant shiver rush through me as his leathery hand touched mine. He didn't whisper a quiet prayer or offer silent blessings. Nor did he wish my family goodness and prosperity like the beggars in Fiji had always done. As he stared unblinking, tremors ran through both of his hands. He licked the hot chocolate off his lips and smirked devilishly. It was his smirk that reminded me of Uncle Baldev, and instantly I felt my breath grow still in my lungs. There was a bitter taste at the back of my throat. I left the man abruptly, but the sound of his hollow laugh followed me into the distance.

I looked around me as I hurried away. In this Christmas season, lights blinked in every store. Most of the displays glowed with gaudily decorated trees. I was a speck in a large crowd, small and invisible. I wished fervently that I had listened to my mother, that I had not left the gold snake charm behind on the windowsill. A small part of me longed for the comfort of the smooth metal resting gently in the palm of my hand.

Yet gradually we became accustomed to the strange sights and sounds that were Canada. The Sky Train schedules, bus routes, and downtown streets were soon imprinted on our minds. By the time we moved into our own flat, we could already navigate Vancouver almost as quickly as Kirtan's sister and her husband.

We had also learned what streets to avoid when we set out for a stroll. East Hastings spelled bad news; it was here that scantily dressed women walked the streets in stiletto heels, and bags of white powder and green herbs were exchanged freely for rolls of crisp bills. Police cars blazed through the narrow streets there, sirens shrieking, chasing unknown ill-doers. On

East Hastings, the concrete walls were painted with obsceni-
ties and crude displays. The public called it "graffiti," the art of
the untamed, said Kirtan's brother-in-law.

Some argued that this graffiti was a movement. But it did
not fill me with hope. Though the air might be the clearest of
clear, every time I walked by East Hastings my heart would
start to beat at a fierce speed and my breath would come in
gasps. I was twelve again, waiting for darkness to overtake
me. If I fell, would anyone help me? Or would the untamed
crowd of East Hastings pounce on me and carry me back to
its graffiti-plastered dens? It wasn't until I had left the area far
behind that my chest would once more release, allowing my
breath to flow freely and easily again.

During my first year in Canada, while Kirtan was busy
balancing the books of a Canadian company, I boarded the
bus that was going in the opposite direction of East Hastings
and went down to Stanley Park—where the tourists, with
cameras draped around their necks or video cameras tightly
gripped in their hands, roamed the paths in white sneakers
and flat shoes. Lines of people with little children impatiently
awaited their turn to enter the aquarium, where they could
gaze at the beluga whales swimming in circles in a large tank
or watch dolphins eat fish out of their trainers' hands. Inside
the Aquarium, noisy sea otters sat on rocks in a small pond,
their noses up in the air like the sister-in-law of Manjula's
first suitor. Barely noticing the crowds around them, they sat
flapping their tiny flippers and making high-pitched squeals.

I never watched the sea creatures do their tricks, however,
for I longed for something quieter and more intimate, somewhere far from the chattering crowds. I would walk along the

natural paths in the wooded area, observing the details on the totem poles and staring at the high, triangular pine trees that reached for the clouds. I would stand on the seawall and dream of home, as I watched the calm seas.

A familiar breeze would blow through my hair, though the air was crisp and even chilly, not pungent with warm salt-iness. I couldn't take off my shoes and hop over the seawall. There were no sandy beaches or yards of shell-scattered shores, no small crabs that disappeared into holes in the sand. Here, six feet of freezing water flowed below, and flying seagulls squawked in the sky. In Vancouver I never heard the pundit chant Sanskrit verses in the far distance, nor the sound of my mother grating coconut on a small wooden board.

It was so cold, so bleak, so bustling. But standing there on the seawall in Stanley Park, looking at the deep ocean grays stretching to the horizon, I felt the smallest fraction closer to home. If I closed my eyes and took a deep breath in, I could almost feel the humid, salty air graze my skin. The scent of jasmine and frangipani flowers blooming in the setting sun did not seem so far away. As I stood and felt the spray of surf, I would reflect upon my old home and this new place that Kirtan and I would slowly make our own. In Canada the smell of curry did not linger in the breeze, but perhaps with time I could learn to love the scent of pine.

What I missed most about Fiji were the holidays. Even though at home I had huffed and sighed sometimes at my mother's celebrations, I still remembered the graceful stories she had told. In Canada, people told stories of baby Jesus and not of Rama, Lakshman, and Sita. Everyone waited for Christmas, never for the lighting of the *diyas* of Diwali, and they indulged in the sound of fire crackling in their fireplaces, never the blast of firecrackers piercing the dark skies.

"Why do we celebrate Diwali, Mummy?" Once again I was five years old, clinging to my mother's sari.

"Questions, questions!" she would sigh, but I always knew she loved to give the answers. "With his faithful brother Lakshman on his right-hand side, the divine king Rama left his jeweled crown on his dying father's pillow," she would begin. "He strapped on his bow and arrow and took out for the woods to rescue his beloved wife, Sita. Even though Sita was a common girl, a common girl whose chastity was in question even in those days." My mother would soak the white cotton wicks in ghee and light them with a matchstick, one by one.

"What does chastity mean, Mummy?"

"Never mind what it means, Kalyana." She would blink her round eyes to brush my question aside. "Do you want to hear the story or not?"

I would nod my head, eager and alert.

"Ravana kept Sita imprisoned in a small hut, in a wooded area. Oh, Ravana thought he could one day convince her to forget about her husband, Rama, and become his kept wife. For fourteen years, God Rama fought lions and tigers, cheetahs and cougars, wolves and hounds, bears and gorillas too. Oh yes, every animal, Kalyana, and more, for he even fought four-limbed and three-eyed monsters, hideous beasts of demonic nature. Yet he defeated them. One by one, the beasts would fall to the ground, panting and weak, then take their last breaths and turn to dust. In the end, after fourteen long years of exile, the victorious divine King Rama killed the demon Ravana and rescued his beloved wife, Sita, and brought her home. That is why we light the pathways, the verandas, and the gardens. It is to help him find his way back home."

I would start to talk about the princes and princesses of my fairy tales, but my mother would shake her head. She would tell me that no, to celebrate Diwali was to celebrate the defeat of evil and the triumph of good, to mark the end of Rama's suffering. "See, Kalyana," she would say, "even a divine force such as Rama was not without trials and tribulations. He, too, suffered, like any other mortal being."

Even now, in the quietness of Stanley Park, I could hear my mother's stories ring in my ear. And in spite of myself, I longed for that day when *diyas* would light the pathways, under the overhanging fruit trees, and, like Rama, I courageously returned home.

28

IT WAS NOT long before Kirtan and I moved into another dwelling, leaving our small flat for a two bedroom townhouse in the outskirts of Vancouver, a place Canadians called "the suburbs." Our larger house was cheaper than our flat, something which mystified even Kirtan.

I was delighted to find that the back door led onto an attached deck and a small patch of green grass. In the middle of the yard, which was surrounded by a brown wooden fence, a crabapple tree stood tall, shading the deck—a reminder of the many fruit trees that lined the back and front yards of houses in Fiji. But soon I realized that, while the fruit from the trees in Fiji were almost always picked by the locals for sale in the markets, the crabapples from the tree in my backyard landed on the ground or on our deck, making a mess. It did not take me long to come to regret this tree. For every time I stepped outside into the backyard, I trod on rotten and squishy crabapples that stuck to my shoes or bare feet and tracked back onto the clean tiled floors of my kitchen. I did not know what to do with the hundreds and hundreds of crabapples that smiled upon me every morning.

One day, full of exasperation and defeat, I was on my deck, contemplating this tree, when our neighbor came out her back door. I had noticed her on her deck before this, standing erect, sipping a hot drink and laughing with her husband. She was petite, with strong shoulders, and she had long, lustrous black hair, small brown eyes, and a warm, charming smile. In so many ways, she reminded me of our Manjula.

"Hello, neighbor," she said, smiling broadly.

I smiled back.

"I'm Angela," she said from over the fence.

I hesitated.

Angela walked closer to the edge of her deck. "I wish I had that crabapple tree in my yard. Then I could have made jam."

I sighed in relief. "Please, come and take them all. I was just standing here wondering what I would do with so many crabapples in my backyard."

Angela climbed down from her deck, and joined me. Still thinking of Manjula, I hurriedly sliced limes and squeezed their juices into a clear jug. I filled it with cold water and ice, then mixed in a few tablespoons of sugar. "Lemonade," I said, pouring the cloudy liquid into a tall glass. I handed it to Angela.

"You mean, limeade?"

I squinted.

"Lemonade is made with lemons, no?" Angela smiled, taking a sip.

"In Fiji, lemonade is always made with limes, never

lemons," I said, and we both laughed at the strange look she gave me. The difference between lemonade and limeade was one of the first small details that Angela made me see differently.

Angela and I spent the afternoon collecting bags full of crabapples, some green and some red. As we chatted and laughed, and she told stories of her adventures abroad, I remembered Mother and Manjula; I remembered Mother and Roni. That afternoon, I realized that I had never before had a female friend.

From that day, Angela came to my house regularly: for afternoon tea; or to collect more crabapples; or to drop off homemade jam—which Kirtan and I loved. Sometimes she came over simply to talk. Angela was unlike any other Indian women I knew. She talked quickly and confidently—in perfect English tinged with a Canadian accent. She walked with an assurance and self-confidence that I had only seen in white-skinned women on Vancouver streets. Often I thought of Manjula, when I gazed upon Angela's small face, and the way my aunt had been: smirking and giggling, breaking tradition, shifting the gears of an automobile as she rode down the bumpy Fiji roads.

Sometimes I wondered what my mother would think of Angela. I thought she might insist that I stay away. For Angela was one of those women to be feared, to be reproached. She was living with a man whom she called her husband, without the pundit chanting Sanskrit prayers over an open fire, without receiving her father's blessing, and without watching her mother's tears of happiness. Yet she lived without shame, without regret. Sometimes, when they were both home on the weekends, she brought her partner over to visit with Kirtan.

Kirtan teasingly called her a coconut. He said she was brown on the outside, but white on the inside. "She's not a real Indian, Kalyana," he would whisper, as if our new neighbor could hear him if he spoke in a normal tone. "That is why she married a white guy named Grog."

"It's not Grog, Kirtan. It's Greg." I would shake my head while he chuckled. In Fiji, "grog" was another term for the popular hallucinogenic drink *yaqona*. I never did tell Kirtan that Angela and Greg were not truly married, like we were. I was not sure what Kirtan would think of my new friend if he knew. In time, I figured, he would come to know on his own.

Perhaps Kirtan was right, and Angela was white on the inside. She would come to the defense of the British so easily, at the slightest provocation. I discovered that she had studied philosophy and religion at graduate schools there, and she had taught in universities that resembled castles. Her parents, she said, still lived in England.

One day, while sitting under the shade of the crabapple tree, drinking limeade, I asked Angela what she thought about the atrocities the British had inflicted on Indian people, and the world. My mother had told me how the British had whipped my ancestors on the ship named SS *Sangola*, how they had raped the Indian women in banana patches and sugarcane farms, in the middle of the night and, sometimes, under the burning heat of a midday sun.

Angela stiffened immediately, as if I had somehow insulted her. Then calmly, she said, "Those were crimes of men against women. It was not just British men who were responsible for the rape of Indian women. Indian men were also guilty of some of the rapes that happened on the plantation farms of

Fiji." She paused for breath, sighed heavily, and then added, "It seems women everywhere, in wars, in famines, in migrations, pay the price with their bodies."

Indian men were also responsible for raping women on Fiji's plantation farms? It made me wonder what else my mother failed to tell me, teach me.

Angela gazed at me gently. "The British did not go around just doing ill in the world, Kalyana. If the British had not intervened and made laws prohibiting *Sati*, Indian widows would still be burned alive with their deceased husbands in India." She sounded sad. "An Indian woman's life was worth something to the British. So they spoke against the practise of widow burning."

I supposed it was true; after all, if it wasn't for the British, we wouldn't have had our roads, our buildings, or even our school systems. Angela reminded me, too, that the British had been responsible for educating women in India, and giving them a voice.

"But they did commit crimes!" I exclaimed.

"Yes, they did use force and manipulation to take over countries and try to turn the whole world into a Christian nation." Angela focused intently on a rotting crabapple on the deck. "But, Kalyana, they did it because they wanted to share their truth, their heaven, with everyone."

Angela looked back at me. I smiled at her feebly, so she sighed and said quietly, "But the British have admitted to these faults and taken full ownership. They no longer bury the truth or rewrite history books to manipulate their legacy." She paused and took a sip of her limeade. "Because of their history, Kalyana, European countries now champion multiculturalism. They advocate for the rights of minorities in all countries. So, out of tragedy and pain and suffering, a new era, a new way of thinking was born. Pain and suffering are a necessary precursor to change, Kalyana."

I took a small sip of my chilled drink. It tasted sweet.

And yet I admired Angela for never hesitating to speak her mind, to express what she felt. Whereas my mother would pass on stories about gods and goddesses of ancient Indian lands, about our tortured past and our place in society, insisting upon them as written or unwritten fact, Angela was not afraid to question these same tales. She was not afraid to challenge ancient conventions. Angela brought to my life something new: She showed me the possibility of speaking my own thoughts, and the power of questioning tradition, and understanding the implications our beliefs and practises have upon women everywhere. It was something that my mother had not given me—and I wondered whether my grandmother had not given it to her either.

My mother wrote me letters frequently, bringing me news both personal and political. Like a schoolgirl, she always used lined paper and wrote her address in blue ink on the right-hand corner. On the left, below the date, she would start formally: "Dear Kalyana." She never used complicated language and always wrote in short, simple sentences. Sometimes it felt as though I were sitting in her living room while she relayed the gossip: news of the neighbors, of Father and Raju, and of her beloved topic, the government.

Dear Kalyana,

How are you and Kirtan? How do you like Canada? Your father, Raju, and I are fine and hoping that you are well on that side of the world.

A new constitution came about in July of last year. It is a good thing that you have left with Kirtan. The new constitution does not allow us rights, even to own land. Even if an Indian is born here, it doesn't matter. All that matters is if you are a Fijian. Too many bad feelings between Indians and Fijians now. Life is not good here at all anymore. But we're surviving. Your father is working hard every day in the shop. Raju now goes there to help him every day. This is good, because one of the workers left for Canada just like you. So we're surviving, bit by bit.

Oh, I should tell you. There is more big news in Fiji. Dr. Anirudh Singh, from the university, burnt a page of the constitution. He made some group called GARD—

With spaces and a different color of pen, my mother elaborated on the important name.

Group Against Racial Discrimination.
A real-life movement. Such an event.
Army got the news of this movement. They captured him—Dr. Anirudh Singh—on the way to work one day. They blindfolded him and took him to the woods. He was beaten for twelve hours, they say. They left him there to die, but he is still alive. Sometimes movements end badly. I feel very scared now—

All the political talk would anger me. Why could my mother speak of nothing else but the doings and undoings of the Fijian and Indian people? Nor did I care about the village gossip: boring news of neighbors' daughters, sons, nephews, and nieces getting married; of people like criminals, their heads hung low in shame, escaping in planes, boats, and sometimes in high-riding automobiles that could travel on water. Perhaps I felt a certain amount of guilt when I thought of those left behind, those who were waiting for some movement the way drought-browned deserts thirst for rain.

What I really wanted to hear was how well the flowers were blooming under the shade of a bougainvillea hedge, or whether the oceans were whispering loudly amidst the sparkle of the evening sun. Now I thought back to the radio she always huddled near, even when I was a child. Perhaps she saw herself as more of a news reporter than a poet. Sometimes, I would read her letters and picture her in the kitchen, chattering and waving a wooden spoon to mark her words. She seemed more wistful, more resigned, than I remembered.

I could hear the plea underlining my mother's voice at the close of each letter. "Write back, daughter," she would say. And I did intend to write her back and send our wishes to her and Father and Raju. But every time I took out a pen and paper, I would sit by the kitchen table and stare at the blank page. Should I start with *Hello*? *How are you?* Or simply, *I miss you, Momma. How is Father? Did Raju find his love?* I wasn't sure what my mother would like me to ask her, if anything at all. I didn't know how to begin. So, after staring at the page for some time, my mind would wander and I would go into the living room and turn on the television set. Or sometimes

I would simply phone Angela and talk about her impending trip to some exotic destination, far away. After that, I would forget all about replying to the letter, until the next time.

Later that winter, when the crabapples died and shriveled up like raisins, Angela took me to an amateur monthly spoken-word event given by her writers' group. At first I was hesitant to follow, without the comfort of Kirtan's protection from the ills and uncertainties of this unknown world. But, in his usual light-hearted manner, Kirtan insisted that I go.

"Come on, Kalyana," Kirtan teased. "You do not need to uphold the Laws of Manu in this land of maple syrup!"

Kirtan loved to quote from this ancient religious text of India, which said that women were nothing without the protection of their fathers, husbands, brothers, and sons. It maintained that women should only walk in the shadows of their men. The same text also said that husbands must cherish their wives, and men must honor all women, for wherever women are loved and revered, gods dance and rejoice.

"But in this household, you must worship me like I am your God," said Kirtan mischievously. "Manu says, Kalyana!" He winked flirtatiously.

I raised my eyebrows. "Didn't Manu also tell husbands to give all their hard-earned money to their wives to do with it as they please, Kirtan? For Manu says it is the wives that run the household, and it is the wives who know where the money will be spent the best." I paused for effect, and then added, "It is strange that men observe only the ancient teachings of scriptures that support their own selfish pursuits and that maintain their own prestigious status in their households and communities, and they gladly ignore all scriptural evidence that gives power to the women of this world! Despicable!"

Kirtan appeared perplexed, but I detected a grin as he turned away. I smiled.

So, ignoring the stern Laws of Manu, at the insistence of my beloved husband, Kirtan, I ventured out with Angela to my first spoken-word event. It was held in a small independent coffee shop that was attached to a store selling used books. The minute I stepped through the door, I left Angela's side and lost myself in the narrow aisles. Books were stacked almost to the ceilings, hard covers and soft covers. Some looked brand new, unread, and others were dusty and dirty, falling apart.

Once again, I was five years old; I was a tiny fish swimming in an ocean of books, free to dart through one aisle and come out the other. I could take out one book and shove it back on the shelf and then remove a second, flipping the bent or crisp pages or looking through the illustrations—just as I had done with my mother at Suva Public Library.

I picked up a small book and looked at the cover intently; it had a young girl standing on a rooftop, wearing a red dress that was blowing in the wind. It made me think of a little girl, alone and lost. How long had it been since I had read a book? I was delighted that Angela had brought me here.

Angela saw me standing at the cashier's desk paying for the book, and hurried towards me, bringing with her a young man and a pretty blonde woman. She introduced them as Peter and Julie, the organizers responsible for welcoming new members and making sure that every event was successful. Julie was the master of ceremonies. I envied that: to be able to step on a stage when all eyes were on you, and to do it confidently and comfortably. It was a skill I knew I didn't have.

"Welcome," Julie said, extending her hand. Peter smiled beside her. I shook Julie's hand lightly, stepping back a little. In that moment, I wished I could disappear.

"Should I book you time on the stage tonight?" asked Julie enthusiastically.

"No. No. No." My heart skipped a few beats, at the thought of having all eyes on me, as I stood mumbling underneath the heat of bright lights.

"Oh, don't worry," said Julie. "No pressure. Whenever you are ready to read let me know." Julie giggled like a teenager, then, spotting other newcomers, she grabbed Peter's hand and left with him.

For most of the evening I sat in a corner with Angela and watched the performances on stage. Emerging writers and poets of all ages and all races, and from all walks of life, had gathered here to showcase their works. Women like Angela eagerly awaited their turns, then strode towards the center of the stage, grabbed the microphone, and without fear of judgment or prosecution, read from their unpublished stories and poems. When Peter's turn came, he jumped up on the stage and, without speaking a single word, through quiet gestures and dramatic actions, told stories of an old man and his dog. He made his small audience cry.

I thought of my mother, telling stories to her small audience in her living room, and I remembered how much I had enjoyed them. Tears flooded my eyes. Even here, in a world so different and so far away, people gathered together, simply to hear each others' stories.

After that first time at the writers' group, I became a devoted member and attended every monthly event with Angela. We met at bookstores, coffee houses, and sometimes simply by the rose garden in a public park. I followed Angela's example, and tasted wine, beer, and cocktails for the first time. When I first drank wine, I scrunched up my nose at its bitterness, expecting it to taste sweet. Angela glowed, sipping from her long-stemmed glass. "It's an acquired taste, Kalyana," she said. "The more you drink it, the more you will like it."

I was not sure that I would ever like wine. But eventually, in time, I did, though I never did develop a fondness for beer. Every time I drank spirits, I thought back to my mother and Manjula, sipping alcohol through straws, claiming they must for the sake of their aching teeth.

Sometimes Kirtan and Greg also accompanied us to the writers' group. It was not long before the friendship between Angela and me developed beyond the writers' circles, and our husbands followed us to many of the international restaurants that Vancouver had to offer. We shared exotic food and wines, conversations and laughs. We ate with silver forks and knives. We slurped soups out of ceramic bowls, and learned to use chopsticks with relaxed expertise. I often wondered what my mother would think if she saw me sitting here in a world so different, with my husband by my side, drinking wine in public, tasting foreign foods, and listening to stories.

"We'll get you on that stage too, someday," Angela would say as we clapped and cheered our support for the emerging stars at every monthly writers' event. But even though I always shook my head, I would remember the times when I had run home from school to write my own stories. What had happened to my imagination, my desire to create? When did I lose that passion to write? I vaguely remembered four old women, encompassing different colors and auras and strengths, beating drums and urging me to dream, in the far, far distance.

29

NAUSEA WOULD not leave me. It haunted me from morning to night. The smell of anything pungent would send me rushing to the washroom. So Kirtan took me to the doctor. We sat in the waiting room, Kirtan holding my hand tightly. Grave concern marked his face.

It was a while before the nurse called me in to see a gray-haired physician. Kirtan stayed by my side, the whole time. The doctor started probing me with a stethoscope, listening to my heart, asking question after question: When did I start feeling ill? Did I feel ill all day or certain times? What were the major symptoms? When was my last period?

It was then that it occurred to me that I had missed my period. The doctor did a small blood test and confirmed what now I already knew: I was very pregnant.

Kirtan was ecstatic. The moment the doctor stepped out of the room, Kirtan embraced me tightly, kissing my cheek. "We're going to be parents!" he whispered in my ear. He sighed loudly; I was not sure if it was panic or he was just overwhelmed. We drove home in silence, yet we still held hands.

As soon as I entered the house, I rushed to the phone and called Angela with my good news. To my surprise, she suddenly became silent, then, after a moment or two, she said quietly, "Congratulations, Kalyana. You have been given a gift. Congratulations." Angela did not say much else about my pregnancy and the upcoming baby, but the next day she stood on my doorstep with a stack of baby books and two jars of pickles.

"I hear pregnant women crave pickles!" she said, with the widest of smiles.

She handed me both jars. Still clutching the manuals on all stages of pregnancy, Angela strode into my living room. She plunked down on my sofa and immediately started flipping through the books, cooing at the pictures of unborn babies and dishing out advice: I should rub oil on my belly, as dry skin could cause stretch marks; I must drink gallons of water every day, as dehydration could cause premature labor; I didn't need to worry about the dark line on my navel, as it was a normal part of pregnancy and would fade with time; I should be careful of spending too much time in the sun, as it could cause brown patches to appear all over my skin. Angela arranged big pillows on the sofa and insisted that I keep my legs on them, as keeping them elevated would stop them from swelling and prevent varicose veins from appearing.

But pregnancy did not come with only warnings. It also came with its own perks: hormones caused my bosoms to swell, my hair to grow lush, and my skin to glow. Angela noticed and complimented me often.

Kirtan also lavished all his attention on me during this time. Even though my stomach had not started showing the signs of a life growing inside, Kirtan still laid his head on my midriff, singing songs and *bhajans* in Hindi, talking to the baby. I never did crave pickles, but desired bright orange *jalebies*—Indian sweets—with an unrelenting fierceness. And Kirtan, even in the middle of the night, like my savior, would rush out and get them. At ultrasound appointments, Kirtan would stand close by me, and gently touch my hand. I had no doubt that he would make an excellent father. Already, I knew he loved our unborn child. I was happy to have both, Kirtan and Angela, on my side.

Kirtan's upstairs office had to be moved downstairs; the second bedroom had to be turned into a nursery; a crib had to be bought; a dresser had to be painted; our whole house had to be baby-proofed. Every minute was occupied with arrangements for welcoming the new arrival in our home. Then a letter from my mother arrived bearing news:

Dear Kalyana,

How are you and Kirtan? Raju and I are fine. Your father is not feeling too good these days. He's saying that his eyes are thirsty to see you. He sits in the chair on the porch and looks out to the road. He has to take blood pressure pills now. Dr. Sudhir Singh gave him the prescription. Raju takes care of the shop completely. Business is not so good anymore, with all the rich Indians gone. People are still fleeing the country. Soon no one will be left here.

I've got some good news. Raju has found a nice Indian girl to marry. We've already met a few times. She's

*a big size, bigger than you. The wedding date is set for
September 21st of this year. I will send you an invitation
closer to the date. I hope you and Kirtan can come down.
It would be nice to see you both again. It's been too long.
Your father will like that, too.*

*I waited and waited and waited for your reply.
Hope nobody is sick in Canada. Try and call sometime if
you can't find the time to write, okay.*

I love you always.
Your Loving Mother,
Sumitri

So! Our Raju, the one who sowed seeds in wild fields
and rowed his boat in feral waters—Raju, *the lover of curves*—
was finally settling down. I was so thrilled to get my mother's
letter bearing this news that I called her on the phone immediately, asking her what I could send for the preparations. It
struck me then that it had been a long time since I had heard
her say "hello."

"My little Kalyana," she said. In her voice, I could sense
the tears filling her eyes.

I still had not told my mother about the baby. Feeling a
twinge of guilt, I relayed my own good news.

My mother was so delighted to hear of my pregnancy
that it seemed to outweigh her disappointment that I would
for the first time not be part of a great family celebration,
a joyous festivity; by that time in my pregnancy, traveling
would have proved difficult. But things were different now,
she said. The duty of a mother was first to her child, born or

unborn, and then to the rest of the world.

Still, she worried. She told me that at this time only a woman would understand what to do and what to say, and I did not have a Manjula or a Roni to lean on in Canada. Only a woman would understand how to rub coconut oil on my hair and wash it, when things became tiresome. I told her about Angela to ease her mind.

I regretted deeply that I would be unable to attend Raju's wedding. How long had it been since I had seen an Indian bride, clothed in gold and red, the colors of passion? In Canada, brides did not walk around the fire of a smoky altar held up by banana leaves and tree stumps. Here, even in the movies and the news, we only saw brides gliding down church aisles and wearing white, the color of purity. A few solemn guests dressed in suits or silk dresses sat still, some looking serious and some smiling slightly. Here there were no band and *baja*, no drums and songs, no old women singing, no children thumping the ground. Here, the little boys and girls dressed in suits and dresses like their parents, and sat quietly or stayed home. They did not dance or cry or run or jump in the aisles. If they did, their mothers or fathers or aunties or uncles immediately removed them from the auspicious occasion. How I suddenly missed the sound of the pundit blowing the conch shell!

After putting down the phone, she must have written me again. Shortly after, I received another letter:

Dear Kalyana,
I am overjoyed beyond belief. Two pieces of good news in one month: a son's wedding and a daughter finally

becoming a mother herself. But so is life. A cycle of good news and bad news, suffering and joy. It is best you stay there and look after yourself. Your body is not your own right now.

How's Kirtan? He must be so happy, jumping for joy, running and screaming down the streets telling everyone. That's what your father is doing down here. Kirtan, a father soon. I still remember when I first met him. Remember? He came over wearing that striped tie and crisp white shirt.

Have you chosen any names yet? It doesn't matter if my first grandchild is a boy or a girl. These days, girls have as many opportunities as the boys. Not like before. And you are in Canada, too.

Make sure you eat well, drink lots of milk, and rub lots of baby oil on your belly. You don't want to end up with stretch marks all over your belly.

Everyone here is well. We are just getting ready for the wedding. Making the guest list for our side of the family and filling out invitation cards. I am sure the girl's family is doing the same. Lots of work. You remember?

Well, I must go and get all the work done. So much to do. Thank goodness Roni is here to help me with everything. Roni says to say, "Namaste."

Your Loving Mother,
Sumitri

As the final days of my pregnancy approached, Angela with the help of Kirtan threw me a surprise baby shower. She decorated the room in pink streamers and lined the counters and tables with cupcakes smothered in pink icing—for we had discovered I was carrying a daughter. She organized games to guess the baby's weight, length, and birth date. And Kirtan supplied the goodies: samosas, pakoras, and chutneys. Angela invited people we knew from the writers' circle and they came, bearing gifts. Peter and Julie were among them.

As I sat in the middle of my living room, taking in the joy and love around me, I began to understand my mother's blessings: For in Kirtan's loyalty and devotion, steadfastness and truth, I saw my father, and in Angela, I found Manjula. I found a sister and a friend.

Aditi was born on a Friday in mid-November of that year. She was four weeks premature.

"Mother of Gods," cried my mother on the phone, overjoyed with the news of the birth of her *poti*, her granddaughter. "That's what her name means, Kalyana. That's what it means." She immediately wanted to know the details. How much had her *poti* weighed at birth?

"Five pounds and eight ounces, Momma."

"Five pounds and eight ounces. No problem. She will grow. In Canada, they have all the technology. Not like Fiji." Then swiftly changing her tone, she said, "If Aditi was born in Fiji, it would have made big news. Her picture would have been published on the front page of *The Fiji Times* and *Fiji Sun*. My *poti* would have been famous from birth. It's Diwali here today," she said. "It's November 13 today."

My mother wanted to know what the birth was like for me. Did I howl and scream as Aditi came into this world? Or did I keep quiet and stay still? I told her that Aditi slid into this world effortlessly and easily. There were no buckets of blood, or, if there were, I was blissfully unaware, for in Canada, pain need not be an essential part of a woman's life where childbirth was concerned. A blue-eyed, yellow-haired specialist inserted an epidural into my spine, eliminating all such suffering.

And yet not all the suffering. Aditi had to stay in the hospital for two weeks. She had an immature brain, meaning that she often forgot to breathe, and the doctors said she must sleep in a glass incubator. She must stay in the hospital under the professionals' care.

I knew that my mother was right. In Canada, Aditi had the support of advanced medical technology; in Canada, Aditi had a chance, and for this I was grateful. But I missed her terribly every night when I came home to a quiet house that did not hold the sounds of a newborn baby. Sometimes I wished I could stay in the hospital lobby all day and all night, close to my child, but when visiting hours were over the nurses would insist that I go home. "Get some rest, Mom," they would say. "Your baby needs you healthy." Reluctantly, my head held low, I would return home with empty arms.

But soon our daughter began to grow and thrive, and at last, the hospital released her into our care. With the passage of time, and perhaps by dint of my constant worrying, she even began sleeping and feeding peacefully, too. She would coo, laugh, and gurgle and spit. She was a spark of joy in our lives.

My mother sent Aditi a pink frilly dress and dried herbs that she claimed a priest had blessed. *The dried herbs will keep her heart beating and her breathing steady through the night,* she wrote on a small piece of yellow paper attached to the packet of herbs. *It will offer her protection.* In a letter, she asked me to put the herbs under the baby's mattress. I put them on the dresser, by her baby powder and diapers.

Upon hearing the news of Aditi's birth, Manjula, too, sent her cards and presents from Toronto. My mother and I were both happy that my aunt had remembered, although Mother once asked me in a letter why Manjula had mailed the presents and not driven over with them. Did her sister not wish to see her *grand-bhatiji*, her own flesh and blood? Accustomed to our island nation, where one could travel by car from end to end in one day, my mother had no concept of the vastness of my new home.

Kirtan, just like my own father, doted on his little girl. He would lie on the middle of the floor beside her blanket, kissing her forehead and counting and tickling her toes. Nor did he feel shame at picking up a broom and sweeping the floors. He would even take on the task of throwing Aditi's spoiled napkins, or diapers as they called them here, in the washer as I slept in our bedroom in the middle of the after-noon, exhausted from my new role as a mother.

In those days, Angela was also a great help. She would bring over home-cooked meals to ease the load on Kirtan and me. For that I was grateful, but especially I liked the gos-sip: of people coming and going in the writers' group; new romances budding and heartbreak tearing members, old and new, apart. It filled my empty days with curious stories.

Whenever Angela arrived on my doorstep, she would stop and gaze into Aditi's eyes and blow gently in her ear. Aditi would giggle and spit, lighting up the room. Watching Angela play with my daughter, made me yearn for the day I would see Aditi play with Angela's child, while we, the proud mothers, would sit in the living room drinking cappuccino and chai.

"When are you and Greg having a baby, Angela?" I finally asked with a smile. "I think now is a good time. Then we can see our children grow up together."

Angela quickly looked away. I saw tears flood her eyes, and my heart sank as she said, "We can't, Kalyana. We have been to every fertility clinic in London, but still no luck. We have one of those rare cases where the cause is not evident."

"I am so deeply sorry," I told her. My heart ached for her. In that moment, I too suffered a loss; I too, would never hold Angela's baby. We would never share that bond, that sisterhood. But still I held out hope. "You never know." I kept my voice encouraging. "If they can't find a cause…"

"If that happens, Greg and I will be overjoyed. But till then, I don't want to go on hoping, you know." Angela paused. "It was the hope, the yearning, that used to kill me, and my mother, every day in England." She sighed heavily then went quiet.

Was that why she had come to Canada? To get away from the memories of it all? I could sense that she did not want to talk about this any further, so I asked no more questions. We sat there for a few moments, observing the silence, feeling the loss.

It saddened me that not every woman was granted the

gift of motherhood. Angela's revelation made me think of the auntie-without-a-name. She, too, must have endured pain, when year after year, season after season, her womb remained empty, her lap stayed bare, and people's accusing eyes followed her far and wide.

My daughter was much too small, and I often worried about her rolling off the bed or choking on her milk. But all my anxiety was needless. With the passing months Aditi fattened, sat up in her car seat, and learned to kick her legs, roll over, crawl, and scream at the top of her now fully developed lungs. She also discovered how to aim spoonfuls of food at the wall and the floors. I took pictures of her every stage and from every angle possible, sticking them in large albums and sending a select few to friends and relatives. I sent the best of the bunch to my mother.

My mother always wrote back immediately, thanking me for her granddaughter's lovely pictures, telling me how happy and blessed she was to receive them and how Aditi's pictures reminded her of the time when I was small. She said we had the same chubby cheeks. As usual, she offered advice: she insisted I feed Aditi an array of curries, to sharpen her mind; and to give her custard, so she'd sleep through the night. And as usual, I ignored her. But she had good news of her own. I could picture the smile that must have lit up her small face when she wrote that Raju's wife, Yashna, was expecting a baby of their own. I was happy for my mother. I knew the joy Aditi had brought Kirtan and me. And I was certain that Raju's son or daughter would bring my mother the same joy, erasing her loneliness.

After Aditi's birth, my mother was on my mind more than ever. Images of her flew back to me from my childhood. When Aditi fell ill and I collected her vomit in my hand, when I wiped away scratches and blisters from her knees and tears from her face, when I gently and carefully trimmed her nails, I thought of how my mother had done the same for me. Sometimes, when I awoke in the middle of the night to comfort my small daughter with tales of Krishna and the five-headed snake, I could almost feel my mother's presence in the room. How long had it been since I had seen her?

My mother, worn out with all my excuses, had stopped asking when we were coming to see her and Papa. Now she just requested pictures. Perhaps she had finally accepted that we were grown and gone, maybe even forever. She seemed to understand that it was through pictures that I could best communicate.

And so, as she asked for more, instead of writing letters I continued to send her photographs. Pictures of Aditi smiling, frowning, scowling, and crying; pictures of Aditi dressed as a pumpkin, a rabbit, a bumblebee, and once as a smiling green frog, hopping among falling leaves. Aditi swaying on a red-and-blue swing set and jumping in the sprinklers, surrounded by *gora* children. Aditi wearing yellow rain boots, standing in a muddy puddle. Aditi sitting on Kirtan's lap, on her first birthday, then her second, and then her third.

My mother, gauging Aditi's size from the pictures, continued to send gifts: Little island shirts, printed shorts, and frilly socks. Once, she sent Aditi a swimsuit. It was white with red hibiscuses printed all over it. Angela marveled at it, and then, to my utmost horror, she suggested that all three of us go swimming. I saw two problems immediately: I did not know how to swim and I did not know how to wear a swimsuit. The women of Fiji swam in the ocean fully clothed, their skirts and dresses ballooning all around them as they bobbed on top of the waves. But Angela persisted and succeeded in dragging me and Aditi to a store whose aisles were lined with different colors and sizes of swimsuits.

"Just choose a color that you think will look flattering on your skin type and wear it proudly," Angela said. I chose a black swimsuit with white borders and a full back. Angela rolled her eyes but accepted my choice, without arguments, without fuss. "Put it on," she said.

Shifting my eyes to the ground, with shoulders slumped and legs heavy, I made my way into the fitting room. I slipped out of my clothes and into the revealing swimsuit. For a moment I felt the ocean breeze rustling through my hair, and the deafening sound of the waves, crashing on the seawall, whistling in my ears. Then I saw my reflection in the mirror in this small room. A hippopotamus looked back at me, jolting me back to reality. My thighs appeared too large and my stomach was fat. I gasped at my nakedness on display for all of the world to see.

"Come on out," yelled Angela when I had remained in the dressing room for over ten minutes. "Kalyana," she bellowed again, a little too loudly for my taste.

Releasing the air trapped in my lungs and bundling up all my courage, I slowly made my way out of the fitting room. At first, I only peeked through the door. The hallways seemed empty, except for Angela standing there, holding onto Aditi's small hand. So I stepped out under the blazing light: A hippopotamus caught in the flood of a hundred headlights.

"Not bad," said Angela, looking me up and down, making me flush. "It's the right style, right cut. All good!" She smiled. It warmed my soul.

"I feel very naked," I said in a small voice.

Angela shrugged. "My advice is to put on your swimsuit, don't look in the mirror, and just walk out there like you are the Goddess of Fiji."

I chuckled.

Later, at the pool, I followed Angela's advice. I did not glance in the mirror, and did all I could to avoid staring at the rows and rows of naked bodies of women, fat and small, young and old, standing under showers and reclining on benches, slipping in and out of their scanty bathing suits. I wrapped a beach towel tightly around my waist, hiding my stomach and my thighs, and, clutching Aditi's small hand, I walked out to the pool. Then throwing my towel onto a bench close by, I slipped into the lukewarm water. I stayed at the edge of the shallow end and held on to my daughter by her waist. Aditi flailed her arms and legs, splashing the water all around me. Angela, comfortable in her bright blue bikini, took out a camera from her bag and snapped a picture of us. I sent it to my mother.

After settling into my new role as a mother, I began to long for the nights I spent at the bookstores and coffee houses,

away from Aditi, listening to poets read aloud the secrets of
their hearts and writers tell stories of the world as they saw it.
There were times, when the evening sun set over the distant
mountains, that a surge of guilt passed through me at the
thought of wanting time alone, time away from my family.
But Kirtan insisted that a woman was not only born to be a
mother and a wife; she was born to follow her passions and
desires, and pursue her dreams. So, on a rainy Saturday, leaving Aditi in the care of Kirtan, Angela and I ventured to the
writers' club, just like old times.

It seemed as if no time had passed. The same people,
the same charm, and the same hazy smoke filled the space.
Perhaps I gained strength from becoming a mother, because
for the first time, I longed to stand in the center of the stage,
amidst the bright lights, and face the clapping, cheering audience. I longed to write. Yet I had often sat down in the middle
of the afternoon when Aditi took a nap and all was quiet, and
still no words had come. Here, through an endless stream of
stories, I could at least feel another artist's joy and pain.

A heavy-set girl with freckles climbed up on the stage and
pulled out a crumpled piece of paper. Angela and I had never
seen her before. The girl looked over the heads of her audience, straight towards the back wall. Upon the first cue, the
room fell silent. The girl stared back at her paper and, in a
husky, uneven voice, she read:

Just About a Rose
Sweet smelling and bloody red
She lies in the midst of thorns unhurt
Greenest of leaves and warmest of the rays

266

Surround her, promising protection
An intruder comes and forces her to part from her home,
Snatches her from what she knows
The leaves fall away, one by one
The clouds swallow the whole sun
The selfish man taints her, for an eternity to come
The redness is lost from her lips
The sweet scent dissipates, in one breath
The rose, crumbles and falls to the earth
It becomes dust.

"This story is just about a cursed rose," she said, hoarsely. People cheered, smiled, clapped, and made noise. Some banged rhythmically on the table, creating music. The hefty girl walked off the stage, pounding her feet and making the microphone squeal.

I sat still, feeling numb. Now I understood why I could no longer write or gather the courage to speak my story. The chains of silence put upon me by my mother were still strangling me, bit by bit, day by day.

30

AS TIME PASSED my mother's letters grew grimmer, often recounting the deaths of people I had known. Cancer had eaten Dr. Timoci Bavadra, she said, many years ago now. It was a sad day for all the supporters of the Labour Party. Kalwant Singh from down the road had died of heart failure. I remembered how the village had taken a collection for him after Hurricane Elsa had flattened his home. Mother said that he had eaten food cooked in too much *ghee*, and it had clogged his arteries.

Uncle Bhatur, a distant uncle I had met just once, had died of unknown causes. He had collapsed in the middle of the wheat field while laying out plots of ground. Yashna's Baba, or father, had also passed away. He had cut his finger, which led to a blood infection. He died in the hospital a week later, at precisely the same time he cut his finger. Auntie Shami had shaken and snored herself to her end. Mother said her snores and shakes must be keeping the gods and goddesses awake in the heavens above.

Tulsi's husband across the street had died in a drunken stupor. He had choked on his vomit and the breathlessness had seized him. His cruel mother had touched a fallen live wire and died of shock. Her body was found burnt to a crisp under the jasmine bush. Gossip on the streets, my mother wrote, was that it was Tulsi's doing, for, a week before the deaths, Tulsi had visited a priest. Perhaps she had summoned a holy man to put a spell on her husband and her slave-driving mother-in-law. Only a mere month later, my mother wrote, Tulsi flew away like a bird to New Zealand to be close to her sister.

So Tulsi got her revenge? I pondered this question.

"Only God knows what the truth is," wrote my mother, "In the end, God sees to everything." With God's good grace, she prayed that they all might come back to the earth in a better reincarnated form, and live a blessed life.

News of the death of my father didn't come in a form of a letter, but in a dream. I dreamed that I sat cross-legged at the head of my bed, rearranging fluffy pillows on my lap. My father came into my room. He had dropped many pounds and looked frail, and there was a sickly purple hue that surrounded his entire body. He slid onto my bed and put his head on my lap. The scent of Vicks filled the air, and I remembered the days of my breathlessness, when the icy heat of the ointment had brought me no relief. Gasping, he took his last breath while looking at my face. I cupped my hands over his cheeks. They felt cold. I closed his eyes. He looked peaceful, resting on my lap.

The next morning I awoke to Raju's phone call. My mother was crying hysterically in the background, speaking to the neighbors and relatives who had gathered in our house, and telling stories of my father's last request: "Rub some Vicks on my back and chest, Sumitri. My lungs are feeling congested.' I didn't know it would be the last time I would be rubbing Vicks on his chest. I didn't know." My mother howled.

There was loud chattering and strange noises. Dishes were falling and breaking. I started crying before Raju broke the news slowly and gently, over the rumble and static. "He went in his sleep," he said. "Exact cause is uncertain."

I regretted fiercely that I had not given Aditi a chance to know him.

And yet I told my mother that I could not afford to come to the funeral. It was true that, with the mortgage payments and only Kirtan working, it would be impossible. I think she understood the truth: that I could not face the thought of my father, frail and weak in death, closed up in a small box. How could I watch his lifeless body succumb to the hungry flames? I wanted to hold onto the memory of the father of my childhood, overflowing with life and showing limitless compassion to all. In my mind, I wanted him to stay that vigorous man who would punch the air fiercely as morning broke. I wanted to picture him going off to work, wearing his khaki pants and white T-shirt; cracking the shells of crabs and prawns with his teeth, slurping the juices; or walking down the street, with his chin up and head held high, making the neighborhood boys stop and shiver. I was glad for my mother that Manjula went to the funeral. I was sure that she would have found solace and strength, leaning on her sister's shoulders.

My father's death marked the end of my nostalgia for the land where the coconut trees swayed freely in the winds, the land that stirred poetic feelings within me. No longer did I feel a connection. Gone were my last few happy memories of Fiji.

After my father's death, my mother wrote fewer and fewer letters. She said that old age was striking her eyes, making her lose sight. She took to speaking with me on the phone occasionally, instead. She provided the same news and offered the same advice, and asked the same questions. But one piece of news, she wrote in a letter: Uncle Baldev, she said, had passed away. Cold had seeped into all his joints, making them brittle as glass; he was bound to the wheelchair in his final months, with no one to care for him. His wife, Mother said, had disappeared years before. No one knew where she had gone, but I knew that, even if they had looked under the stars and the moon or in the shade of a bougainvillea hedge, they would not have found her. Whom would they look for? For nobody knew her name. Uncle Baldev had died lonely and sad, wrapped up in his own vomit and fecal stench.

I thought of Tulsi and her revenge on her husband and mother-in-law. "In the end, God sees to everything," my mother had written then. So this was the end that the gods had devised for Uncle Baldev? This was how the auntie-without-a-name and I would have our revenge? To die alone was sad, but it was without shame. Why did the gods not come down to the very earth, proclaiming to the relatives and villagers the man's evil deeds, the man's crimes? Pain and suffering could be felt both outwardly and within, and it is that which no one can see that wounds the spirit the most. It is she who pays the price for whom life can be unfair.

I banged the cupboards in the kitchen. I dropped cups and plates on the floor; the ceramic dishes splattered all over the clean tiles in a million pieces. I took the doormat of our home and beat it on the crabapple tree outside. I stripped the clean bedsheets off the beds and washed them again and again. Kirtan wondered loudly what was eating me, while Aditi cowered in a corner.

I didn't answer.

I had always followed tradition and kept my mother's letters, just as my mother and Manjula had done themselves. After reading my mother's careful script, I would fold them up and place them neatly in a cardboard box, the stiff paper tied with ribbon. But I did not keep this letter. I read it and threw it into the fire. I watched it burn for a long time.

The following week, I ventured to the monthly spoken-word group with Angela, but I remained invisible among the crowd. I barely heard anyone say their piece; I looked at the stage but saw only blinding light.

On the drive home that night, through the tunnels of cherry blossoms, I remained silent. I did not comment on the works of the rising stars. Nor did I discuss stories and poetry that had touched me.

"When did you stop writing?" asked Angela. There was a gentle quietness in her voice.

"How did you know I used to write?"

"I saw it in your eyes the very first time I met you under the crabapple tree in your backyard. And that's why I invited you to the writers' club." Angela looked at me quickly, then back at the road. "I know there's a whole book inside you, waiting to be written."

I gazed out the car window at the roads covered in cherry blossoms. Light reflected off the bright pink petals, making the dark surface of the asphalt appear lit.

"What made you stop?" asked Angela.

I remained silent. Then, in one instant, I unleashed the dark secret choking me inside. I had to tell someone, anyone. So I told Angela everything: about Manjula's wedding; of Uncle Baldev's doings and misdoings; of the chickens making noise in the Chicken House; of the four old women beating drums and shaking the earth; of the stench of whiskey on his breath; the coconut leaves rustling in the wind; but most of all, I told her about my mother. I told her how she threw my bloody underwear in the fire that night, when the guests had gone home. No one saw anything. No one heard my cries. I told Angela I had not forgiven my mother. I told her that my mother's biggest crime was that she remained silent and hid my shame. She—my own mother—took Uncle Baldev's side.

Angela pulled onto the side of road, struck by my confession. She was deeply moved. She said she had no words to express her anguish, speak her truths. She prayed to God that the vengeance of Mother Kali would fall on my uncle in the hell below, where, she was sure, he now rested. She said all the things I had longed to hear from my mother.

Angela wept with me and for me, on the side of the road that night. And I, having the lonely burden of shame lifted from my shoulders, felt a hundred tons lighter.

After that night, I still called my mother occasionally, although out of a sense of duty more than a true desire. Then one day, out of the blue, I received an envelope in the mail, addressed in her neat handwriting.

I opened the letter with slight trepidation. What had compelled her to take up this old-fashioned habit again? Even now, she wrote in the same archaic way: on lined paper, in blue or black ink, she started her letter with "Dear Kalyana" and ended with "Your Loving Mother, Sumitri." The address and date were tucked neatly in the right-hand corner, as they always had been.

I wondered whether my mother knew that the world had moved forward, that the Internet, like a spider web that went from one end of the ceiling to another, had created an invisible maze of connections from one computer to the next. Few people now exchanged words with a paper and a pen. Even Raju emailed me short notes.

In my mother's letter, she asked why I had not come to Fiji with Kirtan. She had been glad to see him when he traveled back to Fiji to attend his mother's funeral and visit his family, but she was disappointed that I had stayed behind. She said she wanted to see Aditi before her spirit left the earth and joined with her departed husband's. I telephoned her and told her that the reason I couldn't come was money; that we could not afford to travel there as a family on Kirtan's modest income; that it was costing Kirtan thousands of dollars already. His trip had been more than what we could really afford, I said.

But that was not the truth. In Fiji there were still bad memories lurking in the dark shadows of the jasmine bushes.

Here, far from the small island, I could forget. I could pretend. I feared that, were I to visit, these ghosts would follow me across the ocean, through the crowded cities and maple-leaf-covered towns, and into the haunting silence of the room that Kirtan and I shared.

My mother did not understand. She seemed heartbroken. So, out of guilt, I invited her to visit Canada instead.

31

I HAD OFTEN wondered what my mother would think of this and that, if she were to see Canada with her own two eyes. What stories would she gather in her dupatta and take back for her three grandchildren at home? Would she say that, in the land of maple syrup, where *goras* eat *poutine* with forks, men lie with men and women lie with women, and people shrug and look the other way? What would she say about this strange land, where buffalo used to roam and bears infested the forests, this land where women trot the streets wearing pants, tight and loose, short and long? Where teen-aged children, boys and girls, dye their hair red and blue and shout at their parents, where anything goes? Would she throw her hands in the air and look up to the skies, and say, "Oh God, what has this world come to?" Maybe she would pause and sigh and say, "It must be another one of those American movements."

By this time there was a movement of a different kind brewing, making its way across the vast distances and into every home. This movement was one I was desperate to understand. I was also desperate to make my voice heard, though my mother might well have thought it was crazy.

This movement attempted to tear down years of pain, to "break the cycle of silence and wipe away the shame" about childhood sexual abuse. The American talk-show host Oprah Winfrey had initiated the telling of tales, doing away with the shame and secrecy. It seemed clinics and centers were popping up on every street corner to help victims to come to terms with their silent suffering. New laws protecting the rights of victims were being negotiated, while old traditions were being questioned and changed. People lined the streets, carrying banners and making noise. Angela and I were among them.

Watching all of this on the news and on the streets, evening after evening, day after day, I realized that the silence and shame surrounding abuse was not just my lot. It had been shared by American women, and men, too. It was the lot of the rich and elite and the poor and desolate, the experience of the young and the old. I came to understand that it was this single thread, this hidden pain, that bound one victim to another. Just like the blood that linked women of all races, classes, and creeds, so this shared experience made us sisters and brothers on the road to healing.

I wondered what my mother would say about this Afro-haired woman called Oprah Winfrey. Would she say that there is a woman whose hair is as black as the feathers of a raven, who wears dresses made of rubies and diamonds? Would she say that rumor has it when she walks through the streets of America, like the pathways of the heavens, they too turn to pure gold? Or would she say, there's this African-American woman who is stirring up a can of worms with a long wooden stick? There is this African-American woman telling stories that shouldn't be told? What has this world come to and where else is it going to go? Oh, Brother! Is that what she would say while sifting flour in a pot, while picking pebbles from a plate of rice, while wringing wet clothes in a concrete sink?

My mother accepted my invitation. But it was a full year later that she boarded Air Pacific and flew from Nadi to Vancouver to see her sprouting granddaughter. Mother arrived on a chilly day, when the skies were cloudy and leaves bright orange. Amid the dark suits in the airport, she alone reflected the glory of the autumn skies in her pale-yellow-and-orange sari.

I handed her a light-gray fleece jacket. She inspected it closely before she put it on, and then stepped outside, walking slowly beside Kirtan, Aditi, and me. She drank in the reddened leaves covering the ground and the orange leaves blowing in the chilly breeze. I knew this was the first time she had seen the foliage of autumn. She gazed upon it in wonderment.

Mother's hair, now dyed black, was pulled back in a bun, and she wore a gold coin necklace and gold earrings. Although she was slightly hunched over, she showed no other signs of age. Her skin was still supple, and any wrinkles had been kept at bay. For the first time, I began to wonder about the cream my mother had always encouraged me to use on my own face. Perhaps it was sold in Canadian stores, too.

My mother had put her arms around me at the airport, breaking into a smile, and kissed me on my forehead. I could still feel the warmth of her embrace on my skin. She had gazed at Aditi long and hard before she ruffled her hair. Aditi just looked sternly at my mother, this stranger who mussed her hair and pinched her cheeks.

"She looks just like you did at eleven," Mother said, once we were back at our home. She stared closely at Aditi. Did she remember the weight of silence that had been put upon my shoulders when I was my daughter's age? My mother's voice broke across my thoughts. "I am here in time for your birthday, Aditi," she said. "How can I forget? It was Diwali in Fiji on the day you were born. November 13, I remember very well."

"This is your *nani*," I said to Aditi, doing my best to sound cheerful. "That's your grandma!"

Aditi spoke to my mother politely in English. Mother smiled, but her reply was short, just one or two English words. She stood stiffly and pursed her lips, and in her raised eyebrows I was sure I saw a judgment.

I wanted to take her to the Hanging Bridge, to the hiking trails, to chai houses and Indian restaurants. I wanted to take her for a ride in the Sky-Train, for a walk down Robson Street, to stroll with her through Stanley Park. I was desperate to show her my new life: the millions of pigeons on Granville Island and the highest buildings silhouetted across the downtown. But my mother wanted to see none of these things. She wished only to stay in my house, sit at the dinner table, and talk to Kirtan, or to watch me cook and make chai. She told me that I made rotis just like the full moon, nice and round, although she asked for a little more salt and a few more chilies to sprinkle on the chicken curry.

Mother did, however, accompany Angela and me to our writers' group once. I expected her to ask questions, to scrutinize my friend, to offer advice and criticism, but Mother quieted and gave a small smile, not much more. It was as though, upon meeting Angela, she gently and discreetly backed into a corner.

Angela chatted about this and that, in English. She asked my mother numerous questions, and when silence followed, she answered all of the questions herself: How was your trip, Aunty? It must have been long. Were you comfortable on the plane ride? Planes are never comfortable, are they? How long has it been since you saw Kalyana? Kalyana says it has been so many years. You must be happy to see her again, and Kirtan. And meet Aditi. What a beautiful granddaughter you have!

I asked Mother privately why she did not talk to Angela. She told me it was because Angela spoke in English, and her own English was not very good. I told my mother that she could reply in Hindi, for Angela was Indian. My mother only shook her head.

At the coffee house, Mother sat at a far table, invisible. I saw her smile a little when one of the members told a story of a talking teapot. But I observed not much else. I had thought Mother would like to sit among storytellers, listening to their words, but then I realized she would rather have been the one telling the stories. Perhaps that is why she sat in the corner, quiet and unseen.

During her stay with us, Mother suffered bouts of hot flashes. She would be sitting in the middle of the living room, when suddenly she would grab a newspaper off the shelf, screaming for me to open the windows and let the chilly breeze inside. "Oh, my God," she would gasp, her dress drenched in sweat. "This is the curse bestowed upon an aging woman." She would fan harder and faster. "See, Kalyana. A woman is not spared discomfort in old age as well. Instead of blood, sweat is pouring from me like a river."

The cool breeze flowing in through the open windows would dissipate the warm temperature in the room, but not my mother's suffering. She would sit on the floor, fanning and cursing: womanhood and sweat and blood and old age. Sometimes in the middle of the night I would hear her moving in the kitchen, then the crackle of ice in a glass.

Mother had brought spices and tea, Indian sweets, and several tins of canned mutton; shirts and dresses for Aditi and Kirtan that proved to be two sizes too small; and the latest edition of *The Fiji Times* newspaper. Reports of how an Indian temple was burned to the ground covered the front page.

"See what we Indians are suffering through in Fiji, Kalyana. See!" She pointed to the wrinkled paper sitting on our glass coffee table. Then she shook her head in contempt.

"Move to Canada, Mom," I offered. "Kirtan and I can sponsor you."

She fired me a piercing look. "Run away? Never! I was born there, and the ashes from my dead body will mix with the Pacific Ocean. I have as much right to that country as anyone else." Her chest rose and fell as she breathed heavily.

Mother brought years of political news bundled up in her dupatta. Since I had left, she said, Fiji had seen each democratically elected government overthrown by the government succeeding it. There was murder and mutiny and hostage-taking and democracy and military rule, all in quick succession. Domination and submission were entwined within each other. Pain and suffering. Revenge, and more revenge, in the hope of empowerment. Gone were the peaceful days of calmness and stability. Though, in Fiji, my mother said, the flowers still bloomed and the ocean still whispered.

And yet, flowers and oceans were not enough to make it into the paradise it once had seemed. The people did not know who was coming or going, my mother said. Because of the political situation, even Fiji's sugarcane industry was starting to crumble. What would become of the country now? My mother wrung her hands and shook her head. Aditi sat still and stared.

I stacked the newspaper away on a shelf, under the copies of the *Vancouver Sun*.

After two and a half weeks of visiting our little family, Mother decided that she wanted to see Manjula before she left for home. It was then that she witnessed Kirtan and I fight. It was a small stone under in the mattress of a married couple, but the beginning of a new cycle of understanding for me.

It began when Kirtan suggested that Aditi stay with his

sister and brother-in-law after school while Mother and I were in Toronto, since Angela could not watch her. Angela maintained a full-time job teaching religion and gender courses at the university, and she was buried under the crunch of assignments and essays.

I could feel my blood rise, my heart beating faster. Leaving Aditi with her uncle while I was far away on the other side of Canada? That was not possible for me. If my mother had not been able to reach out and save me when I lay calling her name, how could I watch out for Aditi's safety from thousands of miles away?

I protested fiercely. "I don't want her staying with relatives, Kirtan. Why don't you take a few days off work and stay home?"

"He won't do anything. He's not like that," yelled Kirtan.

My mother straightened her back. I could see the question in her eyes and the horror in her face: Does he know?

"I just don't feel comfortable," I said.

"She'll grow up scared of everything if you don't allow her to test her boundaries."

I looked at Aditi's face and her small body. A flood of memories came sweeping in, a tsunami threatening to swallow a whole village.

"What boundaries should she test at this age, Kirtan?" My breathing was labored. "No. You take days off from work and stay home with her. Or I won't go."

So, in the end, without further arguments, Kirtan succumbed. He understood my fears, because after I had confessed everything to Angela that night under the blooming cherry blossoms, I had come home and cried in Kirtan's arms.

He had remembered the day back in Fiji, when I had cut my arm, and he had punched the tree, hurting his knuckles.

Kirtan took the days off work and agreed to stay home with Aditi, while Mother and I traveled to Toronto to see Manjula.

32

WE BOARDED the plane to cross the country together, just Mother and I. At first, all Mother could talk about was me eating *poutine* at the airport. The calories. The lack of nutrients. *Poutine?* Who invented this dish, anyway? Mother had ordered chick-pea-and-masala curry with basmati rice for herself. She did not want to try Canadian food at all, despite my attempts to persuade her. But she criticized as she watched me swallow fry after fry laden in cheese curds and gravy. Some were delicately topped with ketchup, like a cherry plunked on a mountain of whipped cream.

Manjula picked us up at the airport in Toronto. She wore brown corduroy pants, a plain white shirt, and black flat shoes. She stood in front of us, jingling her car keys. "*Kaise,*" she said in Hindi. "How are you?" The two sisters kissed each other's cheeks. An aura of white light surrounded them both. I counted in my head. Ten? Twenty? Or had it already been thirty years since I had seen them together? I was eleven when

Manjula had left, but now I had a daughter of my own a year older than that.

I thought of the years since I had seen my own brother. I missed his punches, his drawl, and his self-assured swagger. Now he was a married man with three children of his own. If he saw me, would he still tease and taunt me? I wondered if he teased his wife or children.

Manjula took my mother's bag from her hands. "Kalyana, you can carry your own bag," she said, chuckling loudly. I had forgotten her odd, hollow laugh. Other travelers twisted their heads to look at us, making me blush in shame as though I were a small child again.

Expertly Manjula hefted my mother's bag onto her shoulder and carried it out to her car. Then she climbed into the driver's seat and took the wheel. Mother gasped. She had become accustomed to Manjula driving back in Fiji, but that was many years ago. Now she shuddered in horror as Manjula wove in and out of the congestion of Toronto traffic, passing buses and gigantic trucks, driven by both women and men.

Trepidation marked my mother's tiny face as she gazed at the skyscrapers and crowds of foreign people swarming around her. "Downtown Toronto is too noisy. Not like Fiji." She nodded her head, looking intently out the car window as she clutched the sides of the seat. "Too much concrete. Toronto needs more trees." How was all this hustle and bustle and the heat and rush of Canadian city life not taking its toll on Manjula? Her sister looked healthy and self-possessed. "It's too much activity for my old bones," Mother said sighing. "My heart is going thump-thump-thump."

Manjula smirked, overflowing with confidence.

Before she took us to her home, Manjula brought us to a nearby mall. A mysterious smile lit up her face. "I want to show you something," she said quickly. We followed her through the sliding glass doors and towards the escalator. My mother hesitated.

Manjula held onto her free hand and said, "It just takes getting used to, Sister. The first time you always feel dizzy. Don't worry. I've got your hand." My mother clutched the rubber handrails of the moving stairs and closed her eyes tightly.

Manjula smiled at me over my mother's head. "How did she handle the escalator at the airports?" she asked.

"We took the stairs," said my mother abruptly. She kept gripping Manjula's hand, occasionally glancing nervously back at me.

At the top of the stairs, we looked down a corridor and saw something that stopped even my mother's voice: Manjula's name across the front of a small store. *Manjula's Alterations* it said behind a blinking light. Manjula nudged us towards the door.

Two middle-aged women, one Indian and one Caucasian, looked up from their sewing machines and greeted us the moment we entered. "My sister and my niece," said Manjula, nodding at us. She hovered over both women, leaning over their machines to inspect their work. "Good, good," she said to the Caucasian woman, and to the Indian one, "Not too tight." She moved into the back room, passing rows of dresses and shirts hanging on a metal rack. She took out her keys and unlocked a gray door, pushing it back so that it swung open into a small room. Her head was held high. "My office," she said to us proudly.

Shelves were stacked with paper and material and patterns. In the corner case, a bucket of needles and different colors of thread sat on the top shelf; beneath it, scissors, patterns, and sewing books were carefully arranged side by side. "I am the boss here," Manjula said, sitting back on a black chair that swiveled like the headmaster's. "I've got three employees. One is on her day off." She shuffled through a few papers, pretending to look for something.

Mother gazed upon her long-lost sister, and it seemed as though she had come to Toronto searching for someone far different. For the old Manjula, the Manjula who speared crabs, tended to vast gardens, quietly cleaned our house, and accepted her inferior place—that Manjula was long gone.

"How's business?" I asked to ease the tension.

"Good. Good," she replied in English, looking up from the documents. "Steady. I have return clientele. Graduation and Christmas seasons are always very busy. People want their dresses adjusted to fit better all the time." She smiled widely. "Peter helped me build my business. I've owned it for sixteen years now."

My mother looked at her sister. Pride was evident in the glow of her gaze.

Manjula rose from the chair. "Let's go," she said with firmness, and headed for the door.

Manjula's home was in Mississauga. "Condo living," she said as she pulled into an underground parking lot. "Peter and I like it better than owning a house." Manjula carried my mother's bags and I brought my own. She was limping, just like old times. I hadn't noticed earlier, when we had been in her store, in the office where she held the reins of business just like my father had. "We just pay a fee and someone else takes care of the outside," Manjula was explaining to my mother. "A house is for people with kids. Ours are all grown up." By "ours," I understood that she meant Peter's boys from his first marriage. As far as I knew, Manjula never had given birth to her own child. Yet, unlike Angela, Manjula, by no effort of her own, but through the grace of fate, had found mother-hood after all.

"What about gardening?" I said. "You used to love to garden."

She laughed. "Oh, that's too much work. I am too old now. And anyway," she said, "in Toronto, the gardening season is short-lived. Gardening months are June, July, and August. That's it. The rest of the time the ground is covered in a sheet of ice. Not like Fiji, huh," she looked at me, and smiled. "In the summer, I grow some flowers in buckets and put them out on the balcony."

She paused in front of the elevator and pushed the big red button. We heard the elevator tumbling down. "I grow my own herbs inside in small ceramic pots, though," she said. "I keep it in the kitchen. It's nice to have fresh herbs all year round."

"Do you speak Hindi at all now, Manjula, or only English?" my mother said, shaking her head.

Manjula chuckled.

As the elevator slid upwards, my mother suddenly col-lapsed, clutching the metal side. Manjula and I both crouched over her in alarm. Mother claimed that her chest felt tight, as if her heart was going to jump forth and fall to the floor in a matter of minutes. "I don't like this elevator stuff," she said. "I don't like being closed up like this, in a moving box. It feels like a flying coffin. Can't we take the stairs?"

Manjula and I exchanged glances of relief. "It's eight floors, Sumitri. Hard to walk up," said Manjula, rubbing my mother's back.

"I feel like I am having a heart attack." My mother, a collapsing brick house, strained to breathe.

The elevator doors slid open as quickly as they had closed. My mother continued gasping unevenly. She had had many shocks today, and not all of them were physical.

Manjula directed us to her condominium. It was clean and comfortable, with everything in its proper place: a vase with fresh daffodils in one corner, an old-fashioned lamp tucked away in another, and white drapes in the living room. A long sofa was pushed up against the far wall, opposite the entertainment unit. It was a three-bedroom apartment that looked out to the city lights in the far distance.

My mother stood near the window, holding her chest. "Oh my God," she said, "You're living in mid-air, Manjula. Why don't you come back to the ground? I feel very scared being this high up."

"Don't worry, Sister. Nothing will happen to us."

"What will you do when a hurricane comes? It will snatch this building up in seconds. It's a long way to the ground, Manjula. It's a long way down."

Manjula playfully rolled her eyes. "Sumitri," she said, "there are no hurricanes in Canada, only in Fiji."

"What about tornadoes? You have tornadoes, don't you?"

"Sumitri, don't worry. They'll warn us way before it hits. We'll have time to move to the ground and find a bathtub to hide in." She chuckled loudly again, not caring if the neighbors heard her. I suppose she was happy. For that, I think, she felt she owed no one an apology or an explanation.

For supper that night, Manjula cooked crab curry, just as she had back in Fiji so many years ago. Peter sat watching hockey on TV, speaking once in a while to comment on the recent political happenings in Fiji. In spite of his age, he still looked attractive. He called Manjula by several nicknames: Manj, Manju, and sometimes he called her Jules, lovingly. It made me think of Raju. It had been many years since somebody had shortened my name in Canada. My heart ached.

"Remember how we used to catch crabs in Fiji?" Manjula intercepted my thoughts as we sat down to eat at the small dining table. The spoons clattered against the glass bowl of crab curry. A silver plate of steaming rotis sat in the middle of the table. "You couldn't wait to have seconds and thirds when we got home and cooked them." Manjula's face lit up with a bright smile.

Snippets of memories flooded my mind: I recalled how Manjula, with alert eyes and a wooden spear in her hand, had stabbed the sand in search of crabs. My job had been to drag the heavy sack filled with squirming crabs across moist sand and shallow waters, but when we were finished and Manjula had hoisted the full sack over her shoulder, I would run ahead and shout back to her, "Slowpoke!" I remembered the lumps of brown meat floating in the bowls later, and how my stomach would churn. I always ended the meal by pushing my full plate away.

"Remember?" my aunt persisted.

"Yep," I shrugged. My memory of eating crabs was evidently much different than hers.

"These are store-bought, from the Atlantic Ocean." Manjula crinkled her nose. "Pacific Ocean crabs, the saltwater crabs, are much better," she said. "If I was in Fiji right now, I would grab a spear and go down to the ocean and catch fresh, live crabs for all of us. It would taste so good." She licked her lips and flirtatiously blinked her eyes.

"You can't fish in the sea anymore," said my mother.

"What do you mean?" Peter said. Manjula squinted.

"New law since the new government." My mother looked sad. "Government says that the sea belongs to Fijians only. Indians are not Fijians, so they are not allowed to take from it."

Manjula gasped. I sat wide-eyed. Peter looked down at his plate.

"Fijians charge forty to sixty dollars per crab. Sometimes more." My mother sighed. "Eating crabs is a luxury now for us Indians." She looked around at the aghast faces and tried to bring cheer back to the table. "It is not all bad. Some folks, Indians and Fijians, are advocating naming all citizens of Fiji 'Fijians' to form unity and one national identity. They say that Indians of Fiji feel no ties, no connection to the land of India. Not anymore. Perhaps change in the name will change our future. It will bring back some of our lost rights." She shrugged then said, "Who knows? I am starting to think that even God doesn't know anymore, either."

Manjula and my mother talked deep into the night. They spoke of the days now long gone, and about the future: Raju's children, my daughter, and Manjula and Peter's grown boys at foreign universities. They reminisced about old crushes, Davindra and Shalendra. How they would spy on them from behind a line of palm trees, by the Suva Point, and from store windows in the middle of Suva town. They hummed their favorite Hindi songs out of tune and snacked on store-bought *barfi* and *galebi*, complaining about the staleness.

Watching Manjula and my mother gab late into the night, made me yearn for Angela's company, while I quietly watched television with Peter, absorbing it all. Manjula told my mother that she went to church every Sunday with Peter, that she was a Christian now. She showed my mother the gold cross Peter had bought for her five Christmases ago. She kept it close to her chest for protection. I wondered what had happened to my small gold charm that I had left behind on the window-sill. Was it still there, collecting grime and dust? Or had it been carelessly chucked in the rubbish bin by the next tenants? I liked to believe that it was now resting on some young schoolgirl's bedside table, keeping her safe from unrelenting fears and all-consuming nightmares of snakes and Surgeon-Superintendents, of knights and dragons, of spiders and tigers.

Manjula said she didn't celebrate Holi or Diwali anymore; she hunted for chocolate eggs in the spring and threw silver tinsel on pine trees and sang Christmas carols in December. She said that she cooked a large turkey for both occasions and invited Peter's whole family to their small condo. At their local church, they sat with friends every Sunday and the adults shared wine and bread.

"Jesus suffered and died on the cross for our sins, Sister." Manjula said this passionately and with absolute conviction. "His suffering brought us mortal beings closer to God."

My mother insisted that all gods were the same. But Manjula shook her head vigorously, saying that there was only one God, and he walked the lands of Israel and Jerusalem along with his Father and the Holy Spirit. "All three are one, Sister!" She glowed.

Manjula tried to convince my mother to convert to Christianity. She said it was a sin to worship idols.

This upset my mother greatly. "We don't stop you from dipping your bread in wine. Why do you try to stop us from burning incense?" She shook her head. "Do you know, Manjula, it is this desire, the desire for religions to convert everyone to one belief, that causes so many problems? The only thing that results from one religion trying to dominate the entire world is pain and suffering. That's all." She sighed, looking a little defeated. "There are several paths that lead to the same river, many roads that go to the same endless ocean."

Manjula looked to the ground. She wanted them to frolic in the fields of Heaven together, she said.

My mother sat back on the sofa, stubbornly. "I'll frolic in the heavens as a Hindu. I was born a Hindu. I will die a Hindu. You go do what makes you happy, Manjula."

Manjula rolled her eyes mischievously. "I will pray for you, Sister," she said, wagging her finger. Mother shrugged, and they both broke into smiles.

Even though Manjula and my mother differed so strongly on their ideas of faith and life, they shared the same loving bond they had years before, when they had shared the work and gossip in my father's house. During our stay in Toronto, I sometimes felt transported back to my old living room, to a time when the record player blared in the background and filled the house with songs of love, of heartbreak, of joy and suffering. Manjula and my mother, side by side, hip to hip, would be telling jokes and stories of neighbors and relatives. They would giggle and laugh as they rinsed dishes or pounded the masala in the stone pot. I remembered them chatting as they grated coconut on wooden boards, rolling rotis, washing drapes, and stirring dhal soaked in ghee.

The playfulness of these two sisters made me yearn for my long-forgotten home. It brought back the memories of the sights and sounds and scents and tastes of the Fiji shores. I remembered strolling beneath the sinking sun under bright orange skies. I thought back to times when I took shelter from pelting rain underneath the banana leaves of a low-hanging tree. For the first time, I thought I might like to visit my homeland again.

Several days later, Manjula drove us to the airport, look-ing heartbroken. Peter and I stood aside as the women said their goodbyes. We knew well that it might be the last time the sisters would be united. But just before we boarded the plane back to Vancouver, Manjula brightened. She hugged me tightly and said, "Thank you, Kalyana. Thank you."

"What for?" I was confused.

"You know," she said, smiling. "You know."

I shook my head.

"For teaching me how to read Ingalish!" She smiled widely. "Without it, I would have never found Peter. I would have never found this life." She locked her gaze with mine and grinned. "I am the princess of the house now!"

With Manjula's words came a sudden realization that my mother had been right: Education was the key to a woman's freedom. Knowledge opened doors, broadened minds, and attracted opportunities—especially for a woman.

After my mother flew away, I enrolled in a recognized online university and took my first semester of three-credit courses, studying South Asian History. I began to write and talk in a Canadian way: spoiled instead of spoilt; learned instead of learnt, dreamed instead of dreamt; and airplane instead of aeroplane. I chuckled when other students strove to be politically correct. They filled their essays with "his or hers," "he or she," and "him or her." I wondered what my teacher from long ago would think of the world now, the teacher who had once accused me of starting a revolution. She had thrown my essay on the ground because I had written "she" instead of "he." Life had certainly progressed. How strange that, even so long ago, my mother had tried to hand me the key.

33

ONE YEAR LATER, on a rainy Wednesday morning, I received the dreaded phone call from Raju. My mother was gravely ill. Her last request was to see me again. "Tell my daughter that no excuses will be accepted," she had said to my brother. "Over the years, I've collected enough money to pay her plane fare down here, if need be."

She had figured it all wrong; I had run out of excuses many years ago. My mother was living her last days, and I knew that to see her once again was what I truly wanted. I packed my bags the same night and boarded the next flight to Fiji. I was going home.

Raju picked me up at the small Nadi airport at seven in the morning. iTaukei men, wearing printed *sulus* and frangipani leis, played guitars and sang traditional songs in the airport lobby, a gesture to welcome the new arrivals. I was surprised to see that none of the brochures lining the airport walls had pictures of the Indian population of Fiji. Even after centuries gone by, we were still an invisible part of the land.

Yet in so many ways, Fiji had changed. The roads were smooth and free of potholes, at least for the most part. Tall buildings sprouted everywhere; beaches looked clean and welcoming; and stories of new million-dollar resorts and casinos were splashed across the front pages of *The Fiji Times* and the *Fiji Sun*. Coffee houses serving hot lattes and espressos and American desserts stood alongside McDonald's, Kentucky Fried Chicken, and pizza franchises. Glass malls stood tall, dwarfing the palm trees far below. Raju said that it was all the doing of Bainimarama. He was for modernization and equality among all people. But what struck me the most was that women, young and old, walked around towns wearing halter tops and brightly colored pants.

But despite these outward signs of Westernization, I noticed some familiar sights. Tall, muscular young men carrying machetes still walked along the side of the road, while island women sold fresh fruits and vegetables under the shade of green tents. Coconut trees still swayed in the warm, humid breeze, and the ocean stretched for miles and miles. Even after all these years, the sweet smell of curry hung in the air.

Raju's hands rested loosely on the steering wheel. He was still thin, but his skin was a few tones darker than before. How much calmer he seemed now than I remembered him! He no longer was interested in cracking jokes, and I wondered whether our mother's illness had worn him down.

He did not talk about her on the road, however, instead asking me about Aditi, Kirtan, and our life in Canada. What did we eat in that part of the world? Curry, rice and roti, what else? And what did we do for fun? What about Indian temples? Did I still pray? I hemmed and hawed, then quieted and looked ahead. Did I still do aerobics?

"Of course not!" I said indignantly, and Raju laughed for the first time.

I told him of our life in Canada, how for seven months out of the year we stayed huddled in front of the fireplace, waiting for either the snow to melt or the rain to subside. What about skiing? He wondered whether Aditi skied. I told him how it mostly rained in Vancouver, and how the ski hills were a long drive away, through the winding and icy mountainous roads. He frowned. I knew it was difficult for him to understand the vastness of the country that had become my home.

Raju spoke of the political situation in Fiji. Houses now had iron bars across the windows and doors. "As if Indians were powerless birds living in cages," he said. He then said that the iron bars were there to keep out the burglars. Raju explained that home invasion had become a common occurrence in Fiji after the original coup. In fact, men had barged into our home twice, taking the laptop and iPod, along with some of Raju's wife's jewelry. Once they had broken in during the afternoon, while Mother was home alone and sitting on the porch.

"Oh my God! Oh my God, Raju!" I clutched the seats. "What did she do?"

Raju chuckled. "She followed them into the house, even though she can't walk without holding onto the walls or the cabinets. She told them to get out of her house." Raju shook his head. "And of course they didn't. They locked her in the bathroom. She stayed there all day, until we came home in the late afternoon."

"Oh my God!" A strange panic had arisen in my chest. "Was she harmed? Was she scared? Why would she follow them into the house?"

"She was a little bruised, but okay in the end." Raju smiled. "Our mother was always a fighter, you know!"

I waved aside his comment. "It was silly to follow them into the house. She should have stayed out on the porch. She could have been seriously hurt. Why did no one tell me about this!" I grunted in frustration.

"I think she feels that she and Dad worked hard for all their material things, and nobody had a right to just walk in and take them."

"Where was she the second time the robbers came in?"

"We were all sleeping, actually. They cut the iron bars and burst in. They went to her room first. They ransacked the room, looking for jewelry and cash. One went through her drawers and stuffed his pockets with the cash. Over a hundred and fifty dollars. She sat quietly on the bed and watched him do this. Afterwards, he looked her straight in the eye and said, 'Where's the money, old woman? Where is it?' She told him that it was in his pocket!"

I had to laugh in spite of myself.

"At this point they started yelling, 'Don't be smart, old woman!' This awoke Yashna and me. Yashna ran to the neighbor's, barefoot, shouting for help. I came out of the room and tried to take one down with a baseball bat. The other two fled at the sight of the stick." Raju paused. "It was quite a night!" My brother sighed. "So many of the good, talented people have left this country," he said. "Even the educated iTaukeis are leaving. Only lots of criminals are left now. But under Bainimarama's rule, maybe the good people will come back."

"Isn't Mom afraid of challenging them like that?"

Raju shrugged. "She was always a fighter, our mother." There was a long pause. I opened my mouth, but Raju spoke first: "Kalyana, that was not the first time our mother lost her mind. It all started on that clear day. The skies were blue like the Fiji flag. Not a hint of storm or wind or noise."

Then Raju said something that would shake my world. On a bright, sunny day, he said, a few months after our father passed away, Uncle Baldev had come to visit her. She had stared at him with intensely dark eyes, and after a few moments of quiet contemplation and silence, she rose from the chair on the veranda, grabbed the cane from my uncle's hands, and beat him with it. She broke not only his fragile, arthritic arm, but his knee, too.

"Blood splattered everywhere as he crawled out of our yard and onto the street," Raju said. He had not been home at the time, but the villagers talked about Rajdev's wife's insanity for months. They said that five men couldn't stop the crazy woman from inflicting pain on the old man that day. The villagers could only conclude that it must have been the loss of her husband that had caused her so much sorrow as to turn her mad. For from what else could a woman draw the strength to beat a man?

I was speechless.

Mother had beaten Uncle Baldev, in broad daylight, in front of villagers and strangers, in front of relatives and friends. She had roared and screamed and inflicted pain upon the man who had once inflicted pain upon me. The woman who claimed the gods determined a man's punishment had dealt a punishment of her own. This anxious and troubled old woman, who had collapsed in a Toronto elevator, who feared villagers' scrutiny and relatives' harsh words, had had the courage within her all along to take a stand against ill-doers. If necessary, she had possessed the strength to crush the shackles that bound her hands in links of propriety and expectation. In the end, she had emerged like Goddess Kali, victorious and strong, dancing upon her oppressors, and like the bird in the elephant story, mighty, powerful, and free.

Raju continued slowly, drawing me away from my thoughts. "What was strange," he said, "was that at the same time that our mother was beating Uncle, villagers say that a whirl of wind, like a twister, arose from nowhere. The veil covering the face of the auntie-without-a-name, who had been standing totally still nearby, gently slipped away. And the villagers noted a small smile, almost invisible, erupt upon her face." He paused. "I even heard that she delivered a kick to the old man herself." Raju eyed me for a moment, then shrugged and gazed out over the road. "Well, good for her if she threw him a kick," he said. "She sure took a lot of beat-ings from him in her odd life."

I sat limply in my seat. It was true, as my mother had once said, that nobody knows the future. Nobody knows where one could end up if one did not give up the fight. And so my mother had found her courage, her voice. Auntie-without-a-name, quiet and subservient, had taken back her power. Even Manjula had discovered her happiness, her self-worth, and Tulsi had flown away to pursue her freedom. How life can change!

But had it changed for me? When would I discover my freedom from the shackles of silence that my mother had bestowed upon me in that cold room where the nailpolishes were lined in perfect rows? When would I find the courage to scream from the mountaintops and tell my tale to the world, without shame, without prejudice, without blame?

I felt a surge of emotions stir within me, but it was not of anger or sadness over what had been lost, or fear of what was yet to come, or even of the pleasure that came from worshipping the Goddess Kali as she trampled upon her enemies. It was of pity. I pitied Uncle Baldev. For there were two kinds of people in this world: those who knew how to give and receive love honestly and courageously, and those who did not. To go through life without learning how to love was the greatest tragedy of all. And perhaps that was Uncle Baldev's greatest punishment.

I followed Raju into our house. It hadn't changed much from what I remembered, although the large front doors were unfamiliar. They now extended across the front of our house and gave it a more modern appearance. A skinny boy, about seven years old, burst onto the small porch. I remembered how my mother used to sit there on a bench, combing her hair and complaining to Roni about all the things that were wrong in this world.

"Daddy," screamed the little boy. "You're home." He paused and stared closely at me. "Ha," he said. "You're from Canada. *Aji*—grandmother—told me about you. *Aji* says that in Canada people fry three pigs, one goat, five chickens, and a dozen eggs and eat it for breakfast. And *Aji* says they eat a pound of potatoes fried in oil and covered in curds and thick brown sauce made from gobs of flour. Powtine." He wrinkled his nose, yet his eyes were bright and eager. "*Aji* says that's why in Canada, where you come from, people are so fat. Is it true?" He didn't give me a chance to respond before shouting out, "I don't believe *Aji*. I think she's making up stories again!"

He shook his head and dashed away, disappearing into his parents' room. I chuckled. I gathered the little boy was Rakesh, the youngest of Raju's three sons. He certainly favored his father, and not merely in his bright-eyed appearance.

Roni met me at the door of my mother's room. Age had not touched her; she looked as charming now as she had when I first met her. Even now she wore a brightly blooming hibiscus tucked behind her ear. It seemed to flash in the dim light of the room. "Kalyana. Little Kalyana—all grown up," Roni said gently.

"Kalyana," my mother whispered. She was sitting up in her bed, propped against a few pillows. I offered a slow, forced smile. *Mother.* She was so frail, so different from the years when she had ruled the house while pretending not to.

"What are these stories I am hearing about you, Momma? I heard you stood up to the thieves like you were a young, strong man." I blinked back tears. As ever, she smelled of coconut oil.

"Kalyana," she said, "my daughter." Her eyes filled with moisture as she kissed my forehead. "I can let go now that you're here. I've seen your face again."

I placed my head on my mother's chest and listened to her heartbeat, holding her hand. Roni reached over and rubbed my head gently. "Don't talk like that, Momma," I said. "Don't talk rubbish."

"This is the cycle of life," she said. "Before, I used to order you around. Now, you get to tell me what to do, what to say, what not to say. If I last any longer, I'll be back in diapers and a nurse will have to be hired to wipe my ass."

"Momma."

My mother sighed. "Cycle of life," she whispered.

I slept soundly and deeply for the first few days, trying to recover from the jet lag. When my mother was sleeping during the afternoon, I sat in my old room and explored the boxes of memories stacked away under the bed my things rested upon. Old poems I had written in primary school, short stories I had written to pass the time; drawings of animals, faces, and trees; the frilly dress I wore right after I was born; and my Enid Blyton books, *The Magic Faraway Tree*, *The Famous Five*, and *The Secret Seven*. The books, now banned from most Canadian libraries and schools, captured a slice of the past, a changing era; they served as a documentary of attitudes and perceptions. Above all, they had meaning to me personally, for they had stirred my maturing imagination. I put these aside. I wanted to take them to Aditi, even though she was far too old for them now.

In the box I also found the romance books I had secretly stolen from Manjula. I remember how I would tuck them into *Archie* comic books and read them in bed. Sometimes my mother would sneak into my room and catch me. "Naughty!" she would cry in Hindi, snatching the book from my hands and scolding me sharply. "Reading adult books. Shameless!" I smiled at this memory.

Raju's wife, Yashna, was a large woman who wore long, colorful dresses: solid blue, red, purple, pink. She said little to me, mostly ordering Raju around the house in a high-pitched voice that hurt my ears. "Raju, get me that bowl from the top shelf...Raju? Did you pick up a box of salt from the supermarket?...Raju? Did you go to the bank and deposit the money I gave you this morning?...Raju? Did you do the evening prayers?" When he ignored her because he was watching Indian soap operas on TV or smoking a cigarette on the porch, she would stealthily make her way towards him and punch him hard on the arm. Raju always jumped, taken by surprise. He would squeal, "Aw! That hurts, Yash!" She would punch him again, harder the second time, and sometimes on his back.

I had to chuckle under my breath. "Raju, I should have been punching your arm all along to prepare you for your fate!" I would say mockingly. Raju didn't laugh or holler or even give a witty retort; he would just purse his lips and shoot me a glowering look. Poor Raju. The wild one had been tamed.

His older two sons, Ramesh and Ritesh, were gone from the house most of the time, just as Raju himself had been in his youth. But Rakesh, the youngest one, hovered near me, staring at me with his piercing dark eyes and chatting incessantly: "*Aji* said that trains fly in the skies in Vancouver, where you're from. Is that true?" He never waited for my answers. He would shake his head and brush the rumor off swiftly. "I don't believe it. Trains can't fly. I think *Aji* was making up stories again. Huh!"

I indulged in memories of the past and visions of the present, but most of my time was spent by my mother's bedside. Like Roni, I held her hand and massaged her feet with coconut oil. Some nights, overwhelmed with loneliness, I crawled beside her and slept on her bed, taking comfort in the steadiness of her breathing and the familiarity of her scent.

Yet sleep would elude me. Often I lay awake at night, recalling the old stories that my mother had told me. How many tales she had recounted in this same room: stories of our heritage, of our past, and of our families. Yet one detail still puzzled me.

One night my mother was also wakeful. I felt I must ask the question that was bothering me: "Is it true that the Surgeon-Superintendent smashed a snake on the very decks on which my grandmother was born?"

"Yes," she said weakly.

"And the snake charmer followed his beloved snake into the depths of the sea?"

Smiling and nodding her head, as though the images flashed across her eyes, she said, "That is why Fiji does not have any snake charmers or snakes. We left him and the snake behind in the sea."

She smiled faintly. "Remember how scared you were of snakes," she murmured.

Suddenly I no longer felt a desire to question her about the facts. I no longer wanted to hear about the snakes and snake charmers lost at sea. The story I suddenly most wanted to hear again was of Krishna's birth—the story that soothed me after my nightmares as a child. But she had never finished the tale. "Tell me the ending of that story, Momma. Of Krishna's birth. Please. I want to hear it."

"You remember that?" she asked, surprised.

"I remember all the stories you told me, Momma." I held tightly to her hand. It felt so tiny and frail in mine.

"I can't tell it the same way I did before. I am too old now. I can't even remember what I had for breakfast. What did I have for breakfast today?"

"The details don't matter, Momma. I just want to hear that story again. Tell me what you remember. Tell me the ending. Remember? King Kansa, the evil ruler, sentenced his sister and her husband to prison because her eighth child was to bring him death, ending his unfair rule. Remember, Momma? He killed all of Devaki's seven children in the cold, hard jail cell. And then her eighth child, Krishna, was born. The guards fell asleep. The cell doors miraculously opened, and Yasudev, Krishna's father, bundled him up and carried him out of the cell and across the raging river. Then the storm brewed in the skies and rain beat down on both, the father and the child…"

"Yes. Yes. Yes. You do remember." My mother smiled. "And then the five-headed snake emerged from underneath the Yamuna River. It shielded baby Krishna from the stormy weather. The river parted ways, making a pathway for Krishna's father."

She coughed and sighed heavily, then continued: "Yasudev followed the divine light to Yashoda's village and placed his precious son beside her. He took her newborn baby—a girl—and placed her in the empty basket and headed back across the river to his wife, who was awaiting his return in the jail cell where the guards still slept."

My mother breathed heavily. I didn't want her to stop, but I could not bear to see her suffer. "It's okay, Momma. If it's too hard to continue, you don't have to."

"No, no, Kalyana. I have already started the story now. I can't stop in the middle of it."

I let her continue. For I knew well that there was nothing she wanted more than to finish telling her story. And there was nothing that I wanted more than to listen.

My mother spoke in a small, shaky voice: "He placed the baby girl by his wife's side. And miraculously, in that moment, the jail cell locked again and the guards awoke. King Kansa got the word that the eighth child, the one that would bring him death, in fact a mere girl, was born. He hurried to the cell." My mother's voice sounded raspy. "Devaki pleaded with her brother. 'Please,' she said, 'the baby is not a boy like the divine prophecy promised. It's a girl, and what harm can a girl bring you?' Her words did not move King Kansa or change his heart. He snatched the girl from Devaki's arms and laughed mockingly. In a gruff voice, he said, 'A girl? A girl is to bring me death?' He threw the baby against the concrete wall, waiting to see her little body crumble to the floor."

Completely absorbed in her tale, I shuddered at the thought of the girl's head crashing onto the concrete floor, a small body covered in a pool of blood. Chills swept up my spine and I thought of tiny Aditi so many years before.

But a smirk formed at the corners of my mother's lips. "She wasn't any ordinary girl, Kalyana," she said. "She was a divine being. Effortlessly she rose to the ceiling, engulfed in a stream of light." My mother was coughing now. "She grew eight arms and carried a different weapon in each of them. She laughed in King Kansa's face and, in a thunderous voice, she roared like a mighty lioness, 'Oh Evil King, you are not mightier than the divine power. You will gain nothing by killing me. The one that will destroy you is elsewhere!' Laughing loudly, she grew wings and, like a bird, she flew away into the skies."

I could envision a baby girl, small and mighty, flying away. She left behind her a trail of blinding light.

My mother sighed again. "King Kansa let Devaki and Yasudev go. And far away, the village of Gokul celebrated Krishna's birth. Yashoda, not knowing the truth, raised him as her very own son! She's known to the world as his true mother. For it's not who gave birth to you that matters, it is who cared for you. It is who loved you." She looked towards my face and moved a stray hair from my forehead. "Nice story, huh, Kalyana?" she said quietly. "Nice story." Then she fell asleep.

Yes, I thought. It was indeed a nice story, and now that I had finally heard the ending, my heart was satisfied.

When my mother awoke again, she was quiet for a while, and then spoke. "Sorry."

I looked at her, confused, still lost in Krishna's tale.

"Sorry," she repeated. "Sorry for what happened to you when you were little. You were so alone. There was so much pain. What a tragedy!" She sighed again. "Kalyana, I am sorry."

I didn't tell her what exactly I had lost. The first old woman, who no longer blew into our living room from the East like a strong cool breeze; the second old woman, who no longer plunked on our sofa in the middle of the day, creating stories that flowed with the fluidity and clarity of water; the third old woman, who burned hotter than the flames of fire itself no longer roared out passionate songs; and the fourth old woman, the mightiest of all, the mother, the protector, and the guard, disappeared forever from the entrance of our home. It was true. I lost my imagination, my innocence, and my faith that hideous day. The old women had never returned.

"I felt so much shame." My mother spoke quietly and slowly.

"It wasn't your shame to bear, Momma. Neither was it mine. It was Uncle Baldev's, it was he who should have—"

"I couldn't protect you. Every time I looked at you, it killed me on the inside. I should have been there to protect you. I, of all people…"

"We can't always be there to protect our daughters or our sons. We can't always walk around knowing who cannot be trusted. We can't know the future or the present. You said that yourself." I sighed this time, mindful of my own struggle. I had learned that I could not protect Aditi from the falls and scratches of childhood, from the heartbreak and pain of a teen love lost, or from the hardships or trials of the world.

I could not protect my mother from the long, slow agony of death. We came into this world to die and to live, to suffer and to rejoice, to smile and to cry. We could not have one without the other. The prince needed his princess and the princess needed her prince. "It wasn't our fault, Momma. It wasn't our fault. Don't you understand?"

"I am sorry." Her voice was weak, defeated. "I am sorry." She coughed loudly. "I should have done something. I should have screamed it from the mountaintops. I should have raged like a storm." Her breathing became labored. She coughed again. "I wish now that I had had that sort of courage, back then. I wish now." She sighed, in exhaustion. "World is changing. Thank God for that." She said this and coughed again, still more harshly.

"Momma, I love you. Get some rest. You need your strength. Should we call the doctor?"

"No point in spending money on doctors now. I am at the end of my journey, Kalyana."

It hurt me deeply to hear my mother speak in such a way. I did not want this time with her to end. Deeply I regretted the letters I did not write and the years I stayed away. I regretted not sitting with her in the veranda in her old age, drinking chai and taking in the evening glow of the setting sun. I regretted missing my father's funeral, not offering her my strength.

My mother drifted in and out of sleep. I sat by her bedside and watched her, holding her small hands. It came to me then that she had never told me stories of her dreams, her hopes, and her desires, and most of all, stories of her own birth. Over the years, it had never occurred to me to ask her.

Did the thunder howl and the winds screech when she was born? Or did the sun yawn and the rainbow smile? Did she enter the world toes first, head last? Or did she come the usual way, with arms clasped across her bare chest? How many buckets of blood marked this auspicious occasion? Did she come crying like a spoiled brat or cooing like a mighty bird? Did she arrive like a queen, head-first and wearing a crown? Did the four old women blow their trumpets and the angels stamp their feet in the heavens above? In the end, I didn't know the answers to the questions that mattered. I didn't know the beginning of the stories I needed the most.

It was a sunny afternoon when she awoke again. She complained of shooting pains down her left arm and asked me to rub it with Vicks. Then she asked me for a cup of warm water with a lemon wedge in it.

"Momma, what was the day like when you were born?"

"Oh, Kalyana, those stories aren't important."

"Yes, they are. I want to know."

"I am too old to remember. My memory is gone now." She kept staring deep into her mug. We listened to the birds chirp outside and the sound of the bees buzzing around the marigold flowers.

"If you hadn't gotten married, Momma, and could be anything you wanted to be, what would you have liked to be?"

"If I had got the chance to complete all my school?" she said weakly, raising her eyes to mine.

"Yes."

She giggled under her breath, then erupted in a coughing fit, spilling the warm water onto the bedcovers. I took the cup from her hands and placed it on the wooden dresser by her bedside. Gently, I rubbed her back.

"If I could have been anything I wanted to be, I would have liked to be..." She gazed up to the ceiling and smiled. "A news reporter."

"A news reporter?"

She nodded. "Yes," she said with absolute certainty. "Yes, I would have liked to be a news reporter, so that I could tell my stories to the world!" She coughed and then turned to me. "But I found joy in being a mother and in being a wife. I have no regrets about that."

My mother was a woman. And regardless of the place of her birth, the color of her skin, and her social circumstances, my mother was like the millions of women who had come before her: she buried her dreams, lived for others, and sacrificed for her children. She tried and failed and succeeded and yet suffered the blame and carried the shame for the misdeeds of others. Like the fourth old woman, whom we all called the mother, she hoisted life's burdens upon her shoulders and stood strong, guarding the entrance. My mother was so much like me.

She woke up twice after that. Once she mistook me for Manjula, who had telephoned to say that her own ill health prevented her from taking the trip. Mother called me Manjula and told me that we would meet on the other side, where she, a Hindu, would frolic in the heavens, with her head held high and shoulders proud. I asked her if she wanted me to call

Manjula. Get her on the phone. My mother didn't respond, falling back into a daze.

The second time she awoke, she mumbled that it was Uncle Chatur. That it happened in her mother's room. It happened every noon hour when her mother went outside to hang the damp clothes. "No, Momma," I said. "It was Uncle Baldev. Remember, Momma. It happened in the coop, outside. It happened only once, on Manjula's wedding day. Remember Momma. You didn't allow it to happen again."

My mother insisted, "No, it was Uncle Chatur. And it happened again and again. And then to you, Kalyana."

She began shivering and complaining that the air felt cold. For me, too, the world seemed suddenly frozen. Mother and me? Uncle Chatur and Uncle Baldev? Was it just the confused ranting of a dying old woman? Or was it something deeper, long-buried memories surfacing like rubbish floating back onto the shore? I could feel the pulsing of my heart, slow and distant within me. Veins and vessels seemed to knot. My lungs felt tight and my body breathless. Was it true that my mother and I had shared one fate and one story? That both of our roads had journeyed through the same past? Had my mother's revenge on Uncle Baldev been on behalf of two hurt little girls?

Mother interrupted my wildly cascading thoughts. "Put more blankets on me, Kalyana. Put more blankets on me. It feels like I am lying in the freezer." She claimed she saw my father, smiling and swirling in a burst of white light. He looked as dashing as the first time she had seen him: so young, so robust. She reached out her hand into the air and clutched his, smiling. It was late in the afternoon.

The sun had started to sink in the far sky when my mother gasped her last breath, her hand outstretched as she smiled. And then she lay back for the final time, and in my arms she silently and peacefully fell asleep forever. My calm shattered, and as I closed her eyelids, I burst into a loud scream.

The members of the funeral procession, led by Raju and me, walked towards the ocean with grave faces and mumbled prayers. The pundit stood in knee-deep water, his white cotton pants soaked, a *lota* full of floating rose petals in blessed water in his left hand and sandalwood incense in his right. He chanted the usual Sanskrit verses, awakening the spirit guides and asking in prayer that they might gently lead my mother's humble soul to the other side. My brother, his head newly shaved bald, stood holding my mother's remains. Ashes and bones, but somewhere the spirit of my mother must still live, hovering above ships, floating over valleys, swinging upon trees.

As the pundit's chants and the relatives' weeping buzzed through the air, I receded to a warm, quiet place in my mind. Kalyana: it was my mother who had given me my name, the meaning of which, she had said, carried the weight of the universe. Blissful. Beautiful. Blessed. The auspicious one. Yet in the end, it was not without suffering. It was not spared pain. *Sumitri*. What did my mother's name mean? I had never remembered to ask her. Did her own mother gift her that, too? There were so many unanswered questions. And so many questions gone unasked.

My heart paused for a moment when I saw Raju's head

dunk under the waves and my mother's ashes spill into the water. Sumitri Mani Seth had become one with the mighty Pacific. Raju dipped his head under the water three times, as the pundit chanted prayers. I stood tearless as I watched her remains be carried away with each rise and fall of the ocean waves. My mother, my protector, my guide; her ashes changed shape and took the form of a five-headed snake.

I flew back to Canada a week later. This time, along with a few of my old poems, books, and short stories, I carried my mother's memories close to my heart. I sat down in front of my computer at home and began to type. If a pen could be mightier than a sword, then my keyboard could be stronger and faster than a machine gun, firing words like bullets onto a bloodless white page.

I wrote the stories my mother had told me: of the great journey of the Indians across the seas; of the mighty gods and goddesses; of the myths and ancient legends; and the tales of women and men. I wrote because I could and I wrote because I must.

The four old women sprang out of nowhere, giggling and dancing, urging me to go on, the colors of their auras once again melding and merging beautifully. And then I felt my mother's warm hand on my back as my fingers flew over the keyboard. The four old women banged the drums and sang the songs of my lost childhood dreams. As words flooded the white page before me, I saw the caterpillar morph into a butterfly.

A little bird was soaring to the skies.

Acknowledgments

I cannot express enough thanks to Patricia Kennedy and Christina Frey, my most amazing editors, for their honesty, patience, and attention to detail. It was such a pleasure to work with both of you.

I also express my deepest gratitude to Margie Wolfe, my publisher, for giving me such a wonderful opportunity to introduce *Kalyana* to the world; and to Carolyn Jackson, for championing my work and overseeing everything, even while on vacation. I am sincerely appreciative of the whole team at Second Story Press for doing such a wonderful job.

Secondly, I am thankful to my whole family in Fiji and my daughter, Laila Blue Khelawan, for always supporting my voice, and encouraging me to write about things that matter to me. To Carmen Wittmeier, I say thank you for the initial feedback on my manuscript. I am fortunate to have friends such as Duchessa Mettimano, Shannon Summers, Hubert Byletzki, Rick Grol, Rudy Friesen, and Shannon and Steve Gaudry—for always believing in my abilities.

Last but not least, to my mother, I say my biggest thank you, for without her educating me on my Indian heritage, and telling me the stories of Krishna and Rama, Kali and Draupadi, Maharajah Akbar and Birbal, and the elephant and the little bird, there would be no *Kalyana*.

About the Author

RAJNI MALA KHELAWAN is an emerging Indo-Fijian Canadian writer. In addition to being a visiting writer at The University of the South Pacific, Fiji Islands in August 2011, Khelawan has been profiled on TV and radio shows such as Bollywood Boulevard, CBC Radio, Omni South Asian News, Asian Magazine TV, and NUTV. Her first novel is *The End of the Dark and Stormy Night*.